LITTLE GREAT ISLAND

"Besides engaging essential issues of life—love, livelihood, environment, greed, decency—this novel has an ingenious narrative structure. *Little Great Island* is told in well-textured prose, full of grounding and intimate details. It's an extraordinary achievement and a pure pleasure to read."

—Ha Jin, National Book Award winner of *Waiting*

* * *

"The power of community and connection in the face of climate change is explored masterfully in this beautiful novel. The soul of an island is at stake, but Kate Woodworth shows with gorgeous prose and a stunning narrative refrain how even though 'we can't change the past, we can change the way we understand it.' *Little Great Island* captures the fragile ecosystems of both our regions and our relationships and how resourcefulness can help heal both."

—Marjan Kamali, bestselling author of *The Stationery Shop* and *The Lion Women of Tehran*

* * *

"In this story, two damaged people seek redemption. The setting (and third central character) is Little Great Island itself, which sits off the coast of Maine. It has pressing problems that are both ecological and social–but it is a special place with a soul, and it nourishes both of these characters. The narrative tenderly unpacks how people process the unexpected things that happen to them, allowing the characters' transformations to unfold organically. It is also a complex love story–not necessarily romantic, but moving nonetheless....the prose evokes an intense sense of place, conjuring a feeling that is both elegiac and hopeful. An uplifting and grown-up novel in which two lost souls find love and purpose."

—*Kirkus Reviews*

"I loved, loved, loved this book about good people and bad decisions, small towns and big corporations, this is also a novel about how deep love—for others and for our planet—can evolve. And, if we are lucky, heal."

—CAROLINE LEAVITT, *New York Times* BESTSELLING AUTHOR OF *Days of Wonder*

* * *

"Put Anthony Doerr's *The Shell Collector*, John Banville's *The Sea,* and Elizabeth Strout's *Olive Kitteridge* into a mixer and out comes Kate Woodworth's deeply beautiful *Little Great Island*."

—SOPHIE POWELL, AUTHOR OF *The Mushroom Man*

* * *

"If you love the novels of Elizabeth Strout and Anne Rivers Siddons... you will love *Little Great Island*. This is one of those novels you will carry inside you forever.

—JENNA BLUM, *New York Times* BESTSELLING AUTHOR OF *Those Who Save Us* AND *The Lost Family*

* * *

"*Little Great Island* is a book about place, and overcoming grief, and how place can heal. A book where people owe something to the land, because the land gives freely of itself to help people, and only asks that we don't destroy it in the process. The island itself —beautiful, struggling, Little Great Island—is a character in and of itself, the central fulcrum around which this story hums with life and purpose."

—WHITNEY SCHARER, AUTHOR OF THE INTERNATIONALLY BEST-SELLING AND AWARD-WINNING NOVEL, *The Age of Light*

"A powerful and satisfying examination of one woman's fight to save herself, her son, and the community she calls home."

—Mira T. Lee, author of *Everything Here is Beautiful*, an Amazon Top 20 Best Literature/Fiction Books of 2018

* * *

"Deftly navigating themes of love and loyalty, forgiveness and redemption, Woodworth welcomes us to *Little Great Island* with open arms. What resonates most about this novel, other than Woodworth's clear and vivid prose, is her ability to reveal one place from many perspectives—year-round locals and summer people alike—giving readers a vibrant, nuanced understanding of a community at a critical juncture of its evolution."

—Shannon Bowring, author of *The Road to Dalton* and *Where the Forest Meets the River*

* * *

"A beautiful book about loss and forgiveness and second chances. About going home again and confronting the ghosts that haunt us."

—Shari Goldhagen, author of *Family Life and Other Accidents; In Some Other World, Maybe;* and *100 Days of Cake*

* * *

"A meditation on loss and a vibrant call to action, *Little Great Island* is, like the waters around Maine's coast, both beautiful and nourishing."

—Julie Gerstenblatt, author of *Daughters of Nantucket*

* * *

"A timely tale, yet timeless in its exploration of the complexities that drive the choices we make toward self-discovery and, ultimately, redemption."

—Femi Kayode, award-winning author of *Lightseekers* and *Gaslight*

"Kate Woodworth's *Little Great Island* takes me home. Woodworth's characters are my fellow islanders. Her lyrical prose paints a picture that's framed by my windows. A work of fiction, yes. But a story of real-world issues and challenges faced by Maine fishing communities. A delightful read for anyone in need of a strong dose of Coastal Maine."

—Linda Greenlaw Wessel *New York Times* bestselling author of *The Hungry Ocean, The Lobster Chronicles* and *All Fishermen are Liars*

* * *

LITTLE

GREAT

ISLAND

A Novel

KATE WOODWORTH

Sibylline
PRESS

AN IMPRINT OF ALL THINGS BOOK

Sibylline Press
Copyright © 2025 by Kate Woodworth
All Rights Reserved.

Published in the United States by Sibylline Press,
an imprint of All Things Book LLC, California.
Sibylline Press is dedicated to publishing the brilliant work
of women authors ages 50 and older.
www.sibyllinepress.com

Distributed to the trade by Publishers Group West
Sibylline Press Paperback
ISBN: 9781960573902
Library of Congress Control Number: 2024941260

Book and Cover Design: Alicia Feltman

Cover art "Stonington from the Road" by William Hallett

LITTLE
GREAT
ISLAND

A Novel

KATE WOODWORTH

For Betsy Burton, for always believing in me
and in the power of community

THE ABENAKI PRINCESS

Little Great Island

It's April on a Down East island—a waning-moon-shaped haven, an isle of spruce and granite and seagull—where a clutch of steadfast families pulls their living from the sea. Out on the water, a chain of lobster boats heads into the fog bank parked on the horizon, their wakes rippling in Vs behind them. In the yards and houses, cats stalk, smokers hack, and coffee brews. Morning sun glimmers on the bent grasses grown long in the slump-stoned cemetery, while in the kitchens the news is of wind speed and tide charts, of dock prices per pound of lobster, of fuel and tariffs and catch predictions, both dire and good.

Clatcher's Market is closed at this hour. Clatcher's Hardware & Marine Center is too. The Blue Buoy's owners are still in their mainland homes. No flag flies at the yacht club. Above The Sweet Shoppe's kitchen, the gray-haired owner lies alone in her bed, contemplating the flour that must be cut with shortening, the bacon that must be fried crisp. In the yellow house on Main Street, a thirty-four-year-old man—dark hair, darker eyes—awakens in the same room he's slept in his entire life and thinks: *four years, ten months, and five days. Bada-boom.*

Outside the village, a rambling red farmhouse with a covered porch peers out to sea. Down the hill, a man with a hitch in his walk carries a battered blue cooler from his weathered Cape to the dock where his lobster boat awaits him: that trusted vessel, the *Alice-Mari*, with its stubborn starter and a wheelhouse that feels halfway between his own skin and home. Behind him, his wife of many decades calls, "Love you, old man," and as he answers, "Love you, old woman," she thinks of the day eons ago when they made love on the bottom of that boat and created a daughter whom she hasn't seen in ten years.

A trio of gulls scatters from their perch, one chord in the morning's sensory symphony of fir, raspberries, blueberries, herons, osprey, woodpeckers, bluefish, harbor seals, sharks, butterflies, bats, asters, and seaweed. Fathoms deep in Maine's Atlantic waters, the lobsters scale rocks and traverse mud fields as they head toward Little Great Island, seeking warmer waters in which to spawn. Across them all comes the blast of the *Abenaki Princess*'s horn.

THE ENTIRETY OF SOUND

Harry

On the ferry's upper passenger deck, Harry Richardson—tall, bearded, and with wind-chapped cheeks—leans on the railing, his arms crossed beneath his chest, his attention on the water thrown aside by the ferry's passing. At forty-one, he has gone gaunt, his khakis with their frayed pocket edges held up by a belt cinched to its final hole. The last few years have plowed furrows across his brow and washed sadness into the blue of his eyes. Gray has found its way into his beard and skin. The sole car on the deck is his—a secondhand Honda Civic, its cargo hold and rear seat packed tight with empty boxes, garbage bags, cleaning supplies, and human ashes. Harry rubs the ring on his little finger, the wedding band of his wife, Ellie, who is—he has accepted the euphemisms of death now that nearly two years have passed—gone. The world around him is lost in cloud.

"Mr. Richardson."

Harry turns his head and, seeing Frank Clatcher, owner of the island's market and boatyard, straightens and extends his hand.

Harry, who has spent weeks on Little Great Island every summer of his life but the last two, knows most of the two-hundred-and-eighty-five full-time residents by name and can, with some accuracy, guess which dog and which child and which vehicle belongs to which family. He knows who to call when his faucet leaks, his electricity fails, his chimney crumbles, or when he wants lobster for dinner. The people of this island are part of his viscera, just like Ellie, who, over time, became woven into every tree branch, every gull call, every ferry horn and breeze from the sea. She should be here, and yet she's gone, and that's the taproot of his problem. If he's learned anything from the past few weeks, it's that it's past time to let go of the constant reminders. Excise them like a tumor and flush them away.

"Frank," Harry says as he shakes the man's hand.

Frank gazes just starboard of Harry's head, the now-familiar look of discomfort settling onto his face. Up until ten days ago, Harry thought his friends, his colleagues, and even he himself had put Ellie's death behind them. But for those confronting Harry's loss for the first time, it's all they can think of, and their first interaction goes one of three ways. Some people want the details to assure them they are different and so cannot be similarly struck down: how her cancer was discovered, where she was treated, how long her remission lasted, whether her diet or her genes or her lifestyle was responsible. Others hug him, their eyes tear up, and they seem unsatisfied that Harry cannot or will not cry too. The third group summons platitudes and then flees. Not one of them has any idea what it's like to watch your young wife die while the septuagenarian in the next hospital room puts on a jacket and goes back to life.

Harry pegs Frank—a man in his mid-sixties with tufts of ginger hair sprouting above each ear—as a runner, and his inner ear supplies the other man's next words before they are spoken.

"So sorry for your loss," Frank says.

"Thank you." Harry turns his attention to Little Great Island's coastline as it comes into view. Beside him Frank fidgets, not fleeing yet, searching for the right words of condolence. But there's nothing that anyone can say or do. Ellie's illness should not have happened. She was too vibrant. Statistical probability was on their side as far as recovery went. Yet she is gone, and what Harry is left with is the understanding that grief is more than sadness. It's a swamp that sucks you back just when you think the footing is firm.

"Up for the weekend?" Frank asks.

"Going to get some work done on the house." Harry doesn't elaborate, doesn't tell the other man that he'd been instructed to take compassionate leave from his teaching duties for the rest of the spring semester. Leave was framed as a gift, explicitly tied to his track record with students and presented with the strong recommendation that he "get some help." He'd tried, but the help—two sessions with a grief therapist who had no solutions not readily available on the Internet—was a waste of time and money. What Harry needed, he realized, was to get rid of all things Ellie. He'll be on the island until the house is emptied, cleaned, and on the market.

"How about your brother and sister?" Frank asks. "They coming up this year?"

"Just me," Harry says. Isabelle, Jonathan, and Harry had equally inherited the family's old farmhouse and the hundred or so acres that surround it when their father had passed away. When Harry broached the idea of selling, they agreed immediately. Isabelle's got an infant and a toddler as well as a demanding job as a New York City lawyer. Jonathan lives in DC, he and his wife work long hours, and their son is on the spectrum. They'd been reluctant to bring up selling the house, Jonathan told Harry, because they know how much he loves it.

"I'm ready to let go," Harry replied.

"Whatever you need, Har," Isabelle said, but he's sure what she really meant was: *For God's sake, move on.*

Right now, Harry should ask how Frank's winter was, how he feels about the summer ahead, but he finds he hasn't got it in him. The ache of Ellie's absence sucks the air from his lungs. But despite knowing, courtesy of grief therapy, that he needs to talk about Ellie's death, there is really nothing more he can say.

The two men keep their gaze fixed on the passing shore: the tangles of rockweed revealed by the receding tide, trees and lawns and houses glittering with the remains of the morning's mist.

"Well, then," Frank says, wiping his palms on his worn Carhartts. He squints at the sky. "Might turn out to be a decent day after all."

"Could be."

The ferry horn blasts a second time. The engines throttle down, and Frank heads to the lower deck while Harry watches the Little Great Island coastline slide by the ferry's port side: stately summer homes with their swaths of grass leading down to weathered docks, flagless poles, empty boat moorings, carless driveways, and the occasional tennis court with the net taken in for the season. Well, naturally everything seems lifeless and abandoned. It's barely April. He knew most of his summer friends wouldn't be on the island this early in the season. They all have jobs, spouses, houses, children in school. All except him.

After a third blast, the captain instructs drivers to return to their cars. *Okay, here we go,* Harry thinks, but it takes him a moment to move. The hunting song of an osprey owns, for a moment, the entirety of sound. The *Abenaki Princess* angles toward the pier, reverses and churns, and Harry gets himself down the stairs and into his car.

IT'S NOT A LIE IF IT COULD BE TRUE

Mari

At the clang of the car ramp onto the deck, Mari McGavin lifts her cheek from where it rests against the scratched and salt-pitted window in the ferry's passenger cabin and regards the ratty-haired head of her six-year-old son, who lies asleep in the protective circle of her arm. The fact of him is the closest thing to a miracle that she knows. Who but God could have brought such perfection from inside her? Who but God would have reached through her clouded thinking and inspired her to grab Levi and run? Who but God could have made it possible to avoid whichever of her ministry brothers was sent after her—because surely someone had quickly noticed her and Levi's absence—and then for the two of them to have travelled this far with virtually no money?

Mari presses her eyes shut. No, none of this can be attributed to God. God was once a background noise and an annoyance. Then a possibility of solace. And now? A false comfort that must be denied. A habit that must be broken. Or maybe a source of strength. Where does God end and her own will begin? Should that juncture be different? How to distinguish between her own wants and God's? And what about Levi? Shouldn't his needs be paramount? Does duty to God supersede the responsibilities of motherhood? Can she blame God for whatever happened to her son? No. The responsibility—the failure—is hers alone.

"Damn it," spits the untamable voice in her brain, the one that's always gotten her in trouble. The one that got her son in trouble.

Opening her eyes, Mari takes in the wood-slatted passenger seats, the life buoy hooked to the wall. All those reminders of who she was before she left the island: ready and willing to live life to the max, was her own opinion. Constitutionally wired to cause trouble was her mother's. "Vain and willful," her husband, Caleb, and the ministry leader, Pastor Aaron, told her repeatedly in her last months at God's Bounty. Disobedient. Possessed by the devil. Pastor Aaron, who looked like a benevolent grandpa and turned out to be a viper.

Whatever. That's all in the past. She's made it back to Little Great Island with Levi. Now she needs to reassure him, get him settled into her parents' house. They both need food, a shower, and sleep. She'll need to find a way to earn money. A lawyer must be hired. Her marriage must be ended.

Leaning forward, Mari shelters her son with her body. They've come a long way, but that was only miles. The distance they have ahead—the trip from her past to some kind of future—cannot be calculated in square feet or kilometers or even in light years. Nevertheless, it must be done.

She lays her lips against Levi's travel-stale forehead and whispers, "Levi, wake up."

Levi's eyes, when he opens them, are bloodshot. His hair, which reaches past his shoulders, is tangled. Smoothing her son's hair back from his face, Mari says, "We're here, sweetheart."

The engine of the only car on the ferry starts up, followed by the mechanical sounds of the ramp being weighted, traveled, and lightened. Whoever brought that car over from the mainland—presumably a seasonal homeowner because the car had Massachusetts plates—is gone now. Mari had managed to avoid the one passenger she's seen—her friend Sue's father, Frank Clatcher—by pretending to be asleep, her face in Levi's body, the one time he walked through the cabin. She and Levi must have looked to him like a pile of secondhand clothes. He wouldn't have recognized her the way she is now.

"Where are we?" Levi asks, his voice muddy as he tries to speak without disturbing the sore on his tongue.

"On the island where Mama grew up. Remember, I told you? We're going to see your grandparents, Grandpa Sam and Grandma Alice."

Levi eyes the ferry cabin blearily. "Where's Papa?"

"He's not here, honey. He's still at God's Bounty." She turns her face to the salt-eroded window, keeping her voice as steady as she can as she names the South Carolina farming ministry where she spent the last ten years. It's the only home Levi's ever known.

"Is he going to come here?"

Fear or hope in her son's voice? Maybe both. Either way, she needs to ensure Caleb never sets foot on Little Great Island.

"We'll see," Mari answers.

"What about Pastor Aaron and Sister Ann?"

"Pastor" comes out as "patter." "Sister" sounds like *teh-teh* due to that sore, the origins of which Levi has refused to explain. When she's asked, Levi has clamped his arms across his chest and glared straight ahead.

"They're back in South Carolina too," Mari tells Levi of the couple who oversees God's Bounty.

Levi says, "I have to tell them sorry. I have to tell Papa."

Standing, Mari pulls Levi to his feet and wraps her fingers through the handles of the plastic bags that hold their belongings. Sleep was impossible on the bus. In twenty-four hours, all she's eaten was an apple.

"It's okay, sweetie," she says. "They know. But they had to stay at God's Bounty. They have work to do."

It's not a lie if it could be true, right? Besides, it's the easiest thing for Levi to understand for now.

"What about God, then?" Levi asks. "Did He stay at God's Bounty?"

"Of course not, sweetheart. He's with us always." Mari keeps her face gentle, her smile reassuring, but Levi has a talent that Pastor Aaron does not and that Caleb has lost: He can see beyond her exterior. Her son can read her soul.

"I want to go home," Levi says.

"It's going to be okay," Mari assures him. "I know this feels strange, but you'll get used to it, I promise."

Unwinding the bags from her fingers, she puts them on the rust-colored floor and crouches next to her son. How to explain to him something she's still struggling to understand? Was she right to flee? To take her son from his father? What happens now? Have they really escaped so easily?

Levi's lips press tight, his eyebrows lower, his arms lock across his chest. His clam look. Shut up inside a shell so thick that Pastor Aaron convinced Caleb they needed to keep him from wickedness with a firm hand. How had she not seen the trouble that was coming? Honestly, she had, but hadn't her own unbridled nature needed taming, and hadn't she benefited from the lessons she learned at God's Bounty? Besides, thought and analysis were luxuries she hadn't had. Beans had to be canned, peaches had to be processed, the bread had to be pulled, golden, from the oven. She'd found it all too easy to tuck her concerns aside, promise herself she'd examine them further at the earliest opportunity. In the meantime, God had to be thanked for His gifts: her wonderful son, her loving and responsible husband, the companionship of her God's Bounty sisters. She had listed her gratitudes and relied on the prayers she'd learned to recite in times her mind was troubled.

Then, in a moment, everything changed.

"You will like Grandma Alice and Grandpa Sam," Mari says now. "They have a vegetable garden. Just like at God's Bounty." Her mother keeps a kitchen garden, not a farm, but Levi doesn't need to know that yet. Rising, she strings the bags along one arm. Pulls a hand from Levi's armpit and clasps it.

"Hens?" Levi asks, no doubt because collecting eggs was one of his chores on God's Bounty. "A pony?"

No hens. No animals. But Mari will change that if it's what Levi needs to be happy.

"You can see the room Mama slept in when she was your age," Mari says. "I had my own room, all to myself. Later in the summer, we can pick blueberries and raspberries. You can go out on the boat with Grandpa Sam when he goes fishing for lobster. You're going to have lots of new friends to play with."

Real play, like kicking a ball around the schoolyard. Decorating Main Street for Halloween with sidewalk chalk. Playing capture the flag and flashlight tag with the summer kids. Surely her island friends have children now. Maybe one of them will be Levi's age, or close enough to be a play-mate. Giddiness tingles her skin; for years, she's tried hard not to miss Little Great Island. Being back feels like being reunited with her heart.

"I don't want to," Levi says.

"I think we're going to have fun."

Levi's expression is doubtful, but he does follow her, step by step. The cabin door is heavy, stubborn, and she sets her shoulder against it out of habit and then braces to grab it, another reflex born of crossings when the wind would catch the door and slam it open. Today, there is only the slightest of breezes.

Levi stalls, so Mari pulls him gently, her body still pressed to keep the door ajar. The outside air is part sun-dried seaweed and part iron. It's threaded through with guano and gasoline, soil and salt and lemon-frosted biscuits, the exhalation of plants and the promise of apples. To Mari, though she hasn't smelled it in a decade, it is nothing less than the smell of home.

THE SWEET SHOPPE

Harry

When his car bumps from ferry ramp to asphalt parking lot, Harry's body sighs with relief the way it always does the moment he reaches the island until he reminds himself that this year is different. This year isn't vacation. It's work. The goal—unrealistic, the Richardson siblings have agreed, but nevertheless worth aiming for—is to have the house listed by early June to take advantage of the summer selling season. The number of buyers for old farmhouses on remote islands in northern climates is tiny, but the pandemic, market factors, remote work possibilities, and a general queasiness about the vulnerability of urban life has created something of a demand. By early August, Harry will have to let the school know if he's returning to teach. By Labor Day, the siblings hope to have the house—which is currently full of generations of stuff—under contract. He'll have plenty, during the next five months, to keep himself occupied.

As he rolls slowly toward the main road, Harry raises an index finger in the traditional island greeting at the manager of the island's ferry terminal in her neon-green vest. Carol bobs her head, acknowledging his arrival in their midst, and

Harry turns his attention to the small village, which seems both intimately familiar and eerily abandoned in comparison to its usual summer bustle. No sign of Frank, who must have disappeared already into his hardware store. A few cars are parked on Main Street, but no people are present. There's no activity at the town office building or post office. The Grange Hall, once the scene of harvest dinners and solstice dances, now sports a collapsed roof and boarded windows. A Siamese cat, tail raised in a question mark, strolls the edge of the road.

Rolling his window down, Harry inhales as deeply as his lungs will bear. The air has a sweetness that's impossible in Boston. *I've got this*, he tells himself, although he doesn't bother to ask whether he means he can get over Ellie's death, ready the house for market, or simply walk through the house's front door. He pulls Ellie's hooded gray sweatshirt from the passenger seat onto his lap.

At the dirt road turnoff to his family's old red farmhouse, Harry brakes. Ellie's not at the house, drinking coffee on the front porch with one of his flannel shirts thrown over her pajamas as a robe. No Ellie, with that slight lisp and impossibly triangular nose. Whose right front incisor was so enchantingly crooked that he'd wanted to kiss her within seconds of seeing her for the first time. Impossible that was more than fourteen years ago.

Maybe breakfast first. There's no food at the house; no one's stayed there since he and Ellie were last on the island three summers ago. Sam and Alice McGavin, the only neighbors on the small peninsula where his family's house stands, have been checking on it. They know he's coming, but he told them not to bother putting food in the fridge. Veering left, he takes the road that circumnavigates the village and is back on Main Street in minutes. Memories rise all around: descending the yacht club steps in the midst of his family as they headed out on a sailing picnic; walking the road around the village over and over with Jonathan and Isabelle when they'd learned their parents were divorcing; Ellie writing postcards at a Sweet Shoppe table, an iced tea with two lemon wedges nearby.

"Hello?" he calls now as he steps through The Sweet Shoppe's door. The café's floors are wide pine, the tables and chairs tidy and ready for the day. Everywhere is the smell of baking. "You open?" Harry asks loudly enough that Lydia Smith, The Sweet Shoppe's owner, might hear him if she is still in her bedroom upstairs.

"Coming." Lydia shuffles from the kitchen, her diminutive body covered by an apron streaked with flour. Her hair is a thicket of curls that clings to her scalp, her face a weave of wrinkles and sunspots behind a pair of oversized wire-frame glasses. Beneath the loose hems of her jeans, Lydia's feet are stuffed into a pair of battered slippers. Harry can't remember a time when she wasn't old, and here she is, still old.

"My stars," Lydia says. "It's Harry Richardson." Craning forward, she peers out the windows behind him. "Did it turn into summer while I was in the kitchen?"

"No. I'm up early this year. Just got off the boat and realized I was desperate for coffee."

"You sit down, then. I haven't got it started yet, but it'll just take a minute."

Harry chooses a seat near the window and watches Lydia while she works. She must be well into her seventies by now.

"You want a pastry?" Lydia asks, then shakes her head. "Listen to me, asking if Harry Richardson wants a pastry. You always did love a sweet. I've got some lemon scones about ready to come out of the oven if you aren't in a hurry."

"No hurry," Harry says. Facing the farmhouse is seeming more difficult by the minute.

"Mild winter," Lydia says. "'Cept for those storm tides. I suspect you saw about them down to Boston. Water right up to my door there." She nods toward the back of the building. "Boatyard got flooded more than once. Frank's shop's damaged. The Buoy too. Don't know what's going to become of us, what with all the flooding. How was it down by you?"

"Fine," Harry says, although he doesn't remember. Hours outside the classroom, the ones once spent with Ellie, went now to historical research and playing tennis so assiduously that he's compromised both knees.

"Lobstermen were out well into December," Lydia says. "Longest fishing season I can recall. Too bad it didn't translate into much of a catch. The worst in twenty-five years."

"Climate change?" Harry asks, and Lydia shrugs.

"Who knows?" she says. "That's a bigger problem than a bunch of lobstermen can fix. And now there's all this business with the whales."

Harry nods, having read about the push to protect right whales from entanglement in lobster-fishing gear. He remains silent while Lydia goes on about young people moving back to the island. They want the quieter life, but there's no affordable place for them to live and even fewer jobs. Harry's students—mostly fifteen- and sixteen-year-olds—have terrible anxieties about their futures. He was always good at reassuring them that adulthood is a welcoming place, but now he's screwed that up as well.

"Other than the storms and the flooding, though," Lydia adds as she puts coffee and a scone in front of him, "winter was pretty quiet." She elaborates on the island news. Someone's dog died. Someone else had Covid. Who's pregnant, who's got a new baby. Harry picks at his scone until she says, "Tom Estabrook's up early this year as well."

Mr. Estabrook had been a good friend of Harry's father—a man of "considerable international influence," Harry's father had always liked to point out. He was known as The Butterfly Diplomat for his tendency to bring up the butterfly effect in negotiations. One person's actions, he'd reminded politicians, business leaders, lobby groups, and NGOs throughout his career, can lead to disaster or, conversely, to clogging the gears of destruction. Mr. Estabrook had taken a liking to Harry early on, singling him out for conversation on the frequent occasions he was at the farmhouse for cocktails. They shared a passion for history, for its lessons and for the insights it gave them into the men and women who made such an impact on the world. Mr. Estabrook also adored Ellie.

"Been here about a week," Lydia continues. She stares out the window for a moment, to where the Siamese cat is now grooming itself at the edge of the road. "Rumor has it he's going to sell the house."

Harry says, "I can't imagine this island without him." True, although right now the question is whether the two houses will compete for the same buyer. The Richardsons' house is closer to town than Mr. Estabrook's. It has more land and better views. Mr. Estabrook's house has been updated and is in better shape.

"Sorry about your wife," Lydia says. "Hell of a thing. She was a nice lady."

Turning to the window, Harry touches a paper napkin to his mouth. A moment passes before he can swallow, and then he gives himself another moment to smooth the napkin across his knee.

"Thank you," he says finally.

"Something wrong with the scone?" Lydia asks. Harry's reduced it to crumbs but barely tasted it.

"No, it's great. Thank you."

"My heart's not in the cooking the way it was," Lydia says. "If the world were a better place, I'd have retired by now. I'm for sure feeling my age." She shakes her head. "Listen to me. Telling you about my problems. You want more coffee?"

Harry holds out his cup, which Lydia tops off. She touches Harry's shoulder with her free hand.

"You just up for the weekend?" she asks.

"The summer. But maybe I'll be back and forth a bit." Not likely. His condo is sublet until August thirtieth. He might put it on the market after that because the condo, like the island, is full of Ellie's absence.

"Well, that's nice," Lydia says. "I'll be glad to see you whenever you come by."

Across the street, Clive, the postmaster, emerges from the post office to stare at Harry's car, then peer at The Sweet Shoppe window. Ah, yes: no secrets on the island.

"I should get going," Harry says.

Lydia looks up from the pastry cabinet, where she has been arranging scones in a row. "You take care, now," she says.

"You too," he says, standing. He feels Lydia watching him as he opens the door and crosses the street, but when he looks back through the plate-glass window, she's already disappeared.

HOMECOMING

Mari

"What are you doing?" Levi asks, because Mari has hesitated at her parents' back door—the same door she went through countless times as a child and as a teen—wondering whether to knock. Her mother, Alice, no more than fifteen feet away, stands at a window with her back to Mari, hand to her hip, and stares in the direction of the barn. After ten years of trying not to think of this paint-peeled Cape house, this kitchen, this person, Mari is surprised by the minute familiarity of her mother: flannel work shirt; baggy, faded jeans; no-nonsense, uncombed haircut. Her mother's barn boots stand on the mudroom floor among the waders and soiled sneakers and snow boots and garden tools and thermoses and gloves of a dozen varieties that are the necessary familiars of her parents' lives. Somewhere in the jumble, even after all this time, there are likely discarded possessions of Mari's own. No doubt the ghosts of her many arguments with her mother still linger in the heat vents, in the pantry corners, on the undersides of chairs.

"Mama," Levi says, impatient. "Why are we just standing here?" Levi is unused to doors that must be knocked on. At

God's Bounty, all property was public, a tenet that Mari had found compatible with her long-held feeling that the concept of land ownership made no more sense than attempting to own a plot of sky or a slice of spring. Many of the worst altercations she'd had while living on Little Great Island stemmed from the absurdity of seasonal visitors attempting to claim ownership of everything from acres of land to the island's way of life when they only spent weeks on the island each year. All Levi knows of ownership and possession is that a closed door offered no more assurance of privacy than an open one, although no one entered Pastor Aaron's home or office unless their presence was requested.

At the sound of Levi's voice, Alice looks up, and Mari watches her mother's expression go from question to surprise to some tangle of feeling that produces both a hand clutching the fabric of her shirt and a flash of horror as she registers Mari's shaved head. By the time Alice has pulled the door open, she is crying. Her mother gathers Mari into her arms, and Mari wishes she could stay there. That she never left. That all the words she and her mother had struck and jabbed each other with had never been spoken. The smell of mother: Dial soap and wood smoke, coffee and freshly turned soil. Squeezing her eyes shut, Mari forces herself to appreciate the moment because it cannot last.

"Sweetheart, just look at you! What happened?" Alice steps back, and Mari sees her mother take in her high-collared blouse, her long skirt, the shortage of luggage, the presence of a child, the absence of a man.

"Can we come in?" Mari asks.

"Sweetie. You don't have to ask." Alice steps aside, her eyes now on Levi.

"Who's this?"

"Levi," Mari answers. "My son."

Alice goes still. Mari holds her breath. "You have a child," her mother says.

"Yes." Mari was never permitted to tell her parents of Levi's birth. She hadn't, in fact, been allowed to communicate with anyone from her past for most of the past ten years. The stricture was for her own good, Pastor Aaron told her. It would keep people like "that heathen"—her father, who had come to God's Bounty once to try to convince her to leave—from interfering with her work. At that point, Mari was head over heels in love with Caleb. She loved working in the fields and with the animals, her schedule and deadlines dictated by the needs of the crops and animals, the weather, the season. She'd had no desire to leave.

Levi stands with his back pressed against Mari, his head bowed and his hands by his side. Dirt rims his fingernails. The clothes he's wearing are at least two sizes too big. His odor is pronounced, even though Mari did the best she could to clean him in the bus station bathroom. He's shaking against her legs, just as he had for most of their bus ride north.

"Boy or girl?" her mother asks.

"Boy." A sideways jab at Levi's appearance is her mother's first response to discovering she has a grandchild? "This is your grandmother," Mari prompts. "Say hi."

"Goo' mor-on, ma'am," Levi says, the best he can do with the words he was taught at God's Bounty to use with a stranger. His voice is faint, his face tipped to the ground. Perhaps, Mari hopes, her mother won't comment on the problem with his speech.

Alice's eyebrows shoot up. "Well, hello to you, too," she says.

Levi stiffens, and Mari puts her hands on his shoulders to reassure him. "It's okay, honey," she says, and then, to her mother, "We've had a long trip."

"Let's get you inside, then." Alice waves them through the mud room, toward the kitchen, and Mari urges Levi forward. Everything about the yellowed linoleum floor, the heavy wood kitchen table with its assemblage of mismatched chairs, and the odor of fish and grease and baking is so familiar that tears flood Mari's eyes. They've made it.

"I can't believe it," Alice says, her eyes on Levi. "I didn't even know you'd gotten married. Is your husband…? Or, I mean, are you marri—"

"Can we do questions a little later, Mom? It's just… Levi's tired."

Alice chews her bottom lip. Mari knows that look means that her mother is certain Mari's insistence on marching to the beat of her own drummer has led to disaster. Well, she isn't mistaken. Not that Mari will admit to that aloud.

"I don't know what to say here," Alice says. Her eyes go to Mari's scalp again, and Mari touches the worst of the abrasions.

"Is Dad around?" she asks.

Wiping her hands down her sides, Alice shakes her head. "Out on the boat."

"How is he?" Mari asks.

Her mother lifts one shoulder. "Too old to be out there all day, but you know your dad."

Mari does. He's a clam, like Levi. A softie hunkered down inside a solid shell. Her mother's the barnacle, armored in a covering that can make you bleed.

"He's going to be over the moon to see you. Sue too." Alice's eyes return to Mari's shorn head in a way that says, *but not with that hairdo.* In the course of Mari's adolescence, her mother saw her with waist-length hair, asymmetric hair, pink hair, green hair, and dreads. Every iteration led to an argument, with Mari claiming her right to have her own hair the way she wanted it and her mother acting as though Mari's magenta dreads were somehow a reflection of her own personal failings.

"She's pregnant," Alice adds. "After a whole host of miscarriages. She's told me any number of times how much she misses you."

Mari missed her childhood best friend too, but she lets the comment pass.

"Go on and take a seat at the table," her mother continues. "Let me pull together something for you to eat. The two of you are skinny as rails."

Alice takes an apron from a hook and slips it over her head. "Eggs?" she asks. "Bacon? Sausage?" When neither Mari nor Levi answers, Alice asks, "How about a couple of pieces of toast to start with?"

"Do you have yogurt?" Right now, toast would be too much for Levi's mouth.

"Yogurt?" Said as though Mari's just asked for the moon.

"An egg, then," Mari says. "But please, let me do it. You don't need to wait on us."

"You sit."

Her mother fixes her with gray-blue eyes, and Mari sits.

Levi reaches for the saltshaker, shaped like a buoy with a red stripe at the top. Red for salt, Mari recalls from childhood. Blue for peppa.

Alice retrieves eggs from the fridge. Over her shoulder, she asks Mari, "You want coffee?"

"I don't drink caffeine anymore."

Alice snorts before asking Levi, "How about you? You want OJ?"

When Levi says "No" to his grandmother, he means, "No, don't talk to me," and not, "No, thank you."

"He can have some," Mari says, although the taste will be unfamiliar. The acidity may burn. Still, he needs the fluid. He refused to eat or drink anything during their entire journey.

It hurts, he said each time she offered food or fluid. "Ih hurs."

"Herbal tea for you, then," Alice says. When her mother puts the steaming cup in front of her, Mari's enveloped by the scent of cinnamon, and she's back at God's Bounty on Christmas Eve. Her gift of hand-knit socks came from her best friend at the ministry, Sister Grace, along with a hand-written note that said, *God loves you and so do I.* The love that seemed everywhere at God's Bounty was such a balm after the impersonal nature of mainland life in both college and grad school. On Little Great Island, everyone knew pretty much everything about everyone else. Folks didn't always like each other, but they found a way to get along. She and Sue had fought physically as small children, slugging and pulling, leaving the occasional bruise and once drawing blood. When they outgrew that, they honed the verbal insults, finding the most tender places. Yet always, within a day or two at the most, they were inseparable again. On the mainland, people didn't say hello or even make eye contact, but God's Bounty felt more like home. Initially, even mild criticism was considered unchristian. It was unthinkable for the brothers and sisters not to smile at one another every time they crossed paths.

"I forgot how much land there is out here," Mari says. Acres of it, sitting unused along the road she and Levi walked from the village.

"Richardson land," her mother says.

"Good farmland." Mari's well-trained eye had automatically considered sun and wind exposure, soil depth versus granite bedrock, and the way land contours would impact drainage. More importantly, like anyone raised on Little Great Island, Mari knows this whole area was once a farm.

"Richardson land," her mother repeats. The McGavins' three acres contain lobster traps, dry-docked boats, tumbled sheds with odd bits of land between them, and the tractor Mari's dad uses to mow the Richardsons' fields. With a glance at Levi, Alice adds, "You back for good?"

Trying to focus on her mother's words is like swimming against a current, and Mari is so, so tired. Bits of prayer crawl into her brain: *I ask...plead...for Thy strength.* She repeats the words silently, a mantra, before the drill of her mother's look stops her.

"We'll talk," Mari says. From what she can tell, Levi doesn't seem to have absorbed the import of her mother's question or her own refusal to answer.

"Levi is a great helper," she adds. "We both want to help you and Dad as much as we can."

"Huh."

Mari could raise hens. Her parents could have better-tasting eggs for less cost. It will help Levi to adjust if he has things to do, and he's familiar with collecting eggs. But those aren't the kinds of issues that can be raised at this time. She and Levi are supplicants now, and besides, she should have learned her lesson when it comes to trying to get others to see things her way. Pushing back on Pastor Aaron's beliefs had become a surefire way to end up on the dirt floor of the prayer shed, with the odor of the toilet pail and the skin-crawling worry about what brand of poisonous insect might be sharing the space.

"Harry Richardson's wife passed," Alice says. "I think he's having a hard time of it."

"I'm sorry." Mari keeps her attention on her son, who is now using a spoon to lever tiny bits of egg between his lips.

Alice wipes her hands on her apron. "Let's you and me go outside," she says.

Levi's head snaps up when Mari stands. "I'll be right there," she says, pointing through the living room. There's a small porch on the ocean side of the house, windows that overlook it. "You'll still be able to see me, okay?"

Levi doesn't nod. He doesn't take his eyes off her, but he doesn't stop her. Her mother begins talking the moment Mari joins her outside.

"What's happened? Have you finally left that place? What about Levi's father? Where is he? Who is he?"

Legitimate questions. Her mother has a right to know. But not now. Not until Levi is fed and cleaned and tucked into bed.

"Is it okay for us to be here?" Mari asks. "We can leave if you want." Not that she has any idea where they might go with no money.

"'Course it's okay. It's only that…it's so unexpected." Alice's look goes to the window, no doubt to check on Levi in the kitchen, hunched over his eggs. "He okay?" she asks.

"Tired."

"He seems …" Alice can't finish the sentence, which is probably for the best.

"He needs some time to settle in. It would help if you could cut us both a bit of slack for a while. It's been a long couple of days."

"Boy could use a bath," her mother says.

"I'll get to it."

"And a haircut."

"Please, give us a little time." Until yesterday, Levi's whole world was two-hundred acres of pasture and crops, and the thirty-two people on it were the ones he knew as his family.

Alice says, "You know me. I don't like surprises."

"We may have to stay a while," Mari replies. "Once Levi's settled, I'll look for a job. I promise."

"You were doing so well," her mother says.

When Mari was first accepted into grad school, her mother confessed there'd been a time she'd dreamed of a college education for herself. "I love your father more than anything," she said. "But I can't help but think about how that other path might have turned out."

"It makes me so sad," Alice adds now, "that you threw away all that opportunity."

"I didn't leave grad school because of Caleb, if that's what you're thinking," Mari says. Or not entirely, at least. "I left because it wasn't right for me."

"You've always thought the grass was greener anywhere but where you are," her mother says, shaking her head. She doesn't have to say "headstrong" aloud for Mari to hear it.

"I made my decisions. I didn't get a master's degree, but I got a magnificent child."

"I can't believe I have a grandson," Alice says. "He's what … five? Six?"

"Six," Mari says. Too big to carry, but she'd lifted him from the prayer-shed floor yesterday, told him to hold on tight. He nearly strangled her. She tried to run, but it was more of a waddle, the plastic bags of clothing she'd managed to cobble together for them slapping her thigh with every step. Levi's silence panicked her, as did that shaking that he could not control. Heedless, she crushed rows of pepper plants and tomato vines, making a beeline for the road. The barn hid them from Home House, but her brothers and sisters were in the fields. She and Levi could have been seen. If there hadn't been a car coming toward them, they never would have made it. Levi hadn't said a word until they were on the bus heading north, and even then, his communication was mostly in the form of head shakes.

Alice says, "Huh," but then her eyes soften. "Your father's going to be so happy," she repeats. "He wouldn't say so, but I know he's always hoped you'd come home."

What about you? Mari knows better than to ask. The answer would be woven through with admonitions and caveats.

"I need to put my son to bed," she says. "I need sleep." Her voice has risen, and it's clear her mother understands what she's really saying is *shut up*, but she's too tired to care.

"But, sweetie, can you at least tell me what happened to your hair?"

A simple enough question, but an answer so convoluted Mari cannot take it on. Work and prayers, chores and pests and weather. Months of her and Caleb orbiting each other as if no one else truly mattered, their days spent increasing efficiencies in the compost piles, convincing Pastor Aaron and the others of the value of cover crops, learning to work the hives. Nights spent finding new ways with each other's bodies. But then came the gradual change in her relationship with Caleb that she chalked up to settling into married life, her pregnancy, the work that exhausted them both. And then the conversion of a disused storage building to the prayer shed, where the tired were sent to find strength and the doubtful to find faith. Then, an eruption. An atonement.

"I just need a little time to get my feet under me," Mari says.

"Before you do what?"

Before she can think. Before she can cope with the questions. Mari presses her mouth shut.

"I just wish you'd never left school in the first place."

"All right," Mari shouts, unable to hold it in any longer. "I'm a failure. I'm a loser. I should let you run my life. Is that what you want me to say?"

"No, I—"

But if Alice finishes, Mari doesn't hear her. Realizing that her raised voice would have been heard by Levi, she glances toward the kitchen and sees that Levi has disappeared.

ALL THE EMPTY PLACES

Sue

In the tiny square of the double-wide's bathroom, Sue Clatcher Greggs—nineteen weeks into her fifth chance at having a child—layers lipstick on her lips, mascara on her lashes.

"The baby's moving," she calls to her husband, Bob, who curls over a bowl of cereal in the kitchen, a can of Coke by his hand. "Want to feel it?"

She waits for an answer, but when none comes, she adds, "I bet the catch is going to be phenomenal this year."

"Could be."

But why wouldn't it be? After all, the baby's still alive, Mari's back, and her brother Reggie's been sober almost five years; miracles do happen.

No further commentary from the kitchen, so Sue continues, "You want me to give you a ride into town? I don't mind waiting." Lie. She is so done with waiting for everything and everybody. Waiting for her dad to turn the business over to her. Waiting for Reggie to get the canned goods put away. Waiting for every supplier on the planet to deliver what they said they'd deliver. Waiting to be a mother. All the babies she lost at eight weeks, at sixteen weeks, at ten weeks—she had waited for them with the happy anticipation everyone told her she'd have, and look where that had gotten her. After this pregnancy, she won't put either Bob or herself through this again. But for this baby, she'll do whatever it takes, including forcing Bob to snap out of his funk.

"Get dressed," she says. "I'll take you down to the boat-yard. You can work on your model." All the way up until she lost that last baby, Bob had loved building model ships. He'd even sold a few. Now, he seems to have lost interest.

"We cannot pay all these bills," Bob says.

"So some will have to wait."

"They've been waiting."

"It's fine, sweetheart."

If she's not out of here in five minutes, Reggie's going to beat her to the store, and she's got to be there first. Even pregnant. Even living halfway across the island when Reggie is walking distance from the market and boatyard. One sucky part of being the little sister is that you have to best your big brother day and night just to stay in the running.

Sue gives herself another layer of blush before leaning back to peer through the open door to where Bob stares into his cereal bowl. Used to be that he called her "princess," which was corny as shit, but she loved it anyway. Used to be that they hung out with friends over at Little Beach on Saturday nights, grilling hot dogs and drinking beer, and Bob would only drink one so she could kick back and get buzzed if she wanted and he could drive her safely home. Sundays, they didn't get out of bed until noon.

"Quit worrying. Everything's going to be okay."

"Can't you skip this ultrasound?"

"No. I need it." Not according to their crap insurance policy, though, so Sue'll have to pay out of pocket the nearly six-hundred-dollars' worth of assurance that there's no reason for this baby to up and die on her like the others. That outlay—twice what she has left from the EMT gig she'd had on the island before she gave it up for this pregnancy—has kicked their savings even further toward the gutter, but what's she supposed to do? The shit side of having medical training: You know every single thing that can go wrong with the human body. The shit side of being an EMT on an island: things don't go bad all that often, which means you're left feeling like the pressure's building up against a dam and your unborn baby is likely to be the first to get clobbered.

"Honey..." Bob says.

Sue eye rolls her reflection. Here comes the yada-yada about the bills again, but she's got an income. Not huge, but something. Baby needs the money more than the truck does, and the boat should be fine. It's new enough that they haven't had to put any money in other than the monthly payments. Fishing season's just getting started. Money will come in.

"It's going to be fine," she repeats.

Shoving his cereal aside, Bob lays his head on his folded arms, and Sue finds him like that when she emerges from the bathroom.

"I'll be back by five fifteen," she says. Not like there's any place she could go after work. The island has three paved roads and a handful of small businesses. The cop is a mainland guy who comes over on the ferry if you call him; the firefighters are part-timers; and if you need a doctor, you've got a handful of EMTs, except in summer when a physician assistant hangs out in the two-room clinic in the village. Other than that, you've got to hope you make it to the mainland in time if your baby all of a sudden makes a premature dive for the exit.

No answer from Bob, so Sue leaves, closes the door soundlessly behind her, and climbs into the truck. When she gets to the paved road, she cranks the volume on the radio, letting the sound of the music overwhelm the cab.

STROLLING THROUGH A
SCRAPBOOK

Harry

"What the hell?" Harry says aloud. *What happened?*
Up until five minutes earlier, he was making headway in the rarely used bedrooms on the third floor. Yellowed sheets and featherless pillows were stuffed into contractor-strength garbage bags. Sailing and tennis trophies were dumped in a box for Isabelle and Jonathan to sort through. Progress made, he determined he could empty a couple of closets on the second floor, but Isabelle and her husband Zach's room flummoxed him. How was he supposed to know if his brother-in-law still wanted this hat or that sweater? It was too easy to imagine Isabelle's long-suffering sigh. Saying, beneath her breath, "Oh, Harry," because he'd thrown away a belt. Or because he hadn't. He'd wandered into his childhood bedroom without thinking, and there were the sheets from the time he and Ellie had ended up in that single bed rather than in the double in the bedroom they ordinarily used. It was the last time they made love on the island. Ellie woke up hours later with the sheets wringing wet.

"Look what you do to me," she'd murmured before turning over and going back to sleep. Neither of them gave that drenching sweat a second thought. Back in Boston, the sweats happened a second time, then a third. They told themselves they were odd symptoms of a cold or allergy. Indeed, the excessive perspiration abated for a while. But then it came back. Who knew that sweating could be a harbinger of aggressive breast cancer?

Now, nearly three years later, Ellie's brush with the lime-green handle is still on the bureau, her hair still in it. Harry had reached for that brush, prepared to toss it in the trash, but his hand started shaking, fingers staccato with a life of their own. The next thing he knew, the front screen door slammed shut behind him, and he was on the front porch.

Get a grip, he tells himself. *You're fine. Walk into the village. Why not?* Arguably, there are few other places to go, especially since fetching his car keys would mean going back inside the house, which is something he cannot imagine right now. But when he forces his feet forward, Ellie's ghost walks beside him. No footsteps, no conversation, no sound of breathing. No fear. But she's there. He feels her. In Boston, in the weeks following her death, Ellie's absence was resonant, but this is the first time he's felt her presence. A repercussion of the rather stiff drink he poured himself last night? Too much time alone? Dehydration?

"Sorry," a woman's voice says, the sound so close that Harry startles, struggles to reorient himself. Ellie's not beside him. She's dead. He's walking the dirt road to the village. He's on Little Great Island, surrounded by bracken and weathered trees.

The woman is draped in baggy clothing, her head covered with a bandana, her cheek and forehead bones jutting as if she's been dieting for decades. Emaciated and hollow-eyed, the woman resembles Ellie toward the end, when both the chemo and the cancer had had their way.

"My God," Harry says. "Mari?" Due to the nine-year age gap between them, Harry and Mari had little to do with each other growing up. Mari had, however, been a regular presence in the Richardson kitchen while her mother, Alice, cooked for parties or houseguests. He remembers her as a kid, long-limbed and big-eyed and always talking. The last time he saw her was before he and Ellie married.

"Hi, Harry," this skeletal Mari replies. "I heard you were on the island."

"Your mom told me you were back." What else should he say? That Alice said she and Sam had been talking about retiring to the mainland, but Mari's return complicated all that? That she worries about Mari's future as well as her past? She also worries about Mari's son, who apparently insists on praying before and after every meal.

"Mom told me about your wife," Mari adds. "May she rest in peace."

Harry nods slightly, already wanting to get moving. He can pick up the mail in the village along with the groceries. He can make headway on the laundry room this afternoon.

Mari says, "I'm sorry I never got a chance to meet her."

"Me too."

Mari glances at his face and switches topics. "You're a teacher now?"

"High-school history."

"You like it?"

Yes? He was good at it, that much he knows. His students learned, and they liked him. Colleagues who observed him talked about how he made the subject seem fresh, about how he got all the kids participating in discussions. But contemplating standing up in front of a classroom again overwhelms him with shame. He'd behaved like a nutcase.

Mari asks, "You going to the market?"

"Yes."

"Walk together?"

"Sure."

He takes off at a fast pace, but Mari keeps up. When he gets back to the house, he'll make a fresh pot of coffee. A good hit of caffeine, and he should be able to get those sheets into the laundry and throw away that brush. This evening, he can do some Internet research on a book about Woodrow Wilson he's been thinking of writing.

"...a farming ministry in South Carolina," Mari is saying, and Harry forces himself to focus.

"I left the island for college in Orono," Mari continues. "Then I went to South Carolina State on a full ride to study sustainable agriculture, but once I got there, I realized I was done with school." She wanted soil and sunshine, Mari tells him. Hands-on learning, not textbooks. Some people she met at a farmer's market invited her to check out their farm, which was big enough to support their community plus generate income from sales. She met her husband at the farm. They had a son.

"Nice," Harry says, although talk about people's children triggers an ache behind his ribs.

When they reach the place where the dirt road turns to asphalt and the buildings of Main Street are laid out before them, Mari stops and faces him.

"My son keeps running away," she says. "Not far. I mean, he's six, and we're fourteen miles from the mainland. How far can he go? Still, he hides, and it terrifies me. I thought I should let you know. In case you find him hanging around on your property or something."

Levi disappeared within the first hour of their arrival on the island, Mari continues. She found him in a shed that was one sneeze from collapsing.

"He's not a crier," she says, as though it's important for Harry to know that. "I think he's a bit traumatized."

"I'm sorry to hear that." Up until he melted down in the classroom—the event that got him sent on compassionate leave—Harry was good at relating to kids. His superpower, a colleague called it. But now he's unsure. Last thing a traumatized child needs is a guy stuck in what the therapist called "complicated grief."

"I have a lot of memories of being in your house," Mari says. "It was like kid central up there. You would all play Monopoly games that went on for days." The two of them swap memories: She recalls baking endless trays of chocolate-chip cookies in the kitchen with her mother. Harry remembers the smell of the cookies arriving warm from the oven to the delight of his friends. She tells him about lifting live lobster from a pail her father brought up from his boat and dropping them into a pot of boiling water. Harry recalls Mr. and Mrs. Estabrook, his parents, and a group of other adults—faces ruddy with gin and tonics, lobster bibs tied around their necks—debating the shortcomings of Clinton's focus on domestic versus foreign policy.

"Being in that house is like living in a scrapbook," Harry says. "I can't take a step without something triggering a memory."

"Scrapbooks only have the good times, though," Mari says. "Houses can trigger sad memories as well as happy ones."

So true. "But you've got to keep moving forward, right?" At least that's what everyone's been telling him.

"Yes," Mari says. "And you've also got to feel the pain."

"Which sucks."

Mari gives him an appraising look. "I agree," she says.

No doubt her understanding of what he's talking about is related to her appearance and to the fact she's back home with her parents, but Harry doesn't want to know more, having learned that even a few drops of another person's misery is enough to overflow his own.

"I've only got a couple of things to grab," he says as they near the market. Getting away from Mari, getting back to work, is beginning to feel urgent. "It was good to see you."

But Mari isn't done with him yet. "I have a favor to ask," she says, and something must show on his face because she laughs. Her fingers graze his sleeve. "No need to panic."

"No, no. I'm not panicked." But his heart is thudding in his ears. "What do you need?"

"You know that vegetable garden you guys have?"

Of course he does. It's a small, fenced plot, situated beside the house to maximize exposure to the sun. Harry used to be sent to the garden before supper to harvest lettuce, beans, zucchini, or whatever was in season. Ever since his parents divorced a dozen years earlier, the garden has been ignored. Ellie had expressed some interest in resurrecting it, but they'd never had the time. Funny how it never seems there is enough time, even when you still believe you have decades of it left.

Now, the garden is a fenced plot full of weeds. What Mari wants is to use the space this summer. She and her son will plant seedlings rather than seeds as it's already late in the season to start the vegetables she wants. They'll weed and water. Harry's welcome to some of the yield.

"My mom's garden is mostly herbs," Mari adds. "Levi and I are both pretty used to eating fresh, organic produce, and you know what the market is like." Harry does know. Everyone who's ever been in Clatcher's Market knows that the produce quality is marginal at best. Everything comes over from the mainland, and none of it is particularly fresh when it arrives.

Mari says, "Plus, Levi kind of needs a project to help him settle in. At least until he starts school and meets some people.

He was kept busy at God's … in South Carolina, where we lived." A slight flush covers Mari's face before she adds, "Bottom line, I want him to be happy here, and he's having a hard time."

Harry's first impulse is to say no. No to the idea of a neighbor using land that he's about to offer up for sale, no to having the intrusion of Mari and whatever past she's dragging anywhere near him. No to having a six-year-old who's already prone to running away get comfortable running in his direction. Isabelle, a lawyer, would freak out; there are a lot of places a child could get hurt. Jonathan wouldn't comment. He'd go for a jog.

"He's a really good kid," Mari says. "I promise he won't bother you."

"I'm planning to—"

"Go back and forth to Boston?" Mari interrupts. "No worries. Seriously. You don't need to do anything. We'll take care of the garden. I can even do a few yard chores for you, like weed or mow."

"Thanks, but—" Harry stops, realizing that it's too early to let anyone know of the plans to sell. The McGavins, as the only neighbors, will be most impacted. Little Great Island is a small community. Even a tiny change is felt by everyone, which means everyone has an opinion. And everyone feels the need to express it. Soon enough, getting the word out about the sale will be useful. Important even. But not yet. Not until the time is right.

Mari says, "You can have whatever you can eat from the garden whenever you're on the island. We can even harvest and clean it for you."

Some afternoons, years ago, Harry would come into the kitchen after whatever activity the family had been doing and find washed lettuce drying on a dish towel. Tomatoes sliced with cucumbers. For the first time in months, his salivary glands react. Ellie would have wanted the garden used.

"It's fine," he says.

"You are the best." Mari touches him again on the sleeve, and when she mounts the stairs to the market, Harry turns around and heads for home.

SUNRISE ON THE OPEN SEA

Mari

Levi, hunched in the deck chair next to Mari, is nearly asleep. Small wonder, Mari thinks. The sky has barely yielded its stars. The hum of the *Alice-Mari*'s engine is a lullaby. The insides of Mari's eyelids feel lined in sandpaper.

Her father, at the helm, is a silhouette against the first shades of dawn. In the two weeks Mari's been home, she and her father have talked lobster and island news and weather. Mari feels all the subjects unspoken between them waiting like a patient audience. Unlike her mother, her father won't push her. As a fisherman, he's used to days of silence, or perhaps his preferred conversation is with the sea. Mari, who'd developed the habit of assuring the newly planted vegetables at God's Bounty that she'd do her best to nurture them, had realized that this bond with the natural world was something she shared with her father. He spoke with the ocean; she with the land. Now the two of them are near a ledge, Little Great Island a half mirage on the horizon, and her father's blue-and-yellow buoys dot the shallows. He throttles back the engine. A quartet of gulls gathers above the stern. The water is as still as glass.

"Ready now," he says, and drops their speed again. As they approach the buoy, he grabs the gaff hook, watches the water, hooks the buoy line, and threads it in the hauler. Although age has slackened him and weather has left its lines, his muscles are still powerful.

"All right," he says. "Here we go."

The choreography of trap hauling comes back instantly. Mari, wide-stanced on the boat's starboard side like her father, watches the ocean until the trap appears, breaks the sea surface, and dangles midair. Her father reaches for it. He pulls it onboard. Even half asleep, her body readies for the rhythm of hauling and rebaiting traps: grab, pull, clean, plunge her gloved hand into the bait barrel to refill the bait bag.

Once the trap's on the boat and opened, her father sorts the catch by eye. Two lobsters too small for market go right back in the water. A good-sized lobster flails claws and legs as her father examines its underbelly.

"Berried," he says and clips a V-shaped notch from the creature's tail before dropping it overboard. The berries are actually eggs, and egg-bearing females are marked and released to help ensure the continuing health of the population. Once the traps are emptied and refreshed, the whole line goes back in the sea, and Mari and her dad head to the next one.

Shapes of other lobster boats become visible in the growing light.

"Mom wants you to retire," Mari says.

"Aye-yup." Her father's tongue probes his teeth. "She's thinking we ought to move to the mainland. Closer to doctors and the like."

"You going to?"

A shrug. "This here is what I want," her father says. "But hell, we're not getting any younger."

"Leave the island, though? I can't picture you on the mainland."

"Made some sense for a while there." Her father chews his lower lip. "Now that you're back, I'm not so sure."

Mari double-checks that Levi is still asleep. "I know you want to know what happened," she tells her father.

"Your story. I'm not going to pry."

But talking with her father is so much easier than talking with her mother. Mari briefly relates her first meeting with Pastor Aaron and Caleb: a couple of farmers selling produce in a parking lot, a parry about organic produce versus maximizing yield that was more flirtation than debate, an invitation from Pastor Aaron to visit the farm. What Mari doesn't mention is how the hair on her arms had stood straight, as if drawn to Caleb by magnetics. The last time she'd felt that way about a guy was Reggie, and that was back in high school.

"I barely noticed the religious aspects."

Her father is heading for the next trap line, but at half speed. No doubt he's giving her time to talk. His head tips slightly, meaning yes, he hears her.

It's true the farm was called God's Bounty, and the head farmer and his wife were addressed as Pastor Aaron and Sister Ann, but what did it matter? Everyone was welcoming. The other people who worked at God's Bounty, who were closer to Mari's age than she'd imagined, were strong and healthy looking from their work in the fields. She spent most of a day there, with Caleb showing her around and asking insightful questions in response to Mari's ideas about crop rotation and water management and fertilization techniques that didn't involve chemicals.

He was the one to dig his fingers into the ground and pour a handful of soil onto her palm. She caught his grin when she reflexively brought the dirt to her face and sniffed it. Inside the cow barn, he stood so close to her that she couldn't concentrate on what he was saying.

"Seemed like there were lots of opportunities to phase in some regenerative techniques, which was something I really wanted to do," Mari tells her father, trying to dismiss her husband's image as the next set of traps comes into view.

"Everyone seemed receptive to my ideas about farming in a way that reduces the negative environmental impact. I truly believed I'd found the life I wanted, one that brought together what I believed and what I'd learned and that could make a difference on an existing farm."

The engine slows again. Her father takes up the gaff hook, but this time he hands it to her, and they switch roles. The traps Mari hauls yield mud, seaweed, a dead crab, and a half-dozen lobster. Two are large enough to keep; the others are returned to the water.

Around the time Mari left for college, her father had brought in four or five hundred pounds of lobster a day. The season's still early, but so far his best day's been sixty pounds.

"All these damn changes," he says, shaking his head: the warming temperatures, the increasing salinity, the extreme tides, the death of one species and the thriving of others. The growth of aquaculture, the wind turbines, the severity of storms, the increase in boat traffic, the encroachment of foreigners, the tempers that burn in every discussion about how best to use and protect the bounty of the sea.

When Mari's father resumes his place at the helm and the line is overboard, he shifts the boat to neutral and swigs the coffee that's been sitting in the mug holder for an hour.

"I'm glad you found the life you wanted," he says. "Even if it turned out not to be with the right people." The set of his mouth tells her he hopes she'll say more.

It would be easier not to have to explain how she—the daughter of this imminently practical-minded man—managed to deny, justify, or overlook all the signs that she was heading into currents too powerful for her to escape. How everything made sense until the moment none of it did. True, there were always prayers before and after meals. Worship services on Sundays. Ministry meetings on Wednesday evenings. Mari had folded her hands and bowed her head because it seemed the polite thing to do. Caleb, next to her, pressed his leg against hers. Fondled her when no one was looking. He insisted there'd be no sex without marriage—it was strictly against God's Bounty rules, and neither of them wanted to risk eviction—but they did everything else every chance they got. And then he went down on one knee and proposed.

"Caleb's a good man, deep down." Positioning herself next to her father, Mari unwraps one of the sandwiches her mother made for their breakfast. The sun is fully risen now, a red-orange ball that stains both sea and sky. Levi will wake up again any minute. There are things that need to get said before that happens.

"But he changed," she adds. "Started believing that he was going to be the next God's Bounty pastor when Pastor Aaron retired." Chewing a mouthful of eggs and toast, Mari considers, swallows, and adds, "I changed too. I thought, with Caleb as eventual pastor, I'd have more influence over the farm, could do more things that were in harmony with the planet. Because of that, I started making even more excuses to myself about things that were happening. Rationalized. Let it go way too far. Didn't intervene when I should have."

Her father is watching the horizon as if something momentous might appear there. His coffee is forgotten in his hand.

"And then we got this biblical run of bad luck," Mari goes on, ironically emphasizing *biblical*, and is rewarded by her father's smile. "Everything from a late freeze to drought to fungus hit God's Bounty." She knew they needed to double down on their efforts at sustainability, that their troubles were the effect of climate change. But that wasn't the way others saw it.

"They blamed you?" her father guesses.

"Not at first. At least, not totally." But Pastor Aaron did start ignoring her advice. Fungicides and pesticides were reintroduced. Mari was consigned to spend most of her time in the kitchen with the other women. Worse, something about the way Caleb made love to her began to seem punishing rather than tender.

"In the end, wanting to farm my way was seen as selfishness."

"Put your trust in Him," Caleb said when she suggested that maybe their best bet was to work smarter rather than simply harder. He told her to stop acting like she knew more than everyone else.

"You're making everything worse," he said.

"Are you saying I'm making things between us bad?"

For a moment he hesitated, whatever it was he'd thought to say caught behind a scowl. "Not everything is about you," he said finally.

All that night, when Caleb didn't come back to their room, she promised herself she'd keep her mouth shut going forward. She would trust in the wisdom of those who had farmed in South Carolina far longer than she had.

Levi stirs and smacks his lips, and both Mari and her father turn to him.

"I guess what I want to know," her father says slowly, "is if you're okay. Now, I mean. With us. You and the boy."

How to explain how impossible it is for her to know? She'd told herself it was okay to be chastised for burned food, lost crops or animals, lack of cleanliness, lack of punctuality. Mari believed, after all, that waste was bad and that cleanliness and order were good. The Earth's resources should be respected and preserved. Communities needed rules and guidelines to function. Change came with a cost. She was the one who had pushed back against God's Bounty's focus on yield outcomes at all costs, and she'd accepted the early condescension and the occasional ridicule she received as part of the process. No one accepted change easily.

But there were things that weren't okay, although she found a way to live with them. There was the night she lost her temper at Caleb after Pastor Aaron had praised him for the new lambing shed. The shed had been Mari's idea. Mari had designed it, figured out ways to get recycled building materials to keep the costs low. Caleb accepted full credit, and when she snapped at him privately, he told her once to keep her voice down. Then he grabbed her by both wrists and forced her to her knees.

"You are my wife," he hissed. "You owe me your loyalty and obedience."

Levi was four then and adored his father. "Don't be bad, Mama," he said.

The next day, she had bruises from where Caleb's hands had been. Tears in his eyes, Caleb swore to God that such a thing would never happen again. Pastor Aaron expected so much of him. He was trying so hard to measure up.

"Our struggles are commensurate with our sins," he said. "Yet we can do all things through him who strengthens us."

Her mistake was to believe that by "him," Caleb had meant the Lord rather than Pastor Aaron.

"You still love him?" her father asks now.

Mari nods. Love doesn't have an off switch. She still has feelings but understands most of the time they will need to be extinguished for Levi's sake and for her own. Still, lying awake at night, she can't distinguish whether it was her inability to be satisfied that drew her to God's Bounty or that caused her to leave. Does she love Caleb, or is he another example of her restless quest for something more, something better, something different?

"He's Levi's father," she adds. "I didn't think I should leave." In the moments the thought occurred to her, she wasn't sure leaving was what she wanted. She reminded herself that Caleb, when his mood was right, would still pick her up and twirl her, making Levi laugh. She might see him coming across the driveway after a meeting with Pastor Aaron and feel that same frisson she'd had the first time she'd laid eyes on him. Even now, her body craves him, as if her cells have acquired an attachment of their own.

But then the yield dropped for a second year. The soil was exhausted. The temperatures too hot. The rain unforthcoming. Pastor Aaron began to damn the outside world more passionately as the ministry's donations dropped. The women weren't allowed off the farm because the influences of the outside world would sully them. Homeschooling was cancelled and the children put to work. Meals became even smaller. Mari suggested that she and Caleb and Levi find a place on a different farm, but Caleb wouldn't hear of it. They could not run from responsibility, he told her. Pastor Aaron needed him. She stopped herself from protesting that she and Levi also needed him because she couldn't afford to anger him. Levi went silent and stubborn when his parents argued, which got him punished. He'd started having nightmares, waking up crying in the night. Was it so wrong to hope that life could become good again?

"I prayed," Mari says, her voice quiet. Levi is still, but he could be awake now. He might be listening. "I didn't know what else to do." Somewhere in the midst of all that praying, she'd even come to believe God really had their well-being in mind.

"And then you left," her father says.

"Yes."

The tiny splash of a fish jumping nearby. A two-stroke engine from someplace far away. The sun has paled and yellowed. There was a moment that started it all. A dropped fork. The sudden silence. The shocked faces. Levi in the prayer shed. The stares of other passengers as she half-carried Levi to a seat on the bus.

"What about him?" her father asks. "You done with all that?"

Is there any chance she'll change her mind and go running back to Caleb, is what her father wants to know.

"It's over," she says. It has to be. "But I don't want to overwhelm Levi by dumping all this on him at once." It's possible that her marriage to Caleb wasn't even legal. The two of them signed something in the excitement of the day, but Mari can't remember what it said. Pastor Aaron had described it as a physical manifestation of God's commitment to their eternal love. She hadn't wondered where that document was or how legally binding it was until Levi fell asleep beside her on the bus heading north.

"Don't you go doubting yourself," Mari's father says. "You got a good heart and a good mind."

I'm not so sure about that, Mari thinks. Look at the mess she has gotten herself into. Look at what she let them do to her son.

"Be good if you could find a way to get along with your mother now you're back."

"I'm trying."

"All right, then," Mari's father says. He pushes the throttle forward, and she stands by the port-side coaming, feeling the breeze slide past. The air smells of fish and coffee. From one of the speakers near the helm, a voice drones about tide heights and times, temperature highs and lows, the prices for herring bait, fresh pogies, and frozen black cod. Her father flicks his glance in her direction for a moment before he speaks.

"Let's see if we can catch us a few more lobster. Bring something home to show for our day."

THE BUTTERFLY DIPLOMAT

Tom

Tom Estabrook, face lined as a felled apple, fights his head through the V-neck of his navy-blue sweater and looks around for his car keys. He's been a lawyer, a diplomat, a justice, the right hand of the Clintons, a patron of the arts, an early advocate for embryonic stem cell research, a husband, and a father, and now he's just a guy who can't find his keys. His tricolor mutt of a dog, named Jussi for an opera tenor in mockery of the animal's propensity for howling, stares at him with baleful eyes.

"The hell are they?" he says aloud. He checks the kitchen counters, the cushion cracks in the living-room couch, and every surface in the sunroom, where he'd spent the morning rereading a pile of articles about the effects of climate change on the Maine coast. The ocean around this island has warmed faster than pretty much every other body of water on the planet. New species of fish are swimming out there, preying on native creatures. Lobsters and clams have shell disease, mussels have disappeared, and monarch butterfly sightings are now rare. The ocean isn't alone in its suffering; invasive plants are taking over the state. In his life, Tom's been most places accessible to people with money and political influence. Every single one has a particular beauty, but right here is his favorite, and it seems to be dying faster than he is. But what's he supposed to do about it when he can't even find his keys?

The sound of a car pulling into his driveway: Alice McGavin, who climbs from her car with her arms full of groceries. Some of these islanders are like rocks you can stand on, Tom thinks. They are so reliable in their way. Kind of people you wished you saw more of in DC. And pretty soon, they aren't going to have a way to live out here. For that matter, he won't be here either. He's top of the list for a retirement center in Boston, his Boston home is sold, and this house is on the market. Sooner rather than later, the island will be returned to what's left of nature, but he won't be here to see it. Humans are the most invasive of species.

"Morning, Mr. Estabrook," Alice says.

"Morning."

When they reach the kitchen, Alice sorts food onto shelves with an efficiency that never ceases to impress Tom. She claims to like this gussied-up kitchen, with its granite counters and acres of cabinets. Efficient, she calls it. Tom finds it soulless. No doubt this business of the world seeming to have lost its moral compass is an artifact of his advanced age, but it feels real to Tom. He's spent his life trying to right wrongs. How can he plop himself in an easy chair at some fancy old folks' home now, when there are so many wrongs that need righting? Well, his kids don't see it that way, and he doesn't want them worried.

"I don't know what Harry Richardson does up there all day long," Alice says.

Tom makes noise to indicate he's listening. Harry. Is that why he needed...what? What was it he was looking for?

"And then he's up all night. I see his light on."

"All night, you say." Tom shakes his head. Richardsons are right on a migratory pathway. If you're patient, you might catch a glimpse of everything from a great cormorant to a belted kingfisher on the stretch of island that leads from their place to edge of the island known as The Cliffs.

"I once saw a juvenile bald eagle learn to fly," Tom says. "But now there's all that damn buckthorn."

Alice is standing a couple of inches away from him, regarding him oddly as he sorts through kitchen drawers. "You lose something?" she asks finally.

"Nope. I'm fine."

Alice fastens an apron around her waist and makes that nasal noise Priscilla, his wife, used to make when she was irked. Alice was worried about a man. Was that it?

"How's that husband of yours?" he asks.

Alice sprays cleanser on his countertops and attacks them with a rag. Her shoulders judder with the effort. "He's okay. It's Mari I'm worried about."

Mari. Tom remembers Mari. Smart kid. Mouthy.

Shoving his hands in his pockets, Tom discovers his missing car keys. Well, imagine that. Sometimes you can look and look without success, and then whatever you were looking for is right there all along.

ROOTBOUND

Harry

Harry stands in the smaller of the house's two living rooms, known as the children's living room, trying to assess where to start the day's cleaning. He's still not ready to face the second floor, although he finally got those sheets off his childhood bed. There have been no more appearances of Ellie's ghost, but he can hear her: water running in the upstairs bathroom, footsteps on the third floor, a muffled voice in the kitchen. No one is ever there. May is bearing down on him. He's made no headway on his Woodrow Wilson project. The lobster boats are out in droves, but the word is that last winter's storms have hurt the fishing, just as they hurt the necessary docks and businesses along the coast. Worry burrs the voices of Little Great Island's lobstermen and their families.

How are you doing? Isabelle texted first thing this morning.

Great! he replied. In return, he got a thumbs-up emoji.

Everything in the children's living room looks the same as it has every summer of Harry's life. Still there are the upright piano with its yellowed keys, the worn wood floor beneath rugs that were old in Harry's youth, the moisture-damaged copies of *The Wonderful Wizard of Oz* and *The Wind in the Willows*. Marathon games used to occur in this room while the adults were on the porch or in the back living room—the *adults'* living room—drinking gin and tonics or Bloody Marys. Sofa cushions still hold the indent of bodies. The same crack transects a corner of the big window that overlooks the street. Mr. Estabrook's foghorn of a voice still broadcasts at a frequency just out of Harry's hearing.

"Richard," Mr. Estabrook used to say to Harry's father after a second cocktail. "You got the best property on the island." How Harry's dad had loved that he'd bested The Butterfly Diplomat on something. And now Mr. Estabrook has beaten the Richardsons to market with his house.

The creak of wooden porch rockers lingers below the surface silence. Ellie's tennis shoes sit askew inside the door as if they had been kicked off moments earlier. In the kitchen, the open shelves are piled with plates and mismatched glassware. The deep double sinks yield the memory of Alice in front of them, rinsing dishes before loading them in the washer, and Mari talking nonstop with her head bent over some picture she was drawing. Harry imagines summers across decades that included Jonathan bringing Umeko to the island to meet the family; Isabelle announcing she was pregnant before she and Zach had even made it inside the house; Ellie, with her hair tucked behind her ears and a flailing lobster in one hand, chatting comfortably with Sam about lobsters' sensitivity to temperature changes and possible reasons why Maine's haul of lobsters had tripled in the past few decades. Even the massive, ancient stove with its eight burners, two baking ovens, and a warming oven is encrusted with memories. Ellie's specialty was fish chowder. She used to stand right there, in front of the stove, her cheeks pinked from a day on the family's sailboat, explaining the steps of cell division to Harry's father, who dubbed her "Harry's brain." For an instant, she is there, refusing to look at him. Refusing to speak.

Shit, shit, shit. Harry balls up the trash bag, throws it across the room. It goes nowhere, has no weight at all. He grabs a throw pillow, something needlepointed by an island woman, and slams it against the coffee table, only succeeding in bashing his finger. A roar builds in his chest, feeling powerful enough to be heard on the mainland. His fist aches to smash against the window. To feel the shatter and the pain.

But there, on the other side of the glass, are Mari and her son. The two of them contemplate the garden plot, which Mari has spent the past few days clearing of weeds. A wheelbarrow full of seedlings is parked beside them. The boy turns and, seeing Harry staring through the window, crinkles his face as though he might cry and leans into his mother. Mari turns, looks, bends to say something into her son's ear.

Even with the little time he's spent in the village, Harry's heard the gossip about Mari and her son. Mari won't tell anyone, even when questioned directly, what living in a cult had been like: why she stayed, why she left, whether she intends to remain on the island. Some people believe the little boy is mute. Others think he's developmentally delayed. Mari apparently went to Lydia for a job, but Lydia turned her down.

"She looks too strange," Lydia allegedly said to someone, who passed it to someone who felt the need to pass it to Sue Clatcher, who worked every job at the market and who was telling everyone who came by.

"She'd scare customers off," Sue told Harry, although Harry's heard plenty of people over the years talking about how Sue, in one of her frequent foul moods, was enough to send shoppers to the mainland for their food.

Mari waves and gestures for Harry to join them, but he shakes his head. He's dressed in flip-flops, a T-shirt, and fog-colored sweatpants, the same clothes he wore yesterday. The same clothes he slept in. He's just nearly smashed a window in front of them, and now he wants to outrun his own skin. He's in no shape to socialize.

"Cleaning," Harry shouts through the glass, retrieving the garbage bag to prove his point. Hard to know if Mari can hear him, but she beckons again. When Harry doesn't move, she says something to her son and heads toward the front door. Damn it. Now he's trapped. Rather than let her see the condition of the house, which has only deteriorated as he's pulled things off shelves and out of cupboards, Harry hurries outside.

"Come help us," she says.

"Sorry. Can't." A tip of his head toward the house is meant to indicate that all sorts of important and time-sensitive tasks await him.

"Too nice a day to be inside."

"I know. But I've got to work."

"Inside work is for later," Mari insists. She's wearing clean clothes and has her shaved head covered with a bandanna, but something in the way she speaks still seems flat. "For after it gets dark," she adds. "Come on." She reaches for his hand, which Harry snatches away instinctively. There was a single mom who put her hands over his in the middle of parent-teacher conferences about six months after Ellie's death.

"I'm here for you," she'd said. "If you need someone to take away your pain." As if that wouldn't have made everything worse.

To Mari, he stammers, "It's...I'm..."

"No excuses. We could use the help. Right, Levi?"

The boy's nod is nearly imperceptible, but Harry's objected as much as he can. If he doesn't help them, he's going to be trapped in the house for as long as they're here. If he does help them, they'll be done that much sooner.

"I like to keep my hands busy," Mari says as she leads him into the garden. "Let my mind do what it wants. Helps me think straight." She shoves a six-pack of plants toward him. Threadlike roots dangle from beneath the plastic tray. Some of the plants have sprouted yellow flowers.

"Best I could do on the mainland without a car," she says. "Dad brought me over on the boat."

"I don't even know what these are, never mind how or where to plant them."

"They're tomatoes," she says. "You can tell by the shape of the leaves. Or by the color. Or by the smell." Holding the tray up to Harry's face, she tells him to inhale.

"It smells like summer," he says.

"Exactly. Turned soil and fresh vegetables and mowed fields. That's what summer should smell like."

"Unless you live in the city, in which case everything smells like city."

"So why would anyone do that?"

To have a job you love. To live with the woman you love. Harry can feel Levi studying him. "Tomato plants have these little hairs on them, see?" the boy says. So he can speak. No doubt his sudden confidence comes from being with an adult who knows less than he does.

"I can see the differences between these plants and those," Harry says, pointing to the tray at Levi's feet. "But that still doesn't tell me what's broccoli and what's Brussels sprouts."

"Well, they have the words on them." Levi points to a sticker on the side of one of the trays. This kid is way ahead of him.

"Eventually you get to where you can tell the difference," Mari says. "I'll set the plants out where I think they should go, and we can plant together."

"How do you decide where they go?"

"You have to know what they like," Levi says. "You have to know who their friends are. Right, Mama?"

"Yes." Mari explains that plant likes and dislikes depend on drainage, sunlight, and spacing. By "friends," Levi means companion planting. Planting dill and basil among tomatoes, for example, helps deflect tomato hornworms. Spinach and Swiss chard benefit from the shade cast by corn. Thyme thwarts cabbage worm. There are combatant crops as well: Cabbage and tomatoes don't get along well at all. Onions stunt the growth of beans and peas.

"On top of all that, there's the pollinators. Certain types of plants attract particular pollinators, and certain pollinators are important to certain crops. Everything is interconnected. It all has to work together."

All three of them have been planting while Mari talks. "Did I overwhelm you?" she asks. "I love this stuff, and it's been a while since I got to talk about it."

"No. It's interesting." In fact, for nearly five minutes, the hard fist in Harry's chest had relaxed. "What's up with these guys?" He points to a row of seedlings sprawled on the dirt.

"Peas. I need to stake them," Mari explains. "Plus, everything's going to need water."

"I'm not very good with plants," he says. Or at keeping things alive.

"No worries. Levi and I will take care of them, and anyway, most of these guys are going to do fine. See how hard they are trying to grow? We only need to give them some space and some water."

Mari pushes another tray into Harry's hands. "No more lollygagging." Pointing with an outstretched trowel, she adds, "Over there. About eight inches apart." As soon as he's back to planting, she's back to telling him about replenishing minerals in the soil and increasing carbon uptake and how great it was to help the needy with the healthy food they grew on the farm where she'd lived.

"Is that why you decided to live there? You dropped out of school to help others?"

Mari shrugs. "A bunch of reasons," she says. "Bottom line, it seemed like a good fit." But then, she says, she discovered that the people she worked with thought climate change was God's will.

"Seriously. Like people had nothing to do with it. It astounds me how willing we are, as humans, to accept any explanation that absolves us of responsibility." Mari glances at Levi before continuing. "The people there listened to me at first." She doesn't reveal what happened later.

"What do you think climate change is going to do here?" Harry asks.

"Hard to say, but it's a decent bet the ocean levels will continue to rise. More flooding along the coast, which at the very least means a constant need to repair and replace the infrastructure critical to the fisheries. The lobsters are probably going to keep moving north to colder water. Or else they'll die. I heard that the only reason there are still any south of Canada is that glacier melt is keeping the ocean cooler than it might otherwise be."

"Are the people who live here year round talking about what to do?"

"They're talking. They know things are changing," Mari answers. It's hard to miss the flooding, the blowdown, the docks missing from the shoreline, the boats torn off their moorings, just as it's impossible for families whose income depends heavily on lobster landings not to notice that the lobster boom of the past few decades has dropped sharply.

"But it's like they can't fully conceptualize that a life that's persisted for so long could be going away forever. Or that all of us have had a hand in destroying it. I'm not only talking about lobster fishing here. All of us *humans*, no matter what we do for a living, can't seem to wrap our heads around the idea of planetary death. We deny evidence rather than accept the need to change. This island offers a unique lifestyle. One that can't be replicated on the mainland. Yes, it's incredibly hard to make a living, but this is what we want. People hate to admit they can't have the life they want."

So true. "Mainland life's not that easy either," Harry says.

"No. It's not," Mari agrees before adding, "A few people are trying to gear up for raising kelp or farming oysters, but that takes money. There are programs that offer funding to farmers wanting to do things more sustainably, but there's a learning curve and a significant time investment. In some cases, there's oversight, meaning you lose autonomy and control. In other cases, you give up ownership, which a lot of farmers don't want to do. They see it as giving up."

For a while, they plant in silence apart from Levi asking his mother a question in a quiet voice, and Harry wonders what made the gregarious daughter of his atheist neighbors join a religious cult. He'd tried three times to find solace in religion when Ellie was dying. Each time was an abject failure. As far as he's concerned, the whole religion thing is hocus-pocus.

"My wife always talked about reviving this garden," Harry says. They'd also talked about having children. Future planning. What hubris that turned out to be.

"I'm sorry."

"I think she would have enjoyed it."

Mari says, "Too bad more people don't have gardens on the island. The soil here is good. It's deep. It holds water."

"Why don't they?"

"You'd have to ask them."

But Harry can imagine the reasons. Life and lobster-ing take time and energy, and if there's any time left over, there's probably better money to be made working for the summer population.

"Stop," Levi says. "Don't hurt them." He points at the tray of plants in Harry's hands, from which Harry has been trying to free seedlings. When Harry looks up at the boy with a question on his face, Mari laughs. Pulling a pair of scissors from a canvas bag she'd dropped earlier in a corner of the garden, she tells him to cut the plastic. But not the roots.

"What are these, anyway?" Harry asks Levi, to see if the boy can answer him, and Levi says without looking up, "Kale."

Which Harry's never even considered eating. "You guys can keep all the kale," he says. "I'm more of pancakes kind of guy."

"You eat pancakes?" Levi asks, aghast.

"'Course I do. Doesn't everyone eat pancakes?"

"But only for special. Right, Mama?"

Harry notices that Mari won't meet his look. "At my house, pancakes aren't only for special occasions," he says.

Levi demands, "But who cooks them?"

Well, no one now. But that doesn't mean he's incapable. "I do."

"No, you do not."

"I do, though. In fact, pancakes are my specialty." Why does this seem so inconceivable to Levi? Does he think men are incapable of cooking? Or does he sense some insufficiency in Harry personally?

Harry adds, "I'll prove it to you."

"How?"

"I'll make you breakfast." Instantly, Harry regrets the offer. Having Levi in the house means having Mari in the house, and having her in the house feels wrong in a dozen different ways. Mari McGavin in the kitchen is the past, the way things were back before he'd even met Ellie, even if Mari is no longer eight. The fact that she is a grown woman and a mother makes the whole thing even worse. Ellie should be the one in the red farmhouse with him. Their child should be the one making his way through a plate of pancakes dripping with syrup.

"When?" Levi asks.

The best answer Harry can give is, "We'll see."

LEAH'S KNUCKLE

Mari

"Want to climb The Knuckle?" Mari asks Levi. The seedlings are planted. Levi's tired from the morning spent in the sun but seems happy. The sore on his tongue no longer bothers his speech. It's time they talked. Levi doesn't agree, but he doesn't disagree, which seems consent enough.

"Do you want to ask me any questions about why we're here?" she asks as they walk the path through Harry's fields toward The Knuckle.

Levi hesitates, then shakes his head.

"How about what happened at God's Bounty and why we had to leave?"

Levi shakes his head again and pulls his hand from hers. The spring wind strokes Mari's face. The need to hire a lawyer keeps her awake at night and chases her in the daytime. It's probably best for her to file for divorce before Caleb does. She can't keep pretending that she can take his son and disappear without repercussions. But lawyers cost money, and she can't find a job, plus Levi needs her full attention right now. Borrowing from her parents has to be an absolute last resort. She knows from overheard conversations that her mother is worried about their retirement savings. One of her mother's reasons for wanting to move to the mainland is so she and Sam can get jobs with regular paychecks before they are too old. Besides, grown children aren't supposed to come back broke and shorn, towing the child of a man they never met and expecting their parents to support them.

"That's Leah's Knuckle," Mari tells Levi, pointing. The Knuckle is part of the Richardsons' property, but everyone on the island climbs it for the exercise, for the view, or simply to remind themselves of all the times they've climbed it before.

"I already know that."

Ignoring his tone, Mari clenches her right hand into a fist and shows Levi her knuckles. "Someone a long time ago thought that little hill reminded them of one of the knuckles on your hand, so that's why it's called a knuckle. Leah was my great-great grandmother, which makes her your great-great-great grandmother. More than a hundred years ago, this whole end of the island was a farm that belonged to my family. Your family."

Back then, the McGavin farm had been more than a hundred acres, occupied by her ancestors, horses, milk cows, cattle, sheep, pigs, and chickens. It had produced wheat, corn, barley, potatoes, peas, beans, wool, butter, milk, and hay. Those early McGavins had fished and farmed, profiting from the mainland's demand for cod and mackerel and from the lamb and beef that were said to be among the best in the country. Everything they harvested or caught sold, along with the pies and sauces the women made from apples and berries. And then the cod disappeared. The Little Great Island economy collapsed.

Levi asks, "Why don't we live in that house?"

She knows he means the big red farmhouse. "We just don't, honey." Economic disparity is more than Mari can explain right now to a child who never laid eyes on currency until he saw her purchase their bus tickets. Truthfully, it wasn't solely the cod's disappearance that forced her ancestors to sell. Trains and trucks became faster and cheaper than ferries for moving food up and down the Atlantic seaboard. The government introduced hygiene standards for meat and dairy that were beyond the capability of any of the island's farmers. Vacationers migrated up from Boston and New York City, looking for alternatives to Cape Cod summers, and fell for the idea of themselves as hardy pioneers when the fog soaked their bread and their bath towels. A sunny day with a sailing breeze was sufficient to convince them they'd discovered the Garden of Eden, and they were happy to buy up the farms and houses the island natives were obliged to sell. The Richardsons bought the McGavins' farm with the exception of the three acres her great grandparents had held onto and, over time, allowed much of their property to go wild. The rest— some twelve acres of cleared land—consists of The Knuckle, lawn, fields, the house, a barn that's been converted to a garage, and a few dozen additional acres of shrubs, spruce, and grasses that lead to the edge of the island, a ledgy area with a lone picnic table known as The Cliffs.

Levi asks, "When are we going to go home?"

"I don't know, honey."

"Is it because of me?" Levi asks. "Is that why Pastor Aaron cut off your hair?"

Mari takes a deep breath. "No."

The morning everything exploded, Mari was sitting between Caleb and Levi on the long benches of Home House's dining table. Caleb, lost in whatever thoughts concerned him, was silent as he chewed his food. The room sang with the chatter and clatter of Mari's God's Bounty family. When Levi's fork fell, Mari hardly noticed, but a split second later, Levi's voice detonated everything.

"God damn it."

The hands of the ministry faithful dove into laps and heads bowed. Everyone was a statue except for Levi, who was in the process of lifting a leg over the bench, freeing himself so he could climb under the table for his fork. Mari stilled him with a hand, gave him a look that brought him back to her side. The profanity was her fault. She'd never subscribed to the notion that a word could be good or bad. It was merely a tool, and she had said as much to Levi, along with the admonition that he only use those kinds of words in private. Not curbing her own tongue had been her first mistake. Her second, she realized as Levi cowered against her side, was a lack of clarity with him about what, exactly, she'd meant by private.

In that horrific silence, Mari kept her hand over Levi's, but her attention was on Caleb. He loved his son. He was a good man. He would find a way to protect them all from Pastor Aaron's wrath. But Caleb was so motionless his breathing seemed stopped.

"The Lord's name has been taken in vain," Pastor Aaron said from the head of the table.

The table murmured a chorus of, "Lord, forgive us."

"Brother Caleb, would you and your family join me in my office, please?" Pastor Aaron asked. His voice, as always, was quiet.

Holding her son's hand, Mari trailed the men down the enclosed breezeway that connected Home House's common rooms to the sleeping quarters, across the dirt drive and into the white clapboard house where Pastor Aaron lived with Sister Ann.

"The evil is unveiled," he said as soon as he was seated. To Mari's horror, his look was directed at Levi and not at herself.

Mari's still not sure how much of what happened next Levi was able to comprehend. His nightmares have lessened.

In the past week, there's only been one instance of him wetting the bed. All good signs, she's promised herself. All signs that the trauma is fading.

From the top of Leah's Knuckle, Mari sees a door open and hears it slap shut at the Richardsons' house. Harry clomps down the steps and makes his way into the fields. For no discernable reason, he stops in the midst of a patch of forage grasses and buckthorn and begins a slow survey of the land around him.

"What's he doing?" Levi asks.

"I don't know."

Levi says, "I want to go home."

By home, she knows he means God's Bounty. Is he craving the familiar? Or exhibiting signs of some kind of Stockholm syndrome? The Internet abounds with theories about how people become enmeshed in cults and the emotional and psychological challenges they face in breaking free. Those explanations both make sense and don't, because how can she have become the person they describe?

Mari says, "Sweetie, we can't right now."

"But how long do we have to stay here?"

Oh, how Mari would love to lie to protect his feelings. But she has allowed herself the comforts of ignoring reality long enough.

"For a long time," she says.

"Forever?"

Mari presses her fingertips into her forehead. Maybe Caleb won't pursue her. Why would he come after someone who has caused him such problems with Pastor Aaron and who gets in the way of him becoming the next pastor? Does he even still love Mari? Wouldn't it be easier to let her go and find a more compliant wife? No. Because of Levi.

"Yes," Mari tells Levi. "This is where we live now."

"I don't want to," he cries. "You're a bad, bad person. Pastor Aaron says so. Papa says so." Pushing past her, Levi quicksteps down the granite, moving too fast for safety. Mari hurls herself after him, calling his name, and sees, from the edge of her vision, that Harry has also given chase.

DEEP NIGHTTIME

Little Great Island

Deep nighttime. Stars blaze in a blue-black sky. Lobster boats doze at their moorings, the bows all facing the wind. The *Abenaki Princess*, in her berth, is lit for safety. Carol Stanley's office is dark. Herring gulls tuck their feet and necks, huddling themselves into sleep. From their ragged regiment in the fields on the island's northeast slope, the ancient and abandoned apple trees have ceased photosynthesis for the night. Children drift in the scent of cooking suppers, and men note the time by the sky color, judge the forecast by the smell of the air.

In the gray-shingled house near the sea, Levi swings his feet on a chair, his mouth moving slightly as Salt and Peppa chase each other in a circle on the kitchen table. Sam sits at the table as well, rubbing the prickling numbness from his arm and fingers. Opposite him, Alice peels the skin off sweet potatoes, her lips pressed together tightly, while Mari chops a handful of parsley into dust.

Harry, in his own house, at his own kitchen table, rereads a sentence about Woodrow Wilson for the third or fourth time while Ellie's ghost walks the upstairs hallway, the floorboards creaking beneath her tread. In The Sweet Shoppe kitchen, warmed by a double-oven stove, Lydia works a sudoku in a book her sister sent from her retirement home in Florida and rehearses, in her mind, the nighttime steps she has taken. The front door is locked. Blinds are pulled across the windows. The oven is off, and the pastries are covered. Frank Clatcher has been told he can wait another damn month for his rent, and if that's not okay, then he can go ahead and evict her. See if that makes him face up to the fact that the reason he's such a pain in the butt sometimes is he's still ashamed, all these years later, that he suggested marriage once and she told him no chance. But for pity's sake, she's more than a decade older than he is, and it's not as if there was anything between them that could be called love or even affection. She draws an eight in one of the empty boxes and stares at it a moment before erasing it, refilling the space with the number two.

Across the island, Tom Estabrook emits a strangled snore from his position on the chair that used to be his wife's, back before she died. The book on his lap is a treatise on the environmental impacts of modern agriculture techniques. His hand still rests on the page detailing the epic increase of reactive nitrogen in the soil, air, water, and rainfall, all of it originating in synthetic fertilizers. Jussi's forepaw twitches.

The garlic mustard flowers, a spider weaves, the stars grow brighter, and a female lobster, freed of her hardened shell, is flipped gently on her back by the male who has won the right to mount her.

THE YELLOW HOUSE ON
MAIN STREET

Reggie

In the yellow house on Main Street, Reggie Clatcher wakes up with last night fouling his tongue and notices a wooden chair on its side in the middle of the room. The sight of it ramps a pain in his shin. Sunlight hurts. His body is freezing. Almost five years, down the drain.

Goddamn Mari McGavin, holding up her hand with the ring on one finger. Telling him what the two of them had was all in the past now, where it needed to stay.

That first sip was so easy. A quick shot. Something to take the edge off because hell, even without hair, Mari has something that gets him going.

Second shot to tamp the anger. One more, because there was always time to quit again if she stuck around or got divorced.

The early May morning keeps on with its stabs of light and noise.

Next door, outside the post office, the postmaster—Clive Stanley—calls to his wife, Carol, to see if she's bought him cigarettes.

"Do I look like your personal shopper?" she replies.

Reggie, shivering beneath his blankets, hears the exchange as if it occurred in his room. His head feels like someone ran a propeller in it all night long.

"You see Mari McGavin was in the village again yesterday, right around the time the boat come in?" Clive says in lieu of answering his wife's question.

"And I care why?" Carol responds.

Curled against the cold, Reggie tucks his hands between his thighs. Pulls his chin to his chest. Tries to work his shoulders to his ears. Never in his life has he had a problem scoring women. He looks good—could have figured that out on his own, but enough girls told him along the way that he was sure of it—and he came up with a way of checking out a girl that hooked them every time. Mari was just another girl, although far and away the hottest girl on the island at the time. That whole year they were together, he kept his eye out for whoever might be next when he was done with her. But when Mari left for college, it was like she ripped the guts right out of him. He wouldn't call or visit for just that reason: He had to prove he wasn't in too deep. But then she was back on the island that Thanksgiving, and it was...holy shit. Like riding a hurricane bareback, and not only the fucking. All of it. Telling her things, like how he wanted to be a boatbuilder on the mainland and not work for his dad. Mari telling him he could do it because he was smart and good with his hands. Even Bob, who'd been his main man at the time and had a thing for model boats, hadn't done much more than grunt when Reggie said they ought to go into boatbuilding together. But with Mari, there were all those stars on the black sky and their breath going to clouds as the inside of the car got colder, and everything he told her seemed possible because she believed it could happen. He was right up against saying that they ought to get married. He actually said the word "love."

Then she went back to college like he was nothing, so he hadn't texted or emailed. He ignored his phone when she called to prove to himself that he could. Everything went to shit after that.

"Winthrops made an offer on Mr. Estabrook's place," Clive says from outside the window. "Younger generation, not Mike and Wendy." No response from Carol.

One car rolls down Main Street, and then a second. A cat sounds its hunger, a tire grinds gravel, a saw whines against a plank of wood. The post-office door huffs closed, and Reggie folds his arm over his face. He closes his eyes, inhales as much air as he can handle, and then forces himself to sit.

IT'S STILL A MAYBE

Harry

Harry got fewer than three hours' notice that Pete and Abby were on the island.

"Kind of a last-minute decision," Pete boomed into the phone, but despite the volume, there was a tentativeness in his friend's voice, a new self-protectiveness threaded into an invitation to dinner. The caution was deserved, because even though Harry can't remember all of what happened when they were together over a month ago, he does know that Pete and Abby confiscated his keys and forced him to Uber home. He does know that the next morning, April Fool's Day, he felt as though the insides of his head had been scraped off a highway on a hot summer day.

Pete said, "Abs and I figured if you could brave the island this early in the season, so could we. So. Dinner? Come at six-ish."

Harry said yes. He and Pete have been friends since freshman year at Groton, and Harry was the one who introduced Pete to Little Great Island that same year. He also introduced him to Abby, whose family had owned a home on the island for a couple of generations. Once Pete and Abby were married and spending a week in her parents' house every summer, Abby had in turn introduced him to Ellie, whom she'd met at college. With all that history, Harry felt he couldn't say no to the invitation, and yet now, sitting in their living room with its two-story window splashed with the colors of sunset, he wishes he stayed home. Home, where he'd found an old copy of Stephen King's *The Shining*, warped and blurred by salty air and the passage of time. Insomnia seems to have moved in with him along with Ellie's ghost, but at least he has Stephen King to keep him company.

"I hope you're hungry," Abby says, setting a plate on the coffee table. Pointing from one round of runny cheese to the next, she says, "Camembert, Roquefort, this one's an Abondance, and that's Reblochon. We aren't eating healthy tonight, but I hope we're eating well. I convinced Pete to bring up a couple of his precious red wines, and I've done my best with *coq au vin*."

Harry feels Ellie's ghostly presence behind him and hears her make some appreciative noise despite the fact she'd never been much of a foodie. Her breakfast, such as it was, occurred while standing at the kitchen counter, thumbing her cell phone with her free hand. Lunches, if she ate them, came from a vending machine at work.

Would she have tried Abby's cheeses? Would she have wished Harry could get himself together to cook something other than canned soup? Would she have called Abby's *coq au vin* "drunk chicken" and kidded that Harry was now going to be known as the drunk chicken as far as the Shaws were concerned?

The day after getting drunk at the Shaws' house, Harry started crying in the classroom. Tears out of nowhere. His kids were dumbstruck until he excused himself and hid in the faculty restroom. The administration knew about the event before he even emerged. Two girls were so upset by his outburst that they had to leave school. By the end of the day, he was put on leave.

"It all looks and smells delicious," Harry says now.

Abby parks herself directly in front of him. "How *are* you?" she asks. "We've been so worried."

"Focused on getting the house in shape," he says.

"You've gotten so skinny."

Harry shrugs. "You know what the food thing is like on the island." There's an awkward moment in which he contemplates Abby's exotic cheese tray, imported from a suburban Boston specialty store. It can be challenging to get certain food items on the island at various times, but it's not like food is in short supply. The problem is that his appetite is gone.

"I'm sorry about last time," he says. "Clearly, I had too much to drink."

"No worries!" Abby proclaims, but that night she had stormed down the stairs in her white quilted robe and ordered him to leave. Shamed him, in short, although he deserved it. There were children asleep upstairs. He'd been shouting.

"You guys are good to me," he says, which produces an awkward silence.

"No problem," Pete says finally.

Scraping a dab of the least runny of the cheeses on a cracker, Harry asks, "So, how goes life in the world of high finance?"

"Things are good."

"*Good* good?"

"Very good."

"That's good."

Banters like this were part of what drew Harry and Pete together more than twenty-five years earlier, but now it's the best Harry can do when it comes to understanding Pete's work. Venture capitalists use money to make money, Pete told him back when he first headed to business school. Over the course of the next fifteen years, the explanation has gotten progressively more laden with jargon: sector dynamics, deal pipelines, post money valuations. The more incomprehensible the explanation, the richer Pete seems to grow and the less Harry understands his friend's life choices. The house Harry's sitting in right now, for example, was the island's number-one gossip topic during its construction. Pete and Abby tore down the farmhouse that had stood in this spot for a century to make room for their new summer home and tripled their sin by building a window-centric behemoth that demanded to be seen by every boat entering the harbor. They'd also ignored the high probability that the more turbulent hurricanes generated by climate change would blow shattered glass everywhere.

Pete was unruffled by the talk. "Other people's opinions are not my problem," he's said, and Harry's wondered at the attitude. As a teacher, he is constantly subjected to the criticisms of students, parents, colleagues, and administrators. He has to listen to what others think of him. A lack of approbation could cost him his job.

A glass of wine takes the edge off the tension. Abby updates him on the twins, who are with her parents for the weekend and who are finishing first grade and doing well. The family went to Vieques for spring break, Pete says. "Lovely spot. Out of the way." Abby is hoping for a wine tour of France in the coming months.

"Dinner," Abby announces. The brass maritime clock on the mantel says it's well after eight. Harry's rationed his wine intake, not wanting to repeat his last mistake, but he's finished two healthy-sized glasses. The cheese he's eaten to dull the effects of alcohol sits heavily in his stomach. As he follows Pete and Abby to the dining room table, he realizes he doesn't want more food. But what choice does he have? He's not going to say or do anything that makes his friends worry even more.

The three of them tiptoe their way through dinner, one fragile conversational topic after another. They've already covered the frailty of an economy built on ocean resources in today's world, the difference Mr. Estabrook's departure from the island is going to make, the dysfunctionality of the Massachusetts Department of Transportation's approach to infrastructure maintenance, and politics great and small by the time Pete asks, "How are things out on your end of the island?"

"Fine," Harry says.

"How's the house?"

"Still a bit of a mess, but I'm making headway." Not a total lie, but progress is slow. He's fallen into a routine of drinking coffee on the front porch until Mari and Levi arrive and then either standing by the garden while they work or pitching in to help them for twenty minutes or so. Two weeks ago, when Levi had taken off running, Harry went after him by instinct. It was clear from the way the boy sobbed while he ran that he wasn't watching out for cars.

"Hey," Harry had called. "Hey!" Then he remembered Levi's name and shouted that, becoming gradually aware that Mari was behind him, calling her son as well. They were practically at the ferry landing when Harry managed to grab hold of Levi's arm.

"Hang on there, buddy," he said, expecting Levi to try to pull out of his grasp. Instead, Levi buried his face in Harry's stomach, both arms encircling Harry's waist. Harry patted the boy's back tentatively until Mari caught up with them, and then he looked to her for guidance, but her expression was impossible to read. Terrified. Guilty. As confused as Harry himself was about why Levi was clinging to him. By the time Levi calmed down, he was too worn out to walk, and Harry ended up carrying the boy back to the McGavin's house. Levi fell asleep in his arms.

"Have you seen Mari McGavin?" Pete asks.

"I have. She and her son have resurrected Mom's old vegetable garden."

"I heard she's run away from a cult."

Was it a cult? Probably. But the things Mari's told him don't seem cultlike: the various needs and behaviors of chickens. Using something called rotational grazing to reduce worm loading in lambs. Every once in a while, Mari stops whatever she's doing to listen to a crow call or a boat engine putter. Sometimes, as far as he can tell, she's simply watching a puff of wind riffle the leaves. She always inhales deeply before returning to her work. Is that a sign of religious fanaticism? Hopefully not, because Harry, discreetly, has started to imitate her. For a few moments afterward, his head and heart feel clear.

"I'm not sure what happened with all that," Harry says.

Abby says, "She waylaid Pete in town. Wanted to know if we needed someone to clean or watch the boys this summer. I got the feeling she's sort of desperate. Small wonder. Who on this island is going to want a Jesus freak lurking around their property, never mind spending time with their children?"

The phrase, applied to Mari, rankles. "She's never said word one to me about religion," Harry says. Mari doesn't, in fact, say much about her personal life. Harry senses there's a lot bothering both her and Levi, but he's not going to pry.

"That wasn't the worst of it," Pete says. Pushing his plate away, he crosses his arms on the table and leans in. "Get this. I tell her 'no, thanks' on the cleaning and babysitting, and she wants to know if she can put sheep on our property. Abs and I hadn't been on the island two hours. We were still trying to get settled in. I had Jack Adams at the house, going through the furnace. And here's this bald religious nut bending my ear about how sheep keep the grass mowed and provide fertilizer and about how she's trying to make a living and support her son. Your poor planning, as they say, is not my problem."

Abby jumps in. "What was she going to do if we said yes? She lives way on the other side of town. Believe me, I don't want to end up taking care of a bunch of sheep for her. That's part of why I never let the twins have a pet. I knew I'd be the one caring for it in the end."

"She did not want to take no for an answer," Pete adds, and Harry remembers ten-year-old Mari, fists on hips, yelling full volume at nineteen-year-old Pete in the middle of the village. Pete's sin had been to leave his trash on one of The Sweet Shoppe's outside tables—a demonstration of egregious privilege and of illiteracy in Mari's opinion, given the very clear signs about the need to clean off tables because of the gulls. His napkin had blown into the street. When Mari told him to pick up his trash, he ignored her. Second time she asked, her voice prickled with fury, but Pete rolled his eyes and asked who was going to make him. Mari shouted loud and long enough to gather a small crowd, but the worst part for Pete was clearly that Abby was watching. He couldn't stand being shamed by a child in front of his girlfriend. Finally, red-faced, he had to throw away the napkin, cup, and spoon he'd left on the table.

"That girl is fucking nuts," he said then, loudly enough for everyone to hear.

Now, Pete continues, "Told me she was trying to pull money together to pay a usage fee. Like that was going to make a difference to us. And then she tried to make me feel guilty that we have land that the year-round population can't use."

"Hello? Private property," Abby says.

"Hello?" Pete echoes. "We paid a lot of money for this land, so I'm not sure why we should let someone else use it for free. Plus, we do pay taxes here. A lot of taxes."

Asking to use the Shaws' property was ill-considered at best, but it hardly seems like a crime. After all, Harry agreed to let her use a piece of his property.

"She's trying to figure out a way to make a living," he says.

Abby stands and reaches for Harry's plate to clear it. "Seriously," she says. "Did Mari offer to come clean up all the lamb poo? No, she did not. Did she offer to spray or otherwise remediate whatever bacteria and ticks and who-knows-what get all over our land? No, she did not."

"I'm sure she would have done those things if you'd asked," Harry says. Abby is pissing him off right now. All Mari did was ask a question.

"The point is, she didn't offer anything." Pete hands his plate to his wife and thanks her before adding, "You know how everyone always called her the wild child? Nothing's changed, as far as I can tell. Still as pushy as ever. Still just as entitled."

"Entitled is not a word I would use to describe her," Harry says. What about people who go to Vieques? People who go on international wine tours? Abby flicks Harry a quick look, as if she heard his thoughts, and his face flushes.

"I'm sure she was fine with a simple no," he says.

Abby snorts, but it's time to drop the subject. Pete reaches to refill Harry's glass. Harry tells him no thanks—his snarky thoughts are a tip-off he's already had more than enough—but Pete pours anyway.

"Can't let this bottle go to waste," he says, and even though Harry swears to himself he won't drink it, he takes a sip. Abby gathers the remainders of dinner things from the table and announces they'll take a break before dessert.

"I'll put coffee on," she says. "You boys catch up."

Although the living, dining, and kitchen areas are all part of one large room, Abby's turned back suggests she's left Harry and Pete to talk privately. The equivalent of men adjourning for a cigar, Harry thinks, not kindly, although there was a time when the men did the dishes and Ellie and Abby chatted.

"Let's go over to the more comfortable chairs," Pete says.

The real reason for his presence here this evening, Harry understands, is about to be revealed. Pete brings both his own glass and the wine bottle with him. Even though Harry attempts to abandon his wine, Pete reprimands him.

"Waste not, want not," he says.

Exhaustion overcomes Harry in the space of a heartbeat. "I really should get going soon," he says. "It's late." Nearing eleven. The roads will be dark and quiet. He's forgotten to leave a light on at the farmhouse for his return. The McGavins have a motion-sensitive light over their barn door, but that's likely to be the only illumination on the whole peninsula unless Mari's up. Two of the second-story windows often glow dimly from the McGavins' house until after midnight. Whenever Harry's been awake and wandering, he's checked for that light. It makes him feel less alone.

Pete interrupts his thoughts. "I've got a proposition for you." That same forward-leaning posture, only this time the wine glass is held in both hands.

"Which is?" Harry braces himself for some suggestion he wants no part of: A date with some friend of Abby's. An entry-level position at some venture capital firm because Pete has decided it's time for him to have a "real" job.

"You floated the idea of selling your place up here," Pete says.

Tentatively, Harry nods. He must have mentioned it the night he got drunk. "It's still a maybe," he says.

"The thing is, I may have someone who's interested."

Harry flinches. "The house isn't actually on the market," he says. "It's still full of stuff." Suddenly he feels as if he's scrambling for purchase on a steep slope. "The sibs and I still have a lot of things to work out."

"This guy's quite interested."

"Someone who knows the island? Who knows the house?"

"No," Pete says. "He's a developer."

Harry nearly spits his wine. "A developer of *what*?" He pictures a strip mall, a cluster of identical houses. No developer in his or her right mind would want property in a tiny community located fourteen miles from the mainland.

"Executive retreats. High end. This guy makes a business, a good business, in this sort of thing." Pete's got more to say about Duncan Development, whose properties are all on islands or in other remote locations. Five-star accommodations. Renowned chefs. Small, exclusive inns that have state-of-the-art meeting rooms and unique recreational opportunities which, according to Pete, could be kayaking, accompanying a lobsterman on daily rounds, or guided nature walks on Little Great Island. "Cross-country skiing or snowshoeing in winter," Pete adds. "Because why not?"

Because the ferry crossing is rough and freezing in winter. Because the island lacks trails. Because it's icy and cold and dark out here, the power unpredictable. You need an iron resolve, a few cords of wood, and the trust and support of the community, not a PowerPoint presentation and a closet full of custom-made shirts.

"Sounds like a nonstarter to me," Harry says, and is on the verge of segueing into thank you and goodnight when Pete adds, "Estabrook snapped up the only residential buyer this island's likely to see this year or next. My guy is actively searching for property. He's got funding. He's ready to move. You really need to give this some thought."

Pete's got a point, so Harry says, "Sure. Fine." But the whole thing is ridiculous. Little Great Island needs an executive retreat like it needs a ballet school. "I'll talk to Jon and Iz."

"You'll get back to me? Soon, though, because Duncan's got options. There are other properties out there."

"Okay," Harry says and manages to get himself as far as the door before Pete grabs him by the shoulder and says, "This is an opportunity, Harry. Don't let it get away."

JINX

Mari

Mari's leaned into her bike pedals, her shoulders bent against the May rain, when Bob and Sue's monster of a truck passes her, spraying water on her legs. The truck pulls over, and the window rolls down.

"Get in," Sue says.

"I'm okay."

"Jesus fucking Christ, Mari. Enough with the martyr bullshit. Throw your bike in the back and get in the damn car."

Mari does, smiling to herself. Sue had learned to swear—from Reggie, unsurprisingly—when she was seven and had taken to it with pleasure. But then, already shivering from the wet and cold, Mari feels a frozen stab in her chest. She presses her head against the car window, needing the solid resistance of it to remind her that she's not in Pastor Aaron's office, not watching her son being led away by his father while she's being told she is expelled from God's Bounty.

Sue interrupts her thoughts. "So, what, you thought you'd go out for a spin around the island? Get a little exercise on this lovely spring day?"

"Something like that."

Sue side-eyes her. "You are so full of shit, Mari McGavin."

"I think we established that a long time ago," Mari says. The two of them have gotten together a half-dozen times since Mari's return. Their friendship returned to normal almost immediately when Sue, eyeing Mari's head, said, "Even in kindergarten, you sucked with scissors."

Now, Sue's pinked lips twitch a quick smile. "True that," she says.

The radio bass is on max, in true Sue style. The windshield wipers flap at the downpour. Mari's thighs are shaking, and Sue must notice because she cranks the heat to high, bumps the fan up as far as it goes.

"Still no luck on the job front?"

"Nope." Mari's gone practically door-to-door asking for work of any kind. She'll clean, she'll babysit, she'll mow lawns or paint walls, but what she suggests most frequently is cultivating and helping to maintain small vegetable gardens like the one she's created on Harry's land. It's easy to throw tools in a backpack and get anywhere on the island by bike. People—summer visitors or island dwellers—could have fresh produce harvested right outside their back door. Why would anyone say no? Yet they do. The Shaws' property is perfect for sheep, but they acted like Mari had suggested hosting the next Woodstock. Why is it so hard for people to agree to responsible use of their land?

"Everyone's afraid you're going to tell them to pray over their eggplant," Sue says.

"The only thing I tell them is that they don't need chemicals."

"That's voodoo enough for some."

Mari says, "I really don't understand my fellow humans."

"Well, don't look to me for explanations. Remember my family."

Sue's mother died young of a heart attack. Mari has faint memories of a huge woman who spent her days picking crabmeat from shells and packing it into plastic containers. There were always candy bars and pastries in the house, along with such exotica as Cheez Whiz, sour cream dip, and potato chips in a variety of flavors. Frank is a Santa Claus, but Mari's seen his temper, and it isn't pretty. After school, Reggie, Sue, and Mari went to the boatyard, where Frank would greet them with snacks, smiles, and questions about their day, but he'd made it clear before Sue was ten that she was responsible for running the household. The businesses would be handed over to Reggie. Frank only grudgingly agreed to the possibility of changing his mind after Sue fled the island for EMT training and then stayed on for nursing school. Even then, Mari suspects, his change of heart was only to make her come back after Reggie developed such fondness for drink; he wanted Sue to deal with her brother.

"Did you ask your dad if he'll hire me?"

Sue laughs. "He says not until you learn to do as you're told."

"I promise to do whatever he says. Or whatever you say."

"Like we haven't all heard that before. Besides, he says you're going to need to be around for a while, act normal. But maybe when the season picks up. You could try asking him then."

They are on the outskirts of the village now, coming from the opposite side from the road that leads out to Mari's place. The houses are blurred by the deluge. Water gushes from downspouts. The ferns and buttercups in the ditches are bent low by the onslaught of rain. In the past two hours, three people have mentioned that it's hours from high tide and the wind's not so bad, so hopefully there won't be flooding.

"Reggie says you told him to go fuck himself," Sue says.

"What I told him is that I'm married and not dating right now."

"Ah, Reggie," Sue says. "Always a reliable source when it comes to the truth. Want me to drop you out at your place?"

"I'm fine getting out in the village. I need to grab some things at the market anyway."

"My dad thinks you broke Reggie's heart. That you are at the root of all of Reggie's problems."

This isn't news to Mari. The way she remembers it, Reggie was the one who dumped her.

"Me? I was surprised to find out Reggie had a heart," Sue continues. "Jury's still out on the brain. You know he's drinking again."

Mari does know, as does Frank, who seems to believe his son will put himself back together any day now.

Sue slows, peers through the windshield in case a jaywalking pedestrian can't hear the truck approaching over the thrum of the rain. "I'm going to park down by the boatyard," she says. "Then I'll walk to the market with you. That okay?"

Mari nods. She can grab her bike out of the back after she picks up the things she needs and ride it home. She can't get any wetter than she already is. As they crawl toward the boatyard, she asks how the baby's doing. Sue seems to have some kind of appointment on the mainland every week. The anxiety of the whole thing, she's confessed to Mari, is making her crazy. The out-of-pocket expenses are sucking their finances dry.

"Everything's good," she says. "Except Bob. We finally pass the halfway point with a baby, and *now* he falls apart. Men."

"Men," Mari agrees.

Sue pulls into a parking place tucked into the recesses of the boatyard and cuts the engine. The sudden absence of the bass is disorienting. Rain thunders against the truck's roof. Around them, yachts are beginning to emerge from their winter shrink wraps, and white plastic bait barrels overflow with trash. Mari, Reggie, and Sue used to get paid a dollar an hour to pick up trash from the boatyard. Sue was the only one of the three of them who saved her money in a piggy bank and didn't immediately buy candy inside the market.

"Levi's going to be so excited," Mari says. "He's already decided that you are making him a best friend." Levi seems intimidated by the children on the island who are his age, and Mari can't decide whether Levi's convinced Sue is growing his best friend because he knows Sue and his mom have always been best friends or because a baby seems like an easier friend than a peer.

"We found out it's a boy," Sue says. "But don't tell anyone. I feel like it jinxes things."

"So why are you telling me?"

"Because you're my BFF. I don't keep secrets from you." Sue's tone indicates there's more, so Mari waits. Sue's clutching the steering wheel. She's staring at the dashboard and is so still she might be paralyzed by fear.

"And because I don't believe in all that God bullshit," Sue continues. "But I know that you do. So I thought, just in case, that maybe you could, you know. Put in a good word."

"Pray for you."

"Or whatever you want to call it."

Mari smiles. "We…they…call it prayer. Many people do."

"Whatever." Sue's suddenly all nervous movement: checking her makeup in the rearview mirror, digging through her purse, pulling her hood over her hair, grabbing the door handle. "I'm going to make a run for it. You ready?"

"I should probably tell you that I don't think God and I are on the best of terms at the moment."

Sue turns to Mari but doesn't look directly at her. Instead, she keeps her attention on the roofline of the abandoned ice-house, a darker form against the smudge of sky at Mari's back.

"Yah, well, right now I'll take any help I can get."

"I'll do my best."

"Whatever." Sue seems finished with that conversation and slides her purse over her shoulder before asking, "What the hell happened to you?"

If only Mari had a good answer to that question. "I fell in love." Caleb feeding her Sungold tomatoes. Putting his hands on her pregnant belly and promising their child he would die for it if it came to that. The feel of his body next to hers at mealtime, in the truck on the way to town. The sight of his strong back as he pulled on his clothes in the morning.

"Yah, but what about the whole Bible bunny thing? How'd you get suckered into that?"

"It seemed right at the time," Mari says. "I guess I was kind of … lost."

Sue huffs disapproval out her nose. "You weren't lost," she says. "You were in grad school, and you threw it all away so you could grow peaches for Jesus."

"I left grad school for a job."

Sue swats a hand in front of her face as if Mari is a particularly annoying gnat, and Mari realizes she's done the right thing by not sharing those last hours at God's Bounty with anyone, despite the promise she and Sue made to each other in first grade to never keep secrets from each other.

"You totally ghosted me. And then you come back with the world's worst haircut. And your kid seems terrified of his own shadow. I mean, what the fuck, Mari?"

"I'm sorry."

"All this stuff was happening," Sue continues. "I wanted you here. I needed you here." She stops, fingers clutching the steering wheel, and throws a look at Mari. "I missed you," she adds. "That's all I'm saying. It's hard to find someone to talk to on this island who doesn't either tell you all the things you're doing wrong or blab your business to the whole world. Or both."

"I'm sorry I wasn't here for you," Mari says. "You really are my best friend. Forever."

More mouth scrunching from Sue. More studying of the chimneys and clouds. "I don't think either me or Bob could survive another miscarriage," she says finally.

"I'll pray for you, if that's what you want."

"And put in a request for a big catch. For everyone, but especially for Bob." One of Sue's eyes narrows in an expression Mari remembers from when they were not much older than Levi. "But that does not mean you get to spew your God shit all over me," Sue adds.

Mari grins. "That jinxes things too?"

"Damned if I know." Sue leans across the truck and hugs Mari quickly. "I'm glad you're back," she says. "More or less. Depending on your behavior. And your hair."

Mari says, "I'm glad too. I really did miss you. A lot." She wishes that Sue would have held her longer, but Sue has grabbed the door handle once again.

"On three," she says, but as soon as she says "one," she's out the door and dashing among the dry-docked yachts and piled lobster traps in yellow, black, and white.

BEHOLD, I HAVE GIVEN YOU SEED

Harry

Levi's voice comes through the open kitchen window as Harry finishes setting the breakfast table. "But why do you have to have money to plant more vegetables if God created everything for man? Why can't we just make the garden bigger?"

"At God's Bounty, we believed God gave the land and the plants and the animals for the benefit of all," Mari replies. "But here, people believe they own land and that they don't have to let anyone else use it if they don't want to."

Harry glances out the window at them. Mari's less skeletal. Her face has acquired some color. Levi, too, looks less like a stray dog. His hair's still long, but it's pulled back now in a rubber band and his clothes are clean and new.

Please let them resolve their conversation before entering the house, he thinks. If Mari wants to expand her garden, he's going to have to say no. Much as he's enjoyed working among the plants with her, her presence on his property has drawn him into conversations he does not want to have. The Shaws still harp on the audacity of Mari's request. Alice frets that Sam won't talk about moving to the mainland now that Mari's back. Clive, in the post office, sniggered to Harry about the island's new prophet of the Second Coming.

Harry knocks on the window, calls out that the food is almost ready, then consults the recipe for the umpteenth time. It's been forever since he fixed food that required the combining of more than two ingredients.

Footsteps clomping the back porch stairs is a sound so familiar that it's a tow rope that pulls the past forward: the three sibs and their spouses in the kitchen, cleaning up after a family meal. Everyone invigorated after a boating picnic and debating their top choices for the best movies of all time.

Ellie in the children's living room, bidding three no-trump in a voice of absolute self-assurance.

Ellie in the bedroom above the kitchen, her fingers over his mouth to muffle his gasp when he came.

"Mr. Harry," Levi says, planting himself in front of Harry. "Mama thinks people have to pay for land, but that's wrong because God said it's ours, right?"

"I'm sorry, buddy. I'm no expert when it comes to God."

Mari says, "I mentioned that I would love to have a bigger garden, but that we couldn't afford to buy any land right now. I said it was your land, not mine. Yours and your siblings'. That got us all caught up in the concept of land ownership and things he learned on God's Bounty." She gives Levi a fond look and continues, "Then I tried to explain different beliefs to him—how very few people believe exactly the same things. And that if nobody else believes what you believe, you have to be able to listen to them. Even if you are sure you are right."

"So why can't we buy some of your land to make the garden bigger?" Levi asks Harry. "You have a lot, and you don't even need it."

This breakfast is going to be a lot harder than he anticipated, Harry thinks. On the other hand, he's constitutionally wired, after years of teaching, to answer any question a child asks.

"It's complicated," he says. "For instance, even someone who has land and needs money won't necessarily take the money for his land because there might be strings attached."

"Strings?" Levi asks.

"Not real strings. That's just a saying that means you have to agree to certain rules if you want the money."

Levi scowls. "That's dumb."

"Maybe a little bit hard to understand," Harry suggests. "But that doesn't make it dumb." A glance at Mari tells him she's glad he's taken over, so he continues. "I don't speak for God, but I can tell you that people can and do buy land all the time. Like we buy groceries at the store. But you need money to buy things, and the thing you want to buy must be for sale."

Harry looks at Mari to see whether his answer meets with her approval. She seems pensive, but the boy is looking at Harry like he's an oracle. Like he's in possession of answers to every question a six-year-old might form. There were five children, seven men, and twenty women living at the cult— or farming ministry, as Mari has informed him it's correctly called. How often had this little boy even seen anyone other than the people living on the farm? Before leaving that place, did he ever hear a conversation among adults who weren't covered in the slick of religious fanaticism? Sheltered kids weren't exclusive to religious communes, however. Harry's had students from tony ZIP codes who were convinced people were poor because they were lazy. Slaves, a girl had once told him, were thrilled to have a place to live and food to eat. They were, in the girl's telling, "like members of the family." Enlightening those kids about reality so they could be sane members of society had been part of his job.

"The Earth evolved over many millennia," Harry says. "Ditto life forms, including plants." Too late he realizes that the boy has probably never heard of evolution. He'd have no idea what a millennium is or what ditto means.

"Okay, maybe we should eat before jumping into the history of agriculture and commerce. You hungry for pancakes?"

"Yes." Levi practically dances in his excitement.

"Go ahead and sit down, then." The table is ready: plates, paper napkins, an assortment of cutlery. He's chosen for Levi the juice glass with oranges painted on the side that was always his favorite as a child. Beneath it all is a red-and-white checked oilcloth, its pattern worn to near invisibility by the passage of time.

"Coffee?" Harry holds the pot up in Mari's direction as she and Levi take seats. He bought cream, milk, and half-and-half to cover all the bases before it occurred to him that Mari might be the kind of person who wants oat milk or soy. The chocolate chips for the pancakes were an impulse buy. Once again, something he'd loved as a child. He's also bought pure maple syrup and bacon that he's forgotten to fry.

Mari says, "I don't drink caffeine."

"Oh."

Mari and Levi both seem to be waiting to see what he'll do next. His heart's beating too loud, too fast. "Don't they, like, revoke your adulthood card if you don't drink coffee?" he asks.

"I don't know. Probably." Mari's got her thumb and forefinger on her knife as though she'd like to flip it over and over out of nervousness, but she doesn't move. A horrible thought strikes him: She might think he's hitting on her. But no. For chrissake, she's married. Never mind that Harry tried dating a handful of times, and every single one was an abject failure. His fault, not that of the poor women who'd made the mistake of responding to the online profile he'd posted at Pete's urging.

"Let me pour you a little," Harry says. He's managed to get his tone into a friendlier register even though he's forcing the coffee on her and he knows it. But for pete's sake, she can drink coffee. She's in the real world, where people buy and sell. They also drink coffee.

"You don't have to drink it," he adds. Mari doesn't respond, so he busies himself fixing her "kid coffee," the mixture of cream, sugar, and a splash of coffee that he and his friends from prep school had consumed. Their "gateway drug" they'd called it as they taught themselves to drink caffeine. Maybe he's corrupting her morals, but it's just coffee and honestly, it would help her if she could try a little harder to fit in, particularly now that the summer crowd is beginning to arrive.

When Mari refuses the coffee a second time, he says, "For a while, after Ellie's death, I kept saying I couldn't feel anything, but the truth is, I was cold all the time. I could not get warm. I basically lived on coffee and hot showers. They were the only things that made me feel vaguely human."

Mari takes the coffee from him but clutches it in her hands without tasting it. "I know my body's on this island," she says. "But I feel like I'm not. I don't know where that thing called *me* is. I think I maybe lost it."

"I know that feeling." Their eyes meet briefly, and then Harry turns away, busies himself ladling pancake batter into the pan.

"No, Mama, no!" Levi shouts.

"Sweetie, it's only a hot drink," she says. "Some people drink it. Some don't. It doesn't mean anything."

"Mr. Harry, you shouldn't give her coffee," Levi says.

After flipping the pancakes, Harry turns to the boy and asks, "So is it your papa or God who doesn't want your mom to drink coffee?"

"It's everybody, only Mama told Papa he was wrong, and he didn't like that because a wife must respect and obey."

Is all this really about coffee? There are too many unknowns for Harry to navigate this conversation. "Your mom seems nice enough to me," he says finally, but Levi shakes his head.

"Maybe we should go home," Mari says. "I'm afraid Levi's not in the greatest mood."

Levi shouts, "No. I want pancakes."

Harry waits for Mari to intercede, but when she doesn't, he tells himself that this is a teachable moment, and Mari's admitted she's not in the best shape to be helping her son adjust. How could she be when she's still trying to adjust herself?

"Maybe your papa was wrong," Harry says, and looks at Mari for permission to continue. She doesn't move, but the way she's staring at him feels like she's been waiting for someone to defend her.

"I'm not saying he was or he wasn't," Harry continues. "I wasn't there. I don't know. But you spoke up when you thought your mom and I were doing something wrong. Don't you think your mom should do the same thing, whether she's someone's wife or not?" The boy's face is pure confusion. "Sometimes, it's one person having the courage to speak up that helps correct an injustice," Harry says. "Like Rosa Parks." He goes on to tell Levi the story of the bus.

"You get to decide for yourself what's right and what's wrong," Harry finishes. "It's part of growing up. And then, if you see someone doing something you think is wrong, you can talk to them about it. Maybe you'll change their mind. Or maybe they'll change yours."

Levi's eyes briefly widen, as if that idea is completely foreign to him—a look that has always prompted Harry to push further in the classroom. "Your mom is pretty smart about a lot of things," Harry tells him, although he's referring to her knowledge of agriculture and the effects of sea-level rise and climate-related storms on coastlines and not to whether she excels when it comes to people.

"And I can tell she's taught you a lot," he continues. "So how do you know she wasn't right when she was talking to your dad? How do you know your dad couldn't have learned something from her if he'd listened?"

"What do you think?" Mari asks Levi.

Levi clamps his arms across his chest and arranges his face into a glare, but there's a lot going on in that kid's head. In the classroom, it's always a coin toss at this point whether to push further or let a kid think through these types of challenges on his own. Harry is piling pancakes onto Levi's plate when the boy finally answers.

"I don't know."

Harry says, "Perfect answer. Good for you." It's so hard for children to be comfortable with not knowing. Who's he kidding? It's hard for adults too. Most people are so loath to admit they don't know an answer that they'll just grab one.

Levi, unsurprisingly, is a big fan of chocolate-chip pancakes and fresh maple syrup. He consumes the first batch of pancakes entirely on his own and asks shyly if he can have more. Mari doesn't speak. Her attention is still focused on her cutlery, although now she's touching the prong end of her fork.

"Any luck on the job search?" he asks after telling Levi he'll make seconds once everyone has had firsts.

"No."

"Are you going to look for something on the mainland?" Some of the islanders commute to the mainland for work. The WiFi's good enough these days that she could work remotely for part of the time.

"What I'd really like to do is start a farm."

"Where?"

"Wherever I can on the island."

Location, Harry realizes, isn't the biggest problem. "How?"

"I know how to farm. I know how to do it efficiently, using ecologically sound methods. I also know how to pursue funding. The only thing I don't have is land, and most of the granting agencies expect you to have a place to plant. It's table stakes."

"You can't use your parents' land?"

"Too close to the waterfront," Mari says. "There are restrictions."

"Do you think starting a farm is practical under the circumstances?" Tilting his head toward Levi, Harry adds, "Wouldn't a steady paycheck be better, at least for now?" Whatever's going on with her husband, it doesn't seem he's sending her any child support.

"Got any ideas where I might find a steady paycheck around here?" she asks, and then, perhaps to temper her sarcasm, Mari adds, "The lobster have always been the glue that holds this community together. If they go, and they *will* go at some point given what climate change is doing to the Atlantic, then the community falls apart. I really, really don't want that to happen. I want to live here. I want my son to grow up here. I want my parents to be able to die here if that's what they want. Farming's what I know how to do. I'm good at it. So I'm going to find a way to do it."

The idea seems nuts, so Harry doesn't comment. Instead, he flips the next batch of pancakes and half listens as Mari tells him she's signed up for a free online seminar designed to let Maine women know of funding opportunities.

"I've done some research already," she says. "To see what kind of money's out there. The grants I've found that help farmers get started aren't huge—a couple thousand dollars at most—but if I got one, I could buy sheep and lease pastureland." She's already ordered a dozen hens and a rooster using money borrowed from her parents, Mari continues. She's negotiating the price of a billy goat. She'll pay her parents back out of proceeds from her egg business. As soon as she can, she'll purchase nannies and raise goats for meat, but the sheep will come first because they generate two revenue streams, fleece and meat.

"Do you think anyone will actually lease land to you?"

"Can I lease some of yours?"

"No." The rapidity of his answer clearly takes Mari by surprise. "I'm sorry," he adds, "But this isn't a good time." Isabelle and Jonathan have decided to talk with Tim Duncan about next steps; Harry's agreed to at least find out if Duncan is serious.

"It doesn't matter," Mari says. "I'll find something."

Maybe. Harry does feel badly for her, but there's nothing he can do.

"Time for your mom to eat something," he tells Levi as he spatulas four pancakes onto Mari's plate.

"You eat too," she says, and she finally gets the knife and fork in her hand long enough to transfer a couple of pancakes onto Harry's plate.

Levi's eyes are on Harry's pancakes, watching the bits of chocolate form tiny puddles at their bases. "Do you eat butter and syrup too?" he asks.

"I do."

"Like me!" This similarity seems to please Levi greatly.

Out of habit, Harry pours more coffee into Mari's cup before filling his own. She lifts the mug to her mouth and sips. Pleasure dances in the corners of her eyes.

"Good?" he asks.

"Like ice cream. Only hot."

Her description makes him smile. Mari's still Mari on the inside, he thinks. She's still got her sense of humor and her smarts. Harry taps his mug to hers and says, "Welcome back to the grownups' tribe," but Levi is outraged.

"You aren't supposed to drink coffee," he protests.

"Sweetie," Mari says. "I'm doing the best I can. God understands that."

"Listen, maybe—" Harry begins, but neither Mari nor Levi pays any attention to him.

"Nothing bad is going to happen." Mari takes another sip of her coffee. "See? Everything's fine."

But everything isn't fine. Levi is in tears and flings himself out of his chair and into Harry's arms.

"Mr. Harry, stop her! The devil is getting inside her!" The boy is shaking beneath Harry's arm. His face is pressed against Harry's chest. Mari's eyes fill with tears and, for a moment, Harry's certain he's going to start crying as well. Ellie always told him he was good with children. He assumed she meant students until his niece and nephews were born, but even they don't throw themselves into his arms the way Levi did.

"I'm drinking coffee," Harry tells Levi as he reaches for his mug. "Is the devil inside me?" He's got devils of his own, and so far they've won every battle. But that's not what this boy needs to hear. Levi shakes his head, but then something changes in his body. He seems to be wondering whether Harry is, in fact, safe. When he pulls away, he looks at Harry carefully.

"Could you feel the devil in me?" Harry asks.

Tentatively, Levi shakes his head. "Only in Mama," he says, but he seems unsure.

"Devil, you get out of this woman, and you leave her alone," Harry says, shaking his finger at Mari. "You go right this minute, or else!"

Mari startles, gasps, presses her hands to her heart. "I think he's gone," she says. She mocks listening, touches her arms and chest. "No, I'm certain of it. He's gone!" Levi's still skeptical and stares intently at his mother when she says she's going to take another sip of coffee to see what happens.

"It's okay," she says triumphantly after swallowing. "I'm saved! The devil's gone."

Levi looks from one to the other of them, and Harry can't tell if he's convinced. One way or the other, the crisis has passed.

"Who's up for more pancakes?" he asks, and both Mari and Levi say, "Me!"

ONE-EYED SEAL

Sam

Sam, at the helm of the *Alice-Mari*, drifts on the tide just west of a rock formation known as Three Sisters. His bib pants are orange, ancient, covered with oil smears and grime. The stubbled skin of his cheeks is engraved with six-and-a-half decades of smiles. His scrambled-egg sandwich, prepared for him this morning like every morning by Alice when it was still too early for speech, lies in the dark of his pocket. He's checked his traps on the northwest side of Little Great Island, the ones that usually do best at this time of year. Every single one of them was empty, but sometimes the lobster are slow to migrate. Yes, there's been talk that the lobster are gone because of climate change, but no one really knows because who can read the mind of a lobster? Who really knows the secret ways of the sea?

For that matter, who knows the secrets of his own child? Not Sam, and that's for sure. He's certain Mari's floating in secrets up to her nostrils. She's been home now long enough that it feels natural that the table is full at supper and that the house sighs with breathing at night. Familiar, even, that his wife and daughter seem always balanced on the edge of a fight.

But getting used to something's not the same as understanding, and one thing Sam's seen already is that things are more complicated for them all now that Mari is back and has a son. Alice wants to know when he's going to retire and if they are still going to talk about leaving the island, but who would he be without their home on Little Great Island? Who would Alice be? Perhaps Mari knows the answer is that they are no one without their island home because, after all, she's back and she's making plans to stay. Reggie's waylaid him in the village a couple of times, wanting to know if Mari's getting divorced and if he could pass on a message that Reggie'd like to go for a drive around the island with her. Even Frank, who's been Sam's best friend since the beginning of time, claps his hands behind his head with his elbows out like wings and says, "Well, there's never a dull moment when Mari's around."

All of this when the summer people aren't even here in force yet. All of this when the lobster are hiding, and when Sam knows for certain that the one thing he won't do is let his family split up again.

But trying to sort that out—how to make a complicated thing easy—is the reason he's been taking his time coming in from checking his traps.

Sam cuts the *Alice-Mari's* engine, lets the boat drift. He keeps his attention to starboard, where the shoulders of the Three Sisters have emerged from the ebbing tide. This isn't a great place for a boat when the tide is receding, but he needs this lap of water against hull, the sway of rockweed on the ocean's surface.

No one who's been on a lobster boat would say you go out on the water to escape your troubles since there's no shortage of trouble when you're on the open sea in a boat that's some thirty-five feet long. Nevertheless, out here, the troubles of land are easy to see from a distance. Aboard the *Alice-Mari*, all problems boil down to the same one: staying alive. And to stay alive, you need a roof, food, and a handful of people to love. People who, if you are lucky, love you back.

The first of the harbor seals surfaces off the *Alice-Mari's* stern. Sam hears rather than sees it: the great exhalation, more woof than sigh. Turning only his head so as not to startle the animal, he sees the sleek-headed creature regarding him, one eye huge and black and knowing. The other is only a scar.

Sam's grandfather once told him, "Even in death, we islanders are always near." The man was blind in one eye from a carving accident as a child. It doesn't take much for Sam to imagine his grandfather has taken to the sea.

More wet bursts of air, and the waters around Sam are filled with silky snouts and expanding ripples. Sam nods, as if in greeting. The sound is of human breathing, but only the seals are present.

The *Alice-Mari* is close to the Sisters' shoulders. The goring rocks are a few feet below. Sam has only a handful of minutes before he must motor to deeper water. When the first seal shoots from the water onto the protruding shelf of rock beneath the Sisters, the sound is less than that of a swallow. One by one, the creatures catapult themselves from the sea, assume their bow shapes, close their eyes in the increasing warmth of the sun. It rarely fails Sam, this form of ocean prayer. He has so many ways to hope.

SHELL, DIRT, HISTORY

Little Great Island

A plot of land, one meter square. At the core is greenstone granite, shaped 545 million years ago, its minerals leached and weathered and stirred with the remains of glaciers that passed fifteen thousand years in the past. Once upon a time, the Red Paint People lived and farmed this fertile soil. Their oyster shells and sturgeon bones, their potsherds and their flesh, are folded into the earth. But the Great Dying came, and the People became this dirt, this soil, which was claimed by the people from the boats. These people from away were restless people called settlers who clear-cut the oak, the beech, the cherry and birch, the ash and maple, the spruce, fir, and white pine to build fishing boats and to make way for pastures and fields.

In this piece of land lies buried a cornerstone hewn from granite. An earthworm plows the dirt. Ladybug footprints line a stalk of purple vetch. The moths have visited the glossy buckthorn. Grasshoppers mate amongst the alfalfa and red clover. A dozen or so monarchs flutter in, cocoon and wait, emerge and fly away. A thrip pauses on a blade of grass. An old man, a lover of birds and, in his younger days, of the idiosyncrasies and foibles of his fellow humans, has witnessed, in one afternoon on this very spot, a red-winged blackbird, a sparrow, a black guillemot, an endangered roseate tern, a raccoon, a house cat, a deer mouse, a goat on a stroll, a dog on a walkabout, a man with a gray-struck beard and his hands in his pockets, a woman with mowed hair who holds her face to the wind, a lobsterman with a hitch in his walk whose shoulders hunch like those of Atlas, and a woman with a thicket of curls and a face woven from wrinkles and worry who sits alone on a rock to eat a simple sandwich, which she shares with the man's own beggar of a tricolor dog.

Unseen: a mink with head raised and ears alert.

Also missed, as the sunlight weakens, the mark of a thick boot with a heavy tread and an extinguished cigarette, dropped among the sedges and the grass.

MY HEART SHATTERS

Mari

Mari, on her way to the post office, keeps the hood of her rain jacket up, her face down as the early June afternoon pours rain, cold and raw. Off in the distance, a foghorn lows. More automobiles fill the Main Street parking than even a week ago. Memorial Day weekend has come and gone, and some of the summer houses are open for the season. Retirees from away are here now, at least temporarily, scheduling dates to get their boats in the water, hauling their porch furniture out of the basement, turning on the water for the outside shower. Not one of them is interested in hiring Mari to cook, clean, or garden, or in letting her use a piece of their land. They have their various reasons or excuses, but all that matters is that every one of them says no. Every day that passes without income is a day that Mari can't hire a lawyer to protect herself and Levi from Caleb. Every afternoon, when her dad comes off the *Alice-Mari*, the slope of his shoulders and the droop of his head tells her the traps remain light. Every night, she lies awake and wonders: stay or go? Little Great Island is the right place for Levi. It's the right place for her. But only if there's a way to survive, and she needs the seasonal visitors to help her.

There's always been a myth about the mutually beneficial relationship between native islanders and summer visitors. The truth is more complicated. There are friendships, there are employer-employee relationships, and sometimes both are the same, although this only works as long as it does. A significant disparity in wealth, social standing, and often in education as well separates the two populations. What unites them is love for Little Great Island, but their loves are different. For people like Mari, this is home. For the summer visitors, it's a nice place to visit, and when they are around, they want everything done their way. The whole world has gone selfish, and now she's got to figure out how to change at least a tiny piece of that.

Fuck.

A word like that at God's Bounty would have gotten her more than a day in the prayer shed, but surely Caleb wouldn't have let his son be confined there that long. Neither Pastor Aaron nor Caleb is a monster. Caleb, when he'd held Levi for the first time, had cried. He would never let harm come to his son.

"Clive?" Mari calls from inside the post office. "You here?"

The post office's bare wood floor lists downhill to the right as it always has. The counter still holds its chained ballpoints beneath a lineup of old island photos, the sepia-toned men and women squinting out at her across decades. Rows of numbered brass doors cover one wall, apart from the window where Mari has stood a thousand times in her life, picking up the mail. Thunder rolls in the distance, possibly as far away as the mainland.

Upstairs, a door opens, and Clive's voice comes clearly. "No, damn you. Get back here." Meowing accompanies his swearing and footfalls. Peering through the window into the office, Mari sees a half-dozen Siamese cats tumble down the stairs—a cacophony of blue eyes and pink tongues, creamy fur and pointed teeth. Clive shuffles across the floor, his legs encircled by cats that chorus their complaints.

"Oh. Hey," he says when he sees Mari. "Be right with you. Let me do something with these guys first." Leaning over, he grabs a couple of cats and tucks them under his arms. In the time Mari was gone from the island, Clive's mustache became dusted with gray. Weight has gathered in his belly so that he seems nearly as pregnant as Sue.

"All of you, out," he says, and opens the back door. It takes a few sweeps with the side of his foot—not kicks so much as shoves—to clear the cats from his office.

"Should have married a woman who wanted babies, not cats," he says.

"Or one who believes in spay and neuter."

"That, too." Clive leans his hairy forearms on the small counter that separates the public and private spaces of the post office and fastens his eyes pointedly on Mari's scalp. Her hair is long enough now for the cowlicks to disrupt it. Before the shearing, it had been a rich, dark blanket that reached to her waist. Sister Ann had claimed to be one of the sisters as she worked beside them, gossiped and laughed with them, but she was the only one who lived with and slept with Pastor Aaron, and they all knew she couldn't be trusted. Fingers gently lifting and separating each hank of hair, Sister Ann had prayed while she scissored and shaved, her voice the volume and cadence of a housewife reciting a recipe. Mari hadn't fought her, telling herself it was only hair and that the sooner the shearing was done, the sooner she could find Levi.

"Well," Clive says. "What's Harry Richardson do with himself all day long out there?"

"I don't see much of him. I think he's writing a book." Clive's a known gossip. Mari learned around the time she began walking to be careful about what she shared. "I got a registered letter to pick up," she adds.

Clive, apparently understanding he'll get no gossip from her, pushes back from the counter and says, "You have to sign."

That Clive had called to tell her that there was a registered letter for her has left her hands shaking and her mind unable to focus on anything other than her mail. It had been silly to assume Caleb would let her go with no repercussions. Still, she'd hoped for more time.

"Here you go," Clive says, pushing an envelope toward her. The envelope is addressed in Caleb's childlike handwriting. Blood floods to Mari's feet, leaving her faint enough that she grabs the counter edge for support. The return address says simply, "God's Bounty." No street number or state is given.

"You sign there," Clive says, pointing.

Mari cannot bring herself to touch it. "What happens if I don't?"

"If you don't sign, I can't let you have it." Clive pulls the envelope away. "Your call."

This moment was always coming, Mari sees now. Once again, she's been too slow to act. Once again, she's put her son in danger. She should have borrowed money for a divorce lawyer the moment she set foot on the island. She should have used the money she spent on chickens to at least get a half hour of a lawyer's time. She should have gotten ahold of a phone to take pictures of the sore on Levi's tongue before it healed. She should have told Sue, or someone, what she knew for a fact had happened so that someone could corroborate her story. Her brain muddles. She isn't strong enough for this fight.

"You going to sign?"

Every cell of her body tells Mari to run from the letter, but if she does, she won't know its contents.

"Yes."

Clive watches as Mari scribbles her name. "You heard about Sue and Bob losing their boat?" he asks. "I tell you what, we're all going to hell in a breadbasket on this island if the lobster are gone for good." He natters on, telling her things she already knows about costs, about scarcity, about the loss and the hardships they're all going to endure.

"I don't know that this whole climate change thing is what they say it is," he continues. "Some of these scientists, they like to make things sound terrible to get attention. You take these big storms, for one thing. But there's always been storms, am I right? So that's not the climate changing. Most likely the problem with the lobsters is those foreigners getting into our waters, stealing our fish."

"Sorry, I've got to run," Mari says and walks out before Clive can say more. The door slams behind her, and the rain resumes its pounding on her hood. Clive and his interest in gossip instantly become the least of her worries. After two months on the island, her time at God's Bounty had started to seem like a television show she watched as a teenager, and now the reality is back. She's going to have to understand the things she can make no sense of: Levi on the ground in the prayer shed. The rope, the tree stumps, the sore on Levi's tongue. His nightmares, loud enough to wake her parents.

The envelope in her hand doesn't feel entirely real and yet, when she opens it, all of God's Bounty will come pouring into her life on Little Great Island.

"God help me," Mari mouths as one of the Siamese, wet and bedraggled, presses against her leg.

Tearing open the letter, Mari notes that Caleb addresses her as Sister Rachel, her God's Bounty name, before reading on:

My heart shatters that you have stolen from me my precious and firstborn Son, Levi. I have, in the weeks since you tore his tender Soul from among us, fasted and prayed, imploring The Lord to overcome the Evil within you so that you might see your sins and return to Our midst. But now I am received of revelation that your nature is such that you cannot fight it on your own. That the Evil forces within you have led you to cleave me from my Son and from you, the woman to whom I pledged Myself before the Lord our God. Thanks be to Him, I understand now that it is my duty to demand Levi's immediate return, as He has revealed that to wait longer would be to risk my Son's immortal Soul, trapped—as he is—in the care of a woman fallen so far from Grace. In good conscience, I can no longer delay. With the assistance of Our Ministry, which understands the dire nature of the need, I am raising the funds necessary to secure full rights, responsibility, and guardianship of Levi, as is only befitting of a Father's relationship with his Son.

As to the future of our union as Husband and Wife, I abide—as always—to the teachings of our Lord and to the vows we made before God, Our Pastor, and Our Brothers and Sisters. We shall be, until death do us part, Husband and Wife. With gratitude to the guidance of Pastor Aaron, I now understand my weakness in succumbing to your temptations. I accept our lifelong union as my punishment and will pray for the strength to forgive should God guide your steps back to my side.

I insist that you do not delay.

In God's Love Everlasting,
Caleb

Crumpling the now rain-dampened letter and stuffing it into her pocket, Mari stands with her back pressed to the post office and a stream of water pouring off the roof and onto her head.

She steps into the rain. The downpour thrums her hood as she walks. Her hands are freezing. Her feet are soaked, but discomfort is something she's learned to ignore when there's a job to be done.

I'M YOUR MAN

Frank

Frank is trying to get the sugar dust off his shirt when he hears the guys in the shop saying hi to a man who answers with an off-island accent. A voice he can almost, but not quite, place. The rest of the box of doughnuts lands in his bottom drawer just as the man, skinny as Mari was when she first came back, comes into his office. One of the Richardson kids, Frank remembers. He'd seen him on the ferry, back in April, and wandering around in the village now and again since then.

"Hey, Frank," the guy says.

"Great to see you," Frank answers, still unable to summon a first name, although he's known this guy since he was too small to walk into the village on his own. All he can think of at the moment is that this poor schmuck's wife died, which is a thing Frank knows about, his own wife having passed when Reg and Susie were small.

"Got a minute?" Richardson asks. The look he gives Frank's office door says he'd like to close it, so Frank tells him to go ahead.

"What can I do you for?" he asks. Problem with one of the Richardsons' boats? Does he need to order something special from the mainland? *Please, please, don't let it be that he's found Reggie passed out up at their place.* Because the truth is, Reggie made himself at home up there for a while last winter when he needed some alone time. What the summer people don't know don't hurt them, but if they do find out— well, the islanders are the ones who get hurt, and Frank's already got enough worries, what with his kids, and with Bob, and with the possibility that the next storm could take half his business right out to sea. Sue's got a baby on the way, so she gets some slack, but Reggie's missed more than a couple of days work, and now Bob's lost his boat. Those guys are grown men. They should be pulling their own weight, paycheck wise. Not leaning on him.

"I wanted to run something past you," Richardson says.

"I'm all ears." He is too, because that's not the way anyone would kick off if they'd found Reggie camping out in a spare bedroom.

"I'm kind of putting out feelers. Nothing about this is remotely close to being definite."

Which means Frank's supposed to keep a secret. This gets better and better. Frank leans back in his chair and puts his hands behind his head while Richardson goes on that his question's related to a real-estate transaction. Frank nods, thinking naturally he'd be the go-to person for that sort of advice. Way back before he even got married, Frank decided he was staying on Little Great Island, and that if he was going to make a living out here, he needed to own property. First place he bought was what's now called The Sweet Shoppe, although back then it was an abandoned eyesore, left over from when the village had been a booming place. He did most of the renovation on his own, learning as he went, and then lived on the first floor with the idea of renting the second. Next came the yellow house when he got married, bought with a little help from his in-laws. There was something of a boatyard next to the ferry landing when he decided to try his hand at business, so he'd bought it decades ago. Then he rented the two-story to Lydia. She talked about starting a little market on the ground floor—a decent idea, so Frank bought up another building in the village not long after his wife passed and converted it into a market before Lydia got her own business up and running. When Lydia threw a fit, he offered to marry her—put all the revenue in one pot, she'd keep an eye on the kids, he'd make sure her bills got paid— but she turned him down so flat you might have thought he was a man with no prospects. So fine, she'd had her chance, business was business, and now he doesn't cut her slack unless his mood is right. It's how things work.

Harry, Frank remembers. Harry Richardson.

Harry says, "We've had someone express an interest in buying our place."

Well, holy hell. Frank wasn't expecting that. But still, what's it got to do with him? "Okay," he says, dragging the word out.

"In order to sell to this buyer, we'd need the property rezoned for commercial use."

Frank gets that tingling in his head that tells him he's got to pay full attention. What kind of commercial? Some people want an old folks' home on the island, but buying Richardsons' land would be more than the island can afford. The occasional idiot has talked about trying to get the Richardsons to donate some of their land so the town can put in a basketball court or a theatre or day care or a restaurant or more apartments where seasonal workers could live. Nothing's ever come of it. Some of the summer people are generous, but some are tight-fisted as hell.

But the fish Richardson has nibbling is someone who specializes in the kind of place top dogs from big companies go for a meeting or two and some R&R. Frank decides to take some notes, make it seem as if he understands what's happening here. He can always sort it out later.

Frank asks, "What do you need from me?" although what he's thinking is, *how can I make this work for me?* Snotty business types aren't going to be coming to him for canned soda and a jar of jam. But if there's going to be meals served out there, he could go for a supply contract for the restaurant. If there's going to be construction, he deserves a piece of that. Word is, there's going to be government money for shoreline businesses needing to protect themselves from sea-level rise; if he can prove he's got a bunch of big-business types relying on him, maybe he can get a bigger piece of that pie.

On the back of an envelope, he lists cargo shippers, lumber sales, food service, staff. After every word, he draws a careful question mark. Building out here requires understanding of the island infrastructure, the logistics of transporting materials and workers from the mainland, the criticality of hiring islanders to keep the peace, and the overall intricacies and delicacies of island politics. Turns out this last is what Harry has cottoned on to.

Harry says, "If...*if* this deal moves forward, it's likely to be contingent on the land being rezoned from residential to commercial." That decision is up to the planning board, which Harry knows. What he wants from Frank is someone—an influential and respected someone—from the island who can help ensure the rezone vote goes through.

"Sure," Frank says as he sketches a careful dollar sign on its own line, telling himself there's economic benefit here at a time he's in need. There's a grandchild in the wings, after all.

"I'm your man." Frank draws two lines under *rezone* before thumping a big period after the word.

ARMAGEDDON

Harry

"Armageddon?" Mr. Estabrook asks when Harry responds to his knock.

"Excuse me?" Harry searches his visitor and his yard for a clue as to what Mr. Estabrook is talking about. The older man has a crumb of something caught in a missed patch of whiskers beside his mouth. His pants, stained, hang on a lanky frame by a faded canvas whale belt that was popular in the eighties. Mr. Estabrook's dog is marking the front of the house every few feet. There's no car in sight other than Harry's own, so Mr. Estabrook, clad in yellow foul-weather gear, presumably walked out here from the village.

"Your vegetable patch," Mr. Estabrook says. "You growing your own food for when the apocalypse happens?"

"That's Mari McGavin's garden," Harry says, although he now works in it as much as Mari and Levi do. It's relaxing to move the hose up and down the rows and to pinch suckers off the tomato plants. Even when the garden needs neither weeding nor water and the sun is already setting, Harry goes out there, just to stand. Just to breathe and listen.

"You've let them use your mother's garden?" Mr. Estabrook asks, raising an untamed eyebrow.

Harry's mother now lives in Florida with her new husband. She gave up her share of the Little Great Island house as part of the divorce settlement, and she hasn't been on the island in years.

"It's fine," Harry says, adding to himself that it would be fine with Isabelle and Jonathan too. He's so certain of that fact that he hasn't bothered to tell them about it. Lately, he's caught himself gazing out a second-story window, only half conscious of the fact that he's looking for a sign of Mari and her son. Somehow his body has learned when the two of them are out scattering feed for the hens, which had arrived a few days earlier. Levi seems to like standing on a bale of hay near the goat's enclosure. From what Harry can tell, the boy's talking to the goat, which they've named Houdini because it keeps escaping. He's thought of going over to tell Mari it's okay to pen the goat on his land. It can act as a four-legged mower. But if the goat, why not sheep? It isn't fair to Mari to let her think she can put animals on his property for any length of time, especially because Duncan's minions have already been to the island to go over the property. They didn't reveal much, but Pete called later to say that "no significant problems stood out." Not exactly a glowing review, but Isabelle subsequently dispatched him to talk with Frank Clatcher about rezoning, despite Harry's protestations that maybe they ought to wait. Maybe the minions felt, as he does, that an executive retreat isn't the right thing for Little Great Island.

"This is so awesome, Har," she said. "Doesn't it feel great to get back in the saddle?"

No.

Mr. Estabrook takes in the front porch with its wooden rockers and wicker table, and Harry remembers all those summer evenings of his youth. All those debates over what to do about Russia, about China, about the Middle East, the World Wide Web, and the crime rates of US cities.

"You sure you want to get involved in her problems?" Mr. Estabrook asks.

"I'm not involved," Harry protests. "She planted the garden to help her son adjust to being here."

"One party utilizing another party's land is a form of involvement," Mr. Estabrook says. "Think landlord-tenant. *Quid pro quo*. Negotiated agreements. Agreed-upon terms."

Is Harry meant to charge Mari rent for growing lettuce? Should he have asked Isabelle to draw up a contract? Mr. Estabrook, in Harry's mind, has spent far too much time negotiating settlements. He's forgotten that sometimes people do things just to be kind.

"We agreed to split the produce," he says. "She gets one week's lettuce, I get the next. Agricultural diplomacy."

Using the term "agricultural diplomacy" is a joke. Harry and Mr. Estabrook both know that agricultural diplomacy includes international free-trade agreements and foreign aid, not splitting heads of red leaf lettuce. The term is an allusion to the kinds of conversations he's had with Mr. Estabrook in the past about how diplomatic solutions lie in the give-and-take. The key to successful diplomacy, Mr. Estabrook has told Harry, is to find first what the parties have in common rather than letting them air their adversarial positions. Eschew dichotomous thinking. Explore the middle ground. Find the compromise.

"The chickens and goat a project for her son too?" Mr. Estabrook asks now. "She going to have a herd of cows out here next?"

"The animals don't bother me." Occasionally Harry hears the rooster crow and finds he likes the sound. The goat mostly stands in its pasture and stares, although Harry's seen the

McGavins scatter both ways on the road to hunt the creature down when it escapes.

"May I come in?" Mr. Estabrook says. "Or should I say we?" He gestures toward the dog.

"By all means." Harry leads the way to the kitchen, and Mr. Estabrook drops himself into a chair. His dog collapses next to him. Mr. Estabrook's cheeks sag away from his bones. The bags beneath his eyes spill downward into bags beneath them. His hair, silver-white, is so sparse that Harry can see scalp beneath it. What's it like for him, growing old alone? Is it harder to lose your wife after decades together? It's impossible to be envious of The Butterfly Diplomat, whom Harry has always loved like a father. Still, in this one area, Harry would happily trade places.

"I know this is all one hell of a thing for you, Harry," Mr. Estabrook says. "But don't you go losing your way. You're stronger than that."

"Thank you," Harry says.

After rummaging in his pocket, Mr. Estabrook produces a worn silver dollar. It's a Peace Dollar, the date on it 1923. Years earlier, Mr. Estabrook revealed that he had a collection of one hundred silver dollars, each one from a different year. His intention, he told Harry, was to give Harry his entire collection. "My kids think they are just dollars," he said. "Only coins instead of paper. You and I, Harry, we know they are pieces of history." The coins are given one at a time but on a random schedule, or perhaps for reasons known only to Mr. Estabrook himself. Some summers, he gives Harry three or four; others, only one. Right now, there are sixty-six of them in a safe deposit box in Harry's bank. They were given to Harry and not to his brother or sister. It matters, being singled out like that by a man whom everyone respects.

Now Mr. Estabrook pushes the dollar across the table toward where Harry stands. "These things are worth next to nothing these days," he says. "No one collects. Everyone unburdens." Giving the coin a final shove, he waits for Harry to take it.

"It's like the past is a mistake we cannot wait to escape from," Mr. Estabrook continues. He shakes his head. "You and I, we know it doesn't work that way."

He might be talking about history in general, Harry thinks. Or about grieving dead spouses. Either way, the man seems sad. Harry asks, "How are you doing, Mr. Estabrook?"

"Getting by." Mr. Estabrook studies the water-stained ceiling and adds, "Getting old. But you know, for the first time in my life, I'm feeling regret. I've realized I'd rather show up dead in my house on this island than spend my days in some old folks' home playing bridge. Too late, though. You probably heard that my house sold. I've got to be out by the end of the summer."

"I'm sorry," Harry says, but is this a word to the wise? Has Mr. Estabrook caught wind of the possible sale of the Richardsons' house?

"I don't believe I'm at the end of my line," Mr. Estabrook continues. "I still think there's life to be lived and a thing or two I'd like to accomplish. But I guess everyone feels that way. Still young inside, but the body will have its say."

Much as Harry would like to make polite noises about Mr. Estabrook still being young, he keeps his mouth shut. Mr. Estabrook knows and observes the protocols for proper social engagement, but he has no patience for interpersonal niceties that evade the truth. Instead, Harry rodeos the proper accoutrements for tea, which, when your guest is Mr. Estabrook, involve the full ritual of cups and saucers—never mugs—along with trays, sugar bowls—cubes, never crystals—lemon slices, milk pitchers, and plates of cookies.

Mr. Estabrook asks, "How about you, Harry? You holding up okay?"

"I'm making do."

"Making do," Mr. Estabrook repeats as he rubs his foot across the dog, who doesn't react. "What's the status on your job? You going back?"

"Still not sure."

"Gotta do something."

"Yes," Harry says. "I know."

Mr. Estabrook nods as if he approves of Harry's answer. "You and me, we're both widowers. The better part of my life is behind me now. It's the way of things. But you're young. You can't hide for the rest of your life."

"I know," Harry says again. "I'm not hiding." He's not socializing beyond his time in the garden with Mari and Levi, but that seems to fulfill his needs for now. His summer friends have yet to arrive for their vacations.

"What's your retirement place like?" Harry asks, but Mr. Estabrook ignores the question.

"As to feeling I'm not yet in the grave, there is something I want to accomplish on this island before I'm gone. A legacy, if you will, although I prefer to think of it as my moral duty to a world that is changing so quickly, and not necessarily for the best."

"What's that?" Harry puts cups of tea on the table, along with a small pitcher of milk and a sugar bowl, and takes a seat.

"I got to thinking about what people did to my house, back before we bought it."

Harry nods, remembering Mr. Estabook's complaints about how previous owners had slapped porches and wings onto a Federal-style farmhouse from the early 1900s and then "prostituted" the interior, courtesy of some suburbanite decorator.

Mr. Estabrook continues, "These new owners can do whatever they want. Cut down trees that will take decades to regrow. Put in a tennis court or a lawn they'll cover with fertilizers and pesticides. Start running farm animals all over it, if you catch my drift." He pauses to give Harry a look from beneath shaggy eyebrows, but Harry doesn't react.

Mr. Estabrook continues, "I realized I should have put a conservation easement on my property before I sold it, but I was too late. Didn't think about it in time. But just because it's too late for me doesn't mean it's a bad idea."

"Huh," Harry says. There isn't a land conservation trust on Little Great Island, but he's certainly familiar with the concept from the protected land around Boston.

"You three ought to look into it," Mr. Estabrook says. "All the shorebirds you've got out here should be protected. These views too. Everything would stay as it is right now—the existing house can be occupied—but the easement ensures all this magnificent land can't be built up in the future."

In an ideal world, it's the right thing to do, but the timing is wrong. A conservation easement would kill the Duncan Development deal, meaning Isabelle and Jonathan would never agree. Even if that sale falls through, an easement would diminish both the value and the desirability of the property.

Mr. Estabrook sips his tea. Those once-lively eyes have clouds now. "I would imagine a buyer for this place would insist that Ms. McGavin and her son remove their garden posthaste," he says. "Encroachments and handshake involvements not being particularly popular with those hoping to appeal to the well-heeled crowd."

"You know about Duncan?"

Mr. Estabrook nods. "No secrets on an island."

"Does everybody know?"

"I happen to have received a phone call from your sister, who wanted to tell me how much I'd be missed on the island."

No doubt she'd also been probing for the sales price of Mr. Estabrook's house and an assessment of Harry's state of mind. Isabelle rarely does anything that doesn't have multiple motives.

"I don't think your friend Ms. McGavin is going to be very pleased with you if you sell your property to someone who objects to having farm animals next door," Mr. Estabrook continues.

"I suspect you're right about that."

"These developers can be hard on neighbors they don't approve of. Lawsuits over one thing or another, until the offending neighbor is on the verge of bankruptcy and forced to sell.

"Put your land in a conservation easement now," he finishes. "And Duncan Development goes away. You and your brother and sister will find another buyer, one whose…ethos, shall we say, is more in keeping with the spirit of the island."

It's easy to imagine Tim Duncan, whom Harry's only met in video calls, disapproving of the rooster, of the goat, of the McGavins' ramshackle sheds, the tractor, the baler, and the boat trailers. The executive guests might complain about the sound of Sam's boat leaving in the early-morning darkness or the smell of barnyard. There might be, as Mr. Estabrook has said, a series of lawsuits against the McGavins if they don't decide to leave of their own accord, if for no other reason than driving them away gives Duncan the chance to buy their land, thus getting waterfront access. Harry has no doubt that thought would have occurred already to Duncan.

"A bit more than agricultural diplomacy going on here, I'd say," Mr. Estabrook says.

Harry thinks of Mari, that first time he'd seen her: skinny and ragged. Frightened but not cowed. There's a good chance Mari's got a huge custody battle ahead of her, never mind the need to make a living. No way he wants to make her life even harder.

"I would appreciate it if you'd bring this subject up with your brother and sister at the earliest opportunity," Mr. Estabrook says.

Yes. But what, exactly, can he say? Isabelle's claiming their property is worth more than three million dollars. He can all but hear her demanding shrilly, "You want me to give that up for the birds? I have *children*, Harry. Forgive me if I put their needs ahead of the speckled web-footed whatever."

Ah, yes. Children.

Mr. Estabrook taps the tabletop with one long, wrinkled finger. He shakes his head. Leaning forward, he pats the back of Harry's hand and says, "No one said it was easy to be the butterfly."

ALL THE MONEY IN
THE WORLD

Mari

"A few thousand, you say?"

Mari nods. There's no one other than Frank she can turn to for a loan this size, and she has to act soon. Maybe Caleb is bluffing. Maybe he isn't. Either way, she needs a lawyer, and the ones she's tried all want a retainer up front. They've all told her to prepare for a lengthy battle. She will have to file for divorce in South Carolina and, given that the South is becoming ever more conservative, there will be bias toward shared custody. Caleb's fundamentalist beliefs won't work against him. Her accusations will be useless because she has no proof. The fact that she essentially kidnapped Levi will cause her problems.

"What makes you think I've got that kind of money lying around?" Frank asks. He shakes a bag of Pepperidge Farm Milanos, double chocolate, holds it open to her, and, after Mari takes one, helps himself to a handful. Everywhere in this building, the air is twined with polyurethane, sawdust, the tang of caffeine and sweat. Here in Frank's office, the surfaces are awash with outdated catalogues, invoices, packing lists, and coffee mugs that hold the dregs of yesterday's coffee, or last week's, or however long it's been. Outside this cramped square of a room, in the space Mari walked through to get here, are workstations made of scarred wood, their windows grimy, their walls tacked over with thumbtacked bits of paper and photographs yellowed by time. In the vast center of that room are yachts on trestles, their masts stored elsewhere, their hulls undergoing repair. Tucked in a corner—the same corner where it stood more than fourteen years ago—is the boat Reggie was building. On paper, the design won him an award, which was sufficient for Reggie to imagine a future for himself as a boatbuilder. Now, it's only a thwart and ribs, resembling nothing so much as an animal that's been plucked and gnawed down to its bones.

Mari says, "I don't think that. I know I'm asking a lot." She also knows Frank offered Bob and Sue a loan to save their boat, but Sue refused it.

"He wants more control over us," Sue told Mari. Apparently a three-hundred-dollar loan to help with ultrasound costs had resulted in constant badgering about how Sue should quit work, stay home, tell Bob to get off his lazy butt.

"I've tried everything else I can think of," Mari continues. No one will hire her. Despite her vow, she's had to borrow money a second time from her parents. They gave her a thousand dollars, and Mari knows her father would give her everything they have, but she would never take it. He and her mother have worked long and hard, and what has she done? Walked away from them and from the future they'd wanted for her. Stuck around and made excuses in a place where her son wasn't safe. Ignored the feeling—no, the knowledge—that the anxiety on her sisters' faces wasn't apprehension about crop yield, it was fear about what was happening to all of them.

"If you can't, you can't," Mari says. "I'm fine with that. I just have to, in good conscience, try everything I can think of." She tells Frank about the grants she's applied for, which, if any of them come through, will have to be spent on farm-related expenses. She needs nonrestricted money—Frank's money—for legal fees.

Frank tilts forward across his desk, eyes Mari's cookie, which she's left lying on one corner of his desk. "You heard about this deal the Richardsons are going after out at their place?"

"Deal?"

With a clear gloat on his features, Frank tells her about the Richardsons selling their property to a developer. "Check this guy out," Frank says and thumps on his keyboard before turning the monitor toward Mari. Duncan Development has a website filled with pictures of endless sandy beaches and building interiors that don't look as though they've ever been sullied by a mortal's hands. The marketing copy includes words like *peaceful seclusion*, *total wellness*, *team building*, and *strategy planning sessions*, as well as five-star chefs.

This was why Harry hadn't been willing to consider leasing her a bit of his land? Mari's opinion of Harry Richardson plummets. "Destination weddings?" Mari asks, incredulous. People who get married on Little Great Island tend to be locals or people with history and roots on the island. They know better than to hire bands and florists that need to be transported from the mainland. "Spa services?"

"High-end stuff," Frank says. "Mega money." The company's head honcho, he continues, owns a half-dozen properties scattered along the eastern seaboard from Florida to Rhode Island. All of them are making good money, as far as he can tell.

"What an idiotic idea."

"These high-end business types know what they're doing. They've got scads of worker bees looking for the right opportunity at the right price. Business analysis. That type of thing." Frank turns his computer back around and smiles fondly at the image on the screen.

"I figured that's why you came to me for a loan. You knew I was going to be in the money."

"How are you going to profit from the Richardsons selling to a developer?" Mari asks, and Frank fills her in on the meeting he had with Harry and Harry's request that he "use his influence as the island's foremost businessman" to ensure the planning board agrees to rezone the land from residential to commercial.

"He as much as promised there'd be a partnership of some sort in it for me," Frank says. "Maybe a deal where they buy all their construction materials through the boatyard, plus some kind of arrangement with the market for food."

"But my parents and I live out there." Traffic on the road would increase. There'd be pressure to moor boats off their dock, to allow anyone and everyone to tromp across their property to the waterfront. Would the fields be turned to lawn boosted by fertilizers and chemicals that would seep down the hill, through the McGavins' property, and into the ocean? Would these entitled individuals ride the ferry, or would they insist on a helicopter pad or a landing strip?

Zoning restrictions aren't something Mari'd considered when she'd applied for grants. Is that going to disqualify her? Will she need to apply for a rezone for the chickens and Houdini? She'll never hear the end of that from her mother, who hasn't insisted Mari get rid of the chickens, but who has not been silent about her displeasure. How is Mari ever going to raise lambs if there are a bunch of rich business types across the street?

Frank interrupts her thoughts. "Thing is, you've caught me when I'm feeling a bit on the optimistic side." Helping himself to another cookie, Frank goes on about how the executive retreat is going to save the island's proverbial bacon. There's going to be construction jobs for people like Reggie and Bob and anyone else who sees the handwriting on the wall when it comes to the lobster. A job for Mari, Frank adds as a small bit of cookie breaks off and falls to the floor. "They're going to need housekeepers, servers, folks in the kitchen, folks keeping up the lawn or whatever.

"They're always going to be needing groceries last minute," he continues. "And I'm right here to serve them. They're probably going to have boats out there by you folks." Frank wheels his chair in a half circle. "Something to get folks back and forth from the mainland. A couple of yachts so folks can sail." What he means is his boatyard business is also going to grow.

Every aspect of this plan makes Mari want to throw something, but Frank is fiddling with the dial on his ancient safe, the one he's had sitting in the corner of his office for as long as Mari can remember. From the looks of it, it was probably secondhand when he first opened the boatyard. Her objections to the retreat stall in her mouth when Frank turns back to her, three stacks of currency, each secured with a paper band, in his hand.

"Ta-da!"

As Frank explains why he has so much cash on hand—gearing up for the summer season, and it's not like there's an ATM on the island—Mari wills herself not to accept it. This is blood money, filth. But her hand reaches out and takes the cash.

"Ah, you're crying," Frank says, and he's immediately around the desk, leaning over Mari to hold her in his arms. The smell of him makes Mari cry harder. Frank was her land dad, she used to tell herself. Her father was her ocean dad.

"Don't worry, honey," Frank says. "It's going to be okay."

"No." Mari's wail is half smothered in Frank's shirt. No, Harry can't sell to a damn developer. No, she can't end up as a waitress or housekeeper for the rest of her life. No, it's not going to be okay.

"I missed your pain-in-the-neck self while you were gone," Frank says. "This place was entirely too quiet without you running around, pissing everyone off."

Mari shoulders the tears from her face. "I wasn't that bad, was I?"

"You could be." But Frank's smile is fond. "You and Susie and Reggie, you're the reason I'm doing all this. And Bob, of course. And that baby. You're family, and besides, you're like me. You're willing to shake things up a bit."

"I don't actually mean to cause problems," Mari protests, even as she wonders if there's a way to stop Harry from selling to a developer. Frank waves her objection away.

"'Course not. You're just you being you, and that's what's so great. So tell me, you going to get yourself a haircut with that money?" Frank laughs at his own joke, and Mari does her best to smile. *Get full custody of my son*, is her silent answer. *Hire a lawyer with fangs and claws.*

"I need a divorce," she says.

"That there is a loan." Frank returns to his seat.

"I understand."

"I'll get you on the payroll soon as I can."

"No worries. I'm onto something." There are around six thousand farms in Maine, Mari tells him. The vast majority of those are small, family run. Mari's got experience, a degree, a few grant proposals submitted and is researching more, so why shouldn't her own small farm be viable? To help generate additional income, she plans to offer consulting services to other farmers about sustainability options and ways to keep pests at bay without using chemicals. She'll face some competition, but the people she's found on the Internet who are offering similar services are charging fees beyond what most small farmers can afford. She'll keep her rates lower. She may have to travel some, but much of the work can be done remotely.

"Sounds like a plan," Frank says, but Mari's pretty sure he didn't follow most of it. "Listen, this loan is just between you and me, right?" he asks. "Seems my offering to help Bob and Sue caused the two of them to go after each other. I don't need to be in the middle of arguments just from trying to be nice."

Mari nods, uncomfortable with the secret but under-standing the reason. Even she's had an earful about how fu-rious Bob is that Sue wouldn't take her dad's money to save his boat.

"And Reggie," Frank continues. "Don't let on to him that I've given you a cent. He gets paid a salary to work here, but he's not reliable these days. I'm not giving him another dime until he shapes up."

"I don't...we don't..."

"I know." Once again, Frank makes the swatting motion with his hand. "Probably best for the two of you to stay away from each other anyway."

Frank's eyes shift to the door. His body stiffens.

"Well, speak of the devil," he says, and Reggie's voice from behind Mari's head says, "Hey, Mermaid." It's her fa-ther's nickname for her, but Reggie adopted it when they were dating. Back then, she loved it, but now there's a new tone in his voice, and when he says, "What's going on here?" she can tell, even without turning, that he's already more than a little bit drunk.

SKIPPING STONES

Harry

The rain has stopped, but the air at Little Beach on the northwest shore of Little Great Island is saturated. It's the second week of June and unseasonably warm. The humidity is acute, and mosquitos are everywhere. Still, it's the best place for cell phone coverage in wet weather. After a few dropped calls and poor connections, Harry told Isabelle to call him back in twenty minutes and drove to this small strip of shell-strewn rocks, cursing the siblings' collective decision to get rid of the landline.

The first time his phone buzzes, Harry hears nothing but a mechanical thrumming when he answers and, beyond it, a noise like someone in dress shoes walking on a wooden floor. The second time, the call is dropped within seconds. Harry waits a moment, then initiates the call himself.

"Harry!" Isabelle's voice booms.

"I'm here. Can you hear me?"

"I've only got a couple of minutes," Isabelle says. "I've got a deposition on Monday, and Zach's in trial. It's supposed to be Mei's day off, but I told her when I hired her that she had to be flexible. She's giving me a lot of pushback, which I really don't need right now."

"What about this conservation easement?" Harry asks, having emailed his siblings about it a few days earlier. "I think it's good idea." Sends the right message about the kind of buyer they are looking for. The kind of family who will fit in on the island.

"Harry, we got the offer."

Her words knock a hole in Harry's chest. Duncan and a group of investors had toured the property a week earlier. Harry was told to steer clear of them. Pete had called that evening, triumphant, to say that Duncan loved the island. No mention was made of an offer, however, which Harry took as a sign that Duncan was going to keep looking at other properties. When Harry had said that he was exploring the option of a conservation easement with his siblings, Pete snapped that he was pulling every string he had to make this deal work for Harry. Harry asked for a bit more time. Pete's response was that a little gratitude would be appreciated.

"How much?" Harry asks his sister now.

Three-point-three-million dollars. With his share, Harry could pay off the hospital bills from Ellie's treatment. He could buy a new car. He could buy a new condo or even a house. He could travel. All things he's never consciously wanted, but now they look like the trappings of a new life, and that should feel good. It doesn't.

"Iz, this island isn't the right place for an executive retreat."

"Not our problem. I've had a real-estate attorney go through the offer. It's got the usual contingencies relating to inspections, but only as it relates to the land." Isabelle and the real-estate lawyer have both assumed that the plan is to level the house, so none of its foibles matter. Duncan doesn't even seem to be concerned about water, sewer, or electricity, which Isabelle explains is because all systems will need to be upgraded for commercial property anyway.

"The only real contingency is that the land gets rezoned for commercial use, but I've checked the ordinances, and it shouldn't be a problem now you've got Frank on board, plus the tax revenue is going to be a real win for the island, which means the rezone should sail through the approval process. It's a clean offer," Isabelle summarizes. "The real-estate attorney says to go for it. Jonathan's signing his copy as we speak. I'll sign mine as soon as I track down a notary. Clive's a notary, right? Can you get to him today?"

"Can't we wait a couple of days?"

"Harry, no. For heaven's sake. This is what you wanted. You are the one who got Pete involved. And now it's happening. Be happy. We're going to come up on the Fourth to celebrate."

"Everyone? That's great!" Maybe he can delay signing until after the holiday. Once the family is gathered on the island, everyone will see that they should hold out for more suitable buyers. He's already deciding who will sleep in which room when Isabelle speaks.

"Just Jonathan and me. I thought a sibling reunion would be nice."

Harry runs the pad of his thumb across the ribbed cuff of Ellie's sweatshirt, which he still hasn't managed to move from the car.

"Why can't the kids come?"

"Nanny logistics, sleep schedules, you name it. Plus, I could use some downtime and Charlie is, you know, Charlie." Charlie, Jonathan and Umeko's son, has a spectrum disorder and does best in familiar circumstances with a limited number of people. Isabelle has never figured out how to relate to him.

"I really think we should hold off on this," Harry says. "This isn't my grief talking or whatever you think. It's happening too fast. We should think about what the repercussions are for the island."

"Two against one here, Harry," Isabelle says cheerfully. "And besides, it's for your own good. You'll have a whole lot of money in your pocket. You can start fresh."

"Fresh." His tone is flat. What, exactly, does it mean to start "fresh" at his age?

"What I'm hoping," Isabelle begins and then stops. Harry can't tell from her pause if she's distracted or choosing her words. "Is that we can find some time to talk about the future, now that it looks like the house is going to sell."

"The future?"

"Okay, fine. Your future. Are you going back to Boston? To your job? Are you selling the condo?"

"I don't know."

Isabelle says, "Seriously, Har, I'm worried. Pete says you've been spending a bunch of time with Mari McGavin." The way she says Mari's name makes it clear Pete's had nothing nice to say about her. It's time to end this conversation before Harry loses his temper.

"I'll look at the offer," he says.

"Today. We have twenty-four hours to get back to them."

Harry closes his eyes, rubs his forehead with his free hand. After a pause, Isabelle continues, "Three-point-three million dollars split three ways is a nice chunk of change, Harry. You did this. For yourself. For all of us. Let's have the full-scale Fourth of July party, the way Mom and Dad used to. Jon and I will hit the liquor store in New Hampshire. G&Ts and champagne. Sound good?"

"Sure."

"You okay, Har?"

A simple question. An impossibly complicated answer. "Fine," Harry says finally.

"I wish you'd go back to Boston every once in a while," she says. "At least for a few days. You're awfully isolated up there. I don't think it's a great idea for you to be alone so much."

What she doesn't know, because Harry hasn't confessed it to anyone, is Ellie moves around now in whatever part of the house he isn't in with some frequency. Sometimes she whispers, although he cannot understand what she says. The only time he feels free of her presence is in Mari and Levi's garden.

"I'm okay."

"Who are you hanging out with? Anybody other than Mari?"

"It's still early in the season," Harry replies. "I've seen Mr. Estabrook. I had dinner with Pete and Abby."

"Oh, Harry," Isabelle says. "Ellie wouldn't want you to be miserable."

"I know."

"This sale is a good thing. I promise. You'll see."

Four people have appeared at the far end of the beach, dark shapes in the fog. Harry tries to identify them as Isabelle says, "Maybe we can get out for a sail, if the weather's good. Listen, I have to go. Mei's threatening to leave. Love you." Harry hears the phone thump on something hard and his sister calling, "What about if I pay you time and a half?" before the connection is broken.

The figures on the beach are close enough now that Harry can identify them as the McGavins. Levi has a bright-red pail clenched in one hand, and he leans over repeatedly to grab things, which he then shows to his mother and grandparents for comment. Their presence seems fortuitous. He should tell them about Duncan Development now, before they hear about it from someone else.

Laying Ellie's sweatshirt back on the passenger seat, he gets out and heads toward the beach, where Sam and Alice dip their heads and greet him. Mari gives a single quick nod. Levi, who is still picking up stones and dropping them into a pail, doesn't look up. The boy's head is bent, hair curtaining his face. His shorts look new. His knees are scraped. Something twinges in Harry's chest, and he turns away. Pretends to be studying the ocean.

"My wife found a piece of blue sea glass here one summer," Harry tells Levi when he's certain his voice is steady. "It made her very happy."

Levi wrinkles his nose. "Why?" he asks.

Because blue sea glass is one of the hardest colors to find. Because Ellie believed in good luck omens despite being a scientist. Because she was Ellie.

"Blue was her favorite color," he says, and then asks Levi if he's ever skipped a rock across the water.

"No."

"Like this." Harry selects an oblong rock with the right degree of heft and flatness. In truth, he's never been good at skipping rocks, and four good hops followed by a series of skitters is probably the best he's ever done. This time, however, he gets lucky, and the rock makes six long leaps before disappearing into the sea.

"Nice one," Alice calls.

Leaning over, Levi selects a rock and tosses it. It sinks instantly. He tries twice more and then frowns.

"Like this." Harry throws again, this one less successful than the first. "The most important part is the rock you choose." Moving closer to Levi, he describes the size and shape they are searching for and plucks a few stones from the beach. The older McGavins watch as Levi rejects a few rocks of the wrong size before finding one that's right. Holding it in the palm of one hand, Levi studies it.

"I don't understand," he says, with a note of petulance.

"The next important thing is how you hold it." Harry demonstrates, balancing a stone on his middle finger while holding it between his index finger and thumb. Mari, in baggy foul weather gear, stands watching a few yards away.

For an instant, Ellie is so close Harry can practically hear her breathing. The curve of her calf is nearly visible from the corner of his eye.

"Now what?" Levi asks.

"Lean forward like this." Harry demonstrates, skips his rock, and watches while Levi angles his stone directly into the water.

"You aren't telling me the right way," Levi complains.

"It takes a little practice," Harry says. "Try leaning over a bit more. You want to throw so that it heads out straight over the water." Holding his hand flat, palm down, Harry sweeps it toward the ocean. "You don't want to think of it diving. Think of it flying along the surface."

Levi tries again. The rock clicks to the shore a few feet away, missing the water completely. "Tell me right!" he insists.

Mari moves toward them, but Harry speaks before she can intervene. "You can do it," he tells Levi. Leaning over, Harry cups his right hand over the boy's.

"Pull your arm back this far," he says. "After that, it's all in the wrist." Their combined attempt crashes an inch or so into the waves.

"I don't think it works for us to do it together," Harry admits. He stands back and watches Levi, who devolves into grabbing whatever rock comes to hand and throwing it into the waves. Mari and her parents watch in silence. There's something a bit too studied in their look, but Harry ignores them, absorbs himself in tossing rocks with Levi, the two of them finding a rhythm between throwing the biggest rocks they can find, tossing a handful of pebbles, and trying to drop a shot into the bullseye left by the last stone to sink. The foghorn starts up again, or maybe it had been hooting all along. Wavelets slap the beach. Levi giggles and Harry laughs, and there's a lull in the sound of splashing as Levi scoops rocks into his bucket, then a crash as the full contents of the pail hit the water.

"Seriously," Mari says. "An executive retreat."

Ignoring her, Harry grabs a rock, balances, and skips: four long leaps before it sinks.

"You did it!" Levi cheers, and Harry is in the midst of high fiving him when Mari says, "Do you have any idea what a huge, flaming son of a bitch you are?"

BAKELITE

Mari

Back aches. Sinuses sheathed with the odor of bait from working aboard the *Alice-Mari*. Left heel burning from a blister raised by the poor fit of unfamiliar boots. Hands sore from the endless wringing of mops. For two weeks—ever since that day on the beach when Harry all but fled—Mari has tried to get Harry to talk with her about Duncan Development. He's always had some excuse for why it isn't a good time. Now, despite her exhaustion, she's out of patience.

After a second knock on the farmhouse door, she gazes down the hill: Levi on a hay bale, visiting Houdini; her mother pinning laundry to the line. The *Alice-Mari* is on her mooring, her dad using his "day off" to meet with the planning board about Duncan Development.

"Coming!" When Harry opens the door, he seems surprised to see her. He's unshaven. His eyes are red.

"Can we talk?"

Clearly, he doesn't want to, but he lets her in. It's gotten worse inside the house. Mari sees a grocery bag of freezer pizzas that looks as though it's been there for a while, a dead mouse on a dustpan. Heaped puzzle pieces, scattered dice, a cardboard box poorly packed with mismatched glassware, stacks of yellowed sheet music and books.

"The kitchen's marginally habitable," he says, and so she follows him there, to where there's a single small plate in the deep double sink. Mari's mother said not to bother him. She said what the Richardsons did with their property was none of the McGavins' business. That they'd find a way to deal with whatever happened next door because that's what you do with what life throws at you. You find a way to go on.

"No," Mari'd said. Shouted, maybe. Loudly enough that Levi abandoned the picture he was drawing and scampered up the stairs to their room. He slammed the door, causing the whole house to rattle. But at least he didn't leave the house. Progress, of a sort.

"Coffee?" Harry asks.

"More of your hot ice cream?" Mari hopes for at least an attempted smile, but Harry doesn't react.

"No, thank you," she amends. In the silence, while he pours himself a cup, prayer wanders into her head. *Please, God, make him see reason. Please, God, let me keep my temper in check.*

Harry leans against the giant oven, face tipped to his coffee, and says, "You've come to yell at me about the offer from Duncan Development."

"Yes."

"We signed the offer."

"When?" Not that it matters. Signed is signed. But don't these things have some kind of exit clause? An escape hatch for people with seller's remorse?

Harry sets his mug on the counter, sweeps crumbs onto the floor with the side of his hand. Meaning he signed a while ago. Meaning while he's been saying he doesn't have time to talk with her, he's been avoiding this confession.

"I was under some pressure from my siblings," he says, and Mari erupts in spite of herself.

"Who cares? You know it's a screwed-up thing to do to the environment. That it's a screwed-up thing to do to this island." It's a screwed-up thing to do to her personally, but he owes her nothing. She's only an islander. A woman on the lam from her husband. An escapee from a religious cult.

"I lost sleep over it."

Poor baby. As if she isn't losing sleep every night over her own predicament, that of her parents, that of Bob and Sue, and that of Little Great Island.

"I wish there was something I could do for you. I wish I could help."

Maybe. Or maybe that's guilt talking, but she'll use his guilt gladly if it helps. The lawyer she found on the mainland—young and inexperienced, but her hourly rate was low—took much of the money she'd gotten from Frank. Still no news on the grants, and the only queries she's gotten for consulting work have been from people wanting to hire someone with a grad degree or with experience farming in Maine. Mari's going to need to show the judge her ability to care for Levi's financial, medical, and emotional needs, the lawyer had told her. To feed and clothe him, ensure his education, keep him happy and safe. She needs a farm. She needs the sheep, a larger vegetable garden, and she needs to be available to Levi whenever he needs her. All that means that her farm must be close to home and close to the elementary school, which means it must be on Richardson land.

"When do you close?"

"Late September."

"Let me use a few acres, at least through the summer."

"I don't think I can do that."

"Why not? It's still your land."

"Technically, the land belongs to me, Jon, and Iz in equal parts."

It doesn't matter. They're never around. "Please. I need this. For me. For Levi." As Mari explains her plan, Harry seems to want to look everywhere but at her face. Pastor Aaron, during the last year, had acquired the same habit of avoiding her eyes.

"I've taken out a restraining order against Levi's father," she says. "That's how serious this is. Levi cannot go back to living there, and neither can I."

"I'm sorry, but there's nothing I can do."

"Come on, Harry. Listen to yourself." When he gives her a perplexed look, Mari adds, "Look at this place. It's a disaster. You're a disaster. Don't tell me there's nothing you can do when one look at you and the way you're living says you've given up."

"I haven't…" He can't finish the sentence. "Cleaning out this house is a lot of work," he says. "I haven't been sleeping well."

"Then I'll help you clean. And in return, you'll let me keep sheep on your land until you close on the sale or until I find someplace else to put them."

"I told you, it's not entirely up to me."

"Fine. Then you can pay me to help you. Pay me a lot."

For a long moment, he contemplates the doorway into the children's living room, where no one is standing, and Mari imagines the voices of other children in there, laughing and slapping at cards. Harry's friends, Jonathan's friends, Isabelle's friends. Summer kids. Even under the same roof, there'd been so much that separated her from them. Those kids and their parents had everything. They spent their days in sailboats or playing games. Her resentment had grown over time; at first, she'd been merely content to be in the same house with them.

Turning her attention back to Harry, Mari notices how his T-shirt comes to a gentle V beneath his Adam's apple. There's that smooth, soft spot low on a man's neck. He rubs the exact place where Mari's been staring, and she feels her face flush.

"How much is a lot?" he asks. "Because I don't have a lot of money at the moment."

"Thirty-five bucks an hour." At that rate, it will take months to earn enough for the lawyer's next installment, but it's better than nothing.

"Starting now," Mari adds. "Let me look around, figure out the best place to begin."

After a final gulp of coffee, Harry leads her into the main-floor bedroom. In farmhouses built toward the end of the nineteenth century, as this one was, this room would have been used by the sick or elderly because of its proximity to the kitchen's warmth. The unmade bed is piled with clothing. Women's clothing, Mari judges by the size and colors. Not Isabelle's; Mari remembers her as partial to pastels. This pile has plums and bright yellows and reds.

"Ellie's?" she guesses.

"Yah. I was going to…I brought it all down here to box it up, but…anyway, this is Jonathan's room, so I need to get all this stuff out. He and Iz are coming for the Fourth."

"I'll do it."

Panic flashes across his face.

"I'm not going to throw anything away," Mari assures him. This house has unused bedrooms and closets galore, but she doesn't want Harry to feel like she's shoving his wife into some anonymous part of the house. If she were in his place, Mari would want to know Ellie's ghost or her soul or her memory or whatever remained of her was someplace familiar and comforting, at least until the house had to be cleared out for the new owners.

"Which bedroom are you using?" she asks.

"My parents' old room. The one with the chickadee wallpaper."

"How about we put these things in your old room, then?"

Harry nods in agreement but doesn't move.

"Would you like me to bring them up?" Mari asks. Harry nods again. She can feel him watching as she gathers the clothing in her arms.

"I'll be right back."

Harry's still staring at the mattress.

"Why don't you track down some sheets, and we'll make up the bed?"

After Harry nods, Mari uses the secret staircase, the one that goes from the kitchen to Harry's childhood room above. When she lays Ellie's clothing on the mattress, she does it gently.

"I'm sorry," she says to whatever there is of Ellie that lingers here. A hairbrush on the bureau kicks her heart into high gear. It's the same color and shape as the Bakelite handle on the old-fashioned knife sharpener that was lying on one of the upended tree stumps used for seats in the prayer shed. At the moment she noticed it, Levi was already in her arms. She was thinking ahead, to how she might get them to the road without being seen. All she registered of that knife sharpener was how completely out of place it was. The oddness of it in the prayer shed was probably what had made the image stick.

Back down in Jonathan's bedroom, Mari finds Harry holding a pillow in his teeth while pulling on the case. There are enough sheets piled on the bureau to make up every bed in the house.

"I wasn't sure which ones fit," he says.

It only takes two tries to find the proper sheets and then, the bed made, Mari goes after the woodwork with rags and a can of Pledge while Harry cleans mirrors and windows. The image of that knife sharpener won't leave her alone.

"Levi had a sore on his tongue when I found him in the prayer shed," she says. "I saw that hairbrush upstairs. It made me think about it."

Since she's been back on the island, Mari's forced herself not to think about the past. She and Levi got away safely. That was all that mattered. But now, eyes on the view of spruce trees beyond the window, she allows the memories in. As soon as she was released by Sister Ann, Mari went to Sister Grace, who told her Levi was in the prayer shed. The shed door was locked, the grime-crusted window a foot above her reach. She managed to climb up to it by rolling a rock the size of a bushel basket with a strength that must have come from sheer panic. Through a missing corner of glass, she saw Levi lying in the dirt, his foot tied to one of the stumps as if he were a rabid dog. Bashing the door down bruised her in the shoulders, the hips, and the feet, but she barely noticed. Got the rope off her son with no problem. Levi whimpered in her arms. It didn't seem odd that he wasn't talking; she figured it was fear. Not until she secured him in a seat belt in the back of a stranger's car had she noticed that his mouth hung open strangely. He was drooling. But they had to hurry. Everything had to happen so fast.

Harry is looking at her, a crumpled paper towel in one hand and a Windex bottle in the other. Mari shakes her head. She cannot tell him what happened. She doesn't know.

"How long was he in the shed?" he asks.

Time folded in on itself from the moment Levi's fork dropped. Her son was out of her sight maybe as long as an hour. Probably closer to a half-hour. As Mari's sisters escorted her away from Pastor Aaron's office, she saw Levi crossing the fields with his father on one side and Pastor Aaron on the other. He had a hand in each man's hand. Looking, from the back, like a child going for a walk with his father and grandfather. A scene that should have been heartwarming but instead shot terror through her limbs.

Sister Grace sent the others from the room on one errand or another, pulled three carefully folded bills from her sock, and instructed Mari to grab some clothes for Levi from the community closet and run like hell.

With Levi in her arms, Mari ran behind the barn, through the fields, and down to the road, where she stuck out her thumb. The prim-faced woman who stopped for them said nothing, but when they reached the bus station, she gave Mari all the bills in her wallet and told her she was doing the right thing by leaving.

Harry's face is the color of a beached clam when she's finished telling him about their escape. "Why did the hairbrush remind you of his sore?"

"I don't know. The color maybe. I was panicked. Trying to get Levi away from there. I wasn't paying much attention to anything else.

Harry sets the towel and Windex down on the table. He is standing so close. Can he feel how much she wants to be held and comforted? But what a terrible idea. He's in the midst of ruining her parents' life and her own.

"I don't want to do anything that hurts you or your family," Harry says. "This development is a bad idea. But I don't think there's anything I can do."

"I can't lose my son," Mari says, and then she realizes it's not Harry she needs to help her. It's his sister, Isabelle, the lawyer. Taking up the Windex from where he left it, she says, "That's enough for today."

POOR LITTLE THINGS

Alice

It's midmorning when Alice pins the laundry to the line. Levi, standing beside her while he feeds Houdini a carrot, says, "Can I give him another?" The way Levi tips his face up at her stirs Alice in a way she hasn't felt in years. This little face with its fine sifting of freckles and ears stuck out from behind tucked hair feels like her own heart. It makes her nuts that she missed so many years of Levi's life, makes her nuts as well that Mari subjected this poor, sweet child to all that religious nonsense just to…what? Prove some point? Piss her mother off? It doesn't matter. What matters is that he is here now, where Alice can protect him.

"Sure," she tells Levi. The bag's right there on the ground. "But only one more," she adds.

Levi says, "I used to think that sheep and goats had devil eyes, but Mama says their eyes are that way because it helps them see if anything's sneaking up on them."

"Yup," Alice says as she realizes someone's standing beyond the barn, where their land gives way to the trees. Someone is watching them. People don't act like that on this island. What reason would there be? The figure moves, and Alice guesses that it's Reggie before he lights a cigarette and gives himself away.

"Hello there, Reggie Clatcher," she calls. "Some reason you're skulking around in the shadows like that?"

"Nope." Reggie comes forward. He's got something she can't make out in one hand, and the hand with the cigarette swings by his side. Alice has always loved Frank's kids—poor little things, losing their mother so young and their dad being such a hard worker and an old crank at times. Made them possessive of people, possessive of love. Reggie had coped worse with it all, although few people other than Alice see it that way. He'd attached himself to Lydia, and she was so good to that little boy until she and Frank had a falling out— Frank suggesting a marriage of convenience is what Alice has gathered. After that, Frank told his kids to steer clear of Lydia. Alice has memories of Reggie trick-or-treating when his teeth were half grownup and half little boy. Ears he hadn't yet grown into, mouth like a kiss planted on his face, and the most trusting way of looking at you that Alice had ever seen.

But having a soft spot for Reggie doesn't mean she wants him anywhere near her grandson. Her daughter either.

Reggie stops a few feet away. To Levi, he says, "Hello there, little man."

Levi shifts his feet slightly and straightens his back. "Hello, big man," he says, and as Reggie's face goes from surprise to laughter, Levi adds, "You shouldn't smoke. It's bad for your health."

"Damn right it is," Reggie agrees and grinds the butt out beneath his heel. "Thanks for that." To Alice, he says, "Mari around?"

"Nope." Mari's up at Harry Richardson's cleaning house, but Reggie doesn't need to know that.

"Okay, but…" Reggie pauses. "Tell her I came by. I brought this." He thrusts the object he's holding at her. It's a hand-sized carved rowboat, complete with oars. Alice recognizes it as Bob's handiwork, from back when he first started making model boats and focused on rowboats instead of three-masted ships.

"This is for you, little man," Reggie adds, hauling a bag of candy from his pocket. Levi accepts it gingerly, thanks Reggie in a quiet voice. Then Reggie stands there like he's trying to come up with a reason to stay. Either that, or he hasn't said what he truly came here to say.

"What's on your mind, Reggie Clatcher?" Alice asks.

"Just being friendly," he says. "Do you know why my dad gave Mari a bunch of money?"

Alice does know, but that doesn't mean Mari's divorce is any of Reggie's business.

"Don't know a thing about it," she says.

Reggie squints, tilts his head. "Doubt that," he says before turning on one heel and marching back across the fields. He's got another cigarette lit before he's reached the trees.

"Is he a bad man?" Levi wants to know, and Alice shakes her head.

"He's a little boy in a grown man's body." Smiling down at Levi, she adds, "You'd be surprised at how often that happens."

THE CLASP OF DEATH

Harry

"A huge boon for the island economy," Tim Duncan says. Jonathan, in the comment section of the video call, tells his siblings that something nice needs to be done for Pete Shaw, as he is the person who brought the Richardsons and Duncan Development together. Isabelle replies she'll bring an extra bottle of champagne over the Fourth. Jonathan suggests they owe Pete a case of bubbly. Harry, reading the messages, still stings from Mari's accusation that he's given up when there's more to be done. Everyone, from his siblings to the bereavement specialist, has assured him he did everything in his power to save Ellie. But had he? Should he have insisted on consults with other hospitals? Recognized the danger inherent in the sweating sooner, treated her better, loved her more or differently? Should he have been more supportive of her desire to go through the first steps of IVF so that motherhood would be possible when treatment was done? Or would the delay in treatment or the IVF hormones themselves have only hastened her death?

He texts his siblings to stay on the call after Duncan leaves. *Back to back for the rest of the day*, Isabelle types back.
I only need a minute.
One minute max.

Jonathan writes that he's trying to get a run in before his next meeting. *2Nite work?* he types, and both Harry and Isabelle respond *no*.

Duncan, who's got dark, heavy eyebrows and a long, thin face, is still talking. The retreat will be an economic infusion for the island at a time when it's desperately needed. Tourism already represents a significant portion of island economies, and his developments increase tourist spending "exponentially year over year." Fisheries are in for hard times, given all the reasons Harry already knows by heart. His retreats, Duncan claims, bring in the right kind of visitor dollars: steady jobs, increased tax revenues, infrastructure improvements.

"We're not talking T-shirt shops and ice-cream stands," he says. "Hordes of people spending minimal amounts of money." Rather, Duncan's properties lead to new home construction and new people with an interest in contributing to the island and the means to do so. People who value privacy and nature and so won't pursue "inappropriate growth."

Soy-latte suckers and exotic-breed dog owners, Mari has called them. The village full of sushi and art boutiques. Her rooster crows, as if protesting this vision of the future.

"There are things we haven't discussed," Harry says, and tries to ignore his sister's scowl. She's in full attorney mode for this meeting: crisp white shirt, so bright it shines like a light source; navy blazer; her brown hair flipped impeccably below her shoulders. Jonathan, an IT guy, has inherited their mother's lighter coloring. The crease between his brows looks deep enough to insert a coin.

"Such as?" Duncan asks.

Attitude, Harry thinks. Fitting in. Understanding the delicacy of the relationship between summer visitors and the year-round population. "How are these people going to get on and off the island?"

Duncan grins. "The remote location is a plus for these people, right?"

"I know, but are they going to come over on the ferry? Because it can be hard to get a car reservation." If they eschewed automobiles and came on a private boat, where would they land? "This isn't the kind of place that's going to welcome helipads or landing strips."

"Let's not get ahead of ourselves," Jonathan says.

"Right." Duncan agrees a bit too quickly for Harry's taste, but the man presses on before Harry has a chance to speak.

"Number one, we've got to get this rezone through." Duncan has done his homework, knows that Sam McGavin is town administrator, and that Bob Greggs, Carol Stanley, and Lydia Smith are on the planning board. "How are things going there?"

With his siblings' eyes on him, Harry tells Duncan about his meeting with Frank Clatcher. An influential businessman, Isabelle adds. Someone who is well respected by the islanders.

"Any opposition from the year-round population so far?"

Harry hesitates for less than a breath before replying that there is.

"One person," Isabelle interjects. "Who hasn't even been living on the island for the past decade."

Harry's ready to capitulate, but then he remembers the gentleness with which Mari had gathered Ellie's clothing into her arms. Levi's small hand in his when they'd tried skipping rocks together.

"I'm wondering if we could let her use a few acres of the land until closing," he says. Instantly, Isabelle's attention drops to her keyboard. She makes no effort to disguise the sound of her furious typing.

Harry says, "I think it would help relations with her and her family, who are going to be most impacted by the construction and increase in traffic."

WTF? pops up in a comment from Isabelle. Right behind it is a question mark from Jonathan, followed by a diatribe from Isabelle about letting her handle things.

"Use it for what?" Duncan asks. Even though he keeps his eyes on the camera, Harry is certain, from the other man's posture, that Duncan jotted a note.

"Pastureland. For sheep."

This time, it's Jonathan whose comment is *WTF?*

Duncan says, "We can't stop you, but if you're asking my opinion, it's a terrible idea. From my experience, relationships with neighbors, particularly in these small communities, can be problematic. In this instance, it feels as though if we give them an inch, they're going to go after a mile."

Duncan's voice is controlled, but Harry senses the tension, realizes that he's made himself the first bump in the road to this multimillion-dollar sale. Isabelle is keyboarding so assiduously the tendons in her neck stand out. Jonathan rubs his forehead. Here he goes again, Harry imagines them thinking. Acting nuts. Grief crazy.

Harry says, "Never mind," and then, because that doesn't seem to fully put the matter to rest, he adds, "She'll probably find another solution anyway."

"Great." Duncan is cheery again, talking about reaching out, touching base. When Duncan leaves the meeting, Harry is tempted to do the same. Pretend he forgot that he asked his siblings to stay on. But that wouldn't work. His phone would be buzzing in an instant. His email would ding like a dinner bell.

"What?" Isabelle demands.

"*What* what?" They are eight and twelve again, Harry playing dumb in the face of his big sister's ire.

"This sale was your idea," she says.

"I know."

"It's the right idea."

"I'm not so sure."

"Listen," Jonathan says. "I've got some things going on, workwise. Not worth getting into, but a bit more of a financial cushion would be helpful when it comes to my getting a good night's sleep."

Jonathan's forever wanting more savings, and Harry can sympathize. Umeko works, but only part time. Support and treatment for Charlie is costly, and much of it isn't covered by insurance. On the other hand, Jonathan has always been the one of the three who is most prone to anxiety. Exams used to cause him fits of vomiting. He'd dealt with ordinary school stress by eating and so had been an overweight child. Then he'd discovered exercise and learned that running from his problems could be a literal solution.

"Seriously, Har. What is going on between you and the wild child?" This from Isabelle, who checks her watch.

"Nothing."

"Promise?"

"Promise."

There's a round of "I love yous" and Harry's screen goes blank. It's disorienting, finding himself alone in the bedroom that looks out over the fields toward the mound of Leah's Knuckle after being absorbed in the meeting. Off to his left are the scattered structures of the McGavins' sheds, their barn, their house, and the ocean beyond. How strange to think of a random businessperson sitting in this space, admiring this view. How odd to think of this being a room someone stays in for a night or two, their focus on profit margins and market position, their time on Little Great Island essentially forgettable in the relentless race of life.

But none of that is his problem. Harry flips the lid of his laptop down, yanks the matelassé bedspread over the twisted sheets, and decides that today isn't a day for cleaning. The rooster crows again. Yesterday's rain drips from the trees.

Harry, on his way downstairs, hears a sound that is closer. A sniffle coming from his porch.

At first glance, there's no one, but then there's movement, and Harry sees Levi tucked in a porch corner, curled behind the rocker that was always the one preferred by Mr. Estabrook. The boy's hair has been cut and, although it still reaches well below his ears, it resembles an actual haircut. He clasps a stuffed donkey to his chest.

"Hey," Harry says. Levi doesn't answer. "Any chance your mom knows you're here?" Once again, Levi ignores him, so Harry tries a third approach. "Do you suppose you'd be willing to come out of there and sit on a chair?"

No is the apparent answer, and Harry realizes that he, too, wouldn't mind hiding from the world for a while. Maneuvering the rocker to one side, he slots himself in beside Levi and pulls the rocker in front of them again. Two can't hide as well as one, but it doesn't matter because no one is looking.

"The devil has taken possession of Mama again," Levi says.

"I know what she feels like," Harry says, because possession by the devil seems like as good an explanation as any for what had caused Harry to agree to this sale.

"You do?" Knees and stuffed animal still pressed to his chest, Levi gives Harry the once-over. His forehead creases as he seems to debate whether this man can be trusted. "I do too," he says finally. "But Mama doesn't want to pray anymore. She says that God knows what she needs and wants and that He knows what's right and wrong, and so she doesn't have to tell him."

"What do you think?"

"She's supposed to ask for Papa's forgiveness, and for God's. Because otherwise, she has to be punished."

"Has she been punished before?"

Levi blinks twice and then points upward and asks,

"What's up there?" Harry thinks that he's asking about Heaven, but Levi adds, "When you go up your stairs."

This out-of-the-blue changing of subjects is typical of children, in Harry's experience, particularly when they are trying to avoid the subject at hand. He's had students ask about his personal life when the conversation was meant to be about plagiarism, cry about a sick cat when the real issue was cyberbullying.

Bedrooms, he tells Levi. Bathrooms. Closets and hallways.

"Do you have your own toothbrush?"

"I do."

"That's good. Because actually? You shouldn't share toothbrushes because of germs."

"I know," Harry says before it occurs to him that owning his own toothbrush must be new to this child.

"I have my towels," Levi says. "Grandma Alice has hers and she keeps them in the bathroom. Mama keeps hers in our room. Grandma Alice says Grandpa Sam can't have a towel because he leaves it on the floor." Eyes twinkling, Levi gives Harry a conspiratorial look. "So you know what he does?"

Harry shakes his head.

"He uses Grandma Alice's towel!"

Smiling, Harry says, "Grandpa Sam's a tricky man, isn't he?"

"He tells stories," Levi says. "Sometimes, I'm in the stories."

"That sounds fun. What about your dad?" Harry asks, despite knowing it's unfair to pump Levi for information Mari's been reluctant to give. "Does he tell stories?"

"He tells about God," Levi says, and Harry can't discern if the boy finds that a good thing or a bad one. "Papa's going to be the God's Bounty leader someday," Levi adds finally. He nods his head, as if the sentence sums up his father well enough. "Everybody says so."

"That's nice," Harry says, but only because Levi seems to think so.

"This is Pretty," Levi says, holding up his stuffed animal. "He was my mom's, and she called him Eeyore, but I decided Pretty's a better name because my favorite horse at home was called Pretty. I know this is a donkey, but I like to pretend he's a horse because I like horses better."

"Hello, Pretty," Harry says. "I'm pleased to meet you." He shakes the toy's front leg. Whatever the eyes had been, they are stitched now. The thread has started to fade. Harry jots a mental note to check online for a new stuffed horse.

"When the devil was in me, I said a bad word," Levi says, Pretty pulled tight to his chest again.

"We all do, from time to time."

Levi shakes his head. "I said God's name. In a bad way." His voice is barely audible.

"I'm sure you didn't mean to be bad."

Tears are filling Levi's eyes. Shit, Harry thinks. He is way out of his depth.

"I was supposed to go in the prayer shed for a long time," Levi adds. "I'm not supposed to let unwholesome talk come from my mouth."

"Were you scared?"

Levi sticks his tongue out, his eyes fastened on Harry's, and then retracts it. It's an odd gesture, and Harry can't parse it.

"A papa who loves his child disciplines him," Levi says.

"Did he hurt you?" Harry asks, trying to keep any sense of blame or judgement from his voice.

"I was bad," Levi whispers. A tear falls on the back of his hand.

"Sometimes we blame ourselves for things," Harry says, "but they aren't really our fault."

Levi shakes his head vehemently. "It was me," he says. "I said it." His arms thread across his chest. His brow lowers. This conversation, his body language makes clear, is over.

FIREWORKS THAT SIZZLE
AND CRACK

Little Great Island

The sun on the Fourth of July has passed its zenith. Down at the yacht club, the last of the holiday boat race finishers climbs the ramp holding a spinnaker bag, polarized sunglasses propped on a well-tanned nose. From every flagpole at every island home or business hangs a red-white-and-blue flag. Even the trash cans on Main Street have been outfitted in streamers of crêpe. The parking spots are full. Across Little Great Island, screen doors on the houses slam, car engines grumble, the air acquires the tang of working grills and spent firecrackers. The lobstermen hose their boats and stow their gear, recount their catch as though ten lobster or twelve might have become a hundred or more as they motored homeward. Out on the horizon, the *Abenaki Princess* appears, running deep in the water from the holiday crowds onboard. The sun dips lower. A spider falls victim to the wheel of a car. The market is closed. The post office is locked. No lights shine in the town office, but The Blue Buoy—storm damage repaired—has opened for the season and is filled to capacity while a line of impatient parents and hungry children waits out front. A heavyset woman in a white butcher's apron emerges from The Buoy and leans to write *Sold Out* next to any meal containing lobster on the chalkboard that stands by the door. Complaints file back through the line. Slowly, the crowd disperses.

"It's not the Fourth without lobster," a woman groans.

"What this island needs is more restaurants," grouses her husband. "I do not feel like cranking up the grill."

The Blue Buoy's two owners stare at each other with worry.

The first of the evening's fireworks sizzle and crack in a village driveway. More explosions follow. Dogs howl a symphony of anguish. Birds scatter. Fertilized lobster eggs, hundreds of them, are released to the ocean in a stream. Rockets whistle and a fountain sputters. Toddlers scream. The sun sets in a frenzy of red and orange and yellow.

SHRIMP CURLS AND
SKEWERED SCALLOPS

Mari

Wrights, Parkers, Sheehan-Neilsons. Three houses, each cleaned weekly, is four hundred and fifty dollars a week. Times nine until Labor Day, plus the two hundred Mari's made from cleaning Harry's house and the additional hundred twenty she'll make tonight. With that income and, with luck, another few houses to clean, she'll have money back in savings by the time her lawyer bills her again. All that means that it's okay that she's used the rest of the money Frank gave her to pay for a half-dozen Columbian ewes and a ram, all due to be delivered before the end of the week. Once this party is over, Isabelle has agreed to talk with her, and Mari intends to get whatever free legal advice she can about obtaining custody of Levi. Maybe Isabelle will even agree to represent her; Isabelle's got a far more forceful personality than Mari's current lawyer, and she's got way more experience. Granted, Mari and Isabelle have never actually been friends, but they've known each other forever. Wouldn't it be better to have a lawyer who knows her? Would Isabelle bill her at a friends-and-family rate?

"Earth to Mari," Alice snaps. "Put this platter on the coffee table."

Mari, along with her mother and Sue, are in the kitchen of the red farmhouse, fixing hors d'oeuvres for the Richardsons' party. Plated around them sits their handiwork: shrimp curls that spoon one another around a bowl of sauce; scallops embraced by bacon and impaled on a pick; Roquefort and triple crème Brie and Manchego from the mainland, ready to be sliced and laid on crackers. The party's been going strong for more than three hours, and there must be sixty people scattered throughout the house and porch. Sue is sprawled on a chair, stroking the mound of her belly. Ever since she arrived, she's been talking about her swollen ankles, her sore back, the stone-cold assholery of her brother, who came to work so hungover he could barely walk.

"Hi, best friend." Levi leans close to Sue's baby bump, holds a box of crayons a millimeter from her belly. "Look at my crayons."

"Nice," Sue says grumpily.

Levi scowls at her tone, and Mari gives her a look.

"I haven't felt this baby move since this morning," Sue tells her. "I'm a bit on edge here."

The kitchen is warm. A slick of sweat covers Sue's top lip. Mari, remembering the irritability of pregnancy, reassures her friend that sometimes unborn babies don't move because they're sleeping, but Sue doesn't seem relieved. Instead, she eyes Levi's new crayons, then covers her stomach with her hands.

"Where'd you get a box of crayons like that?" she asks. Levi ignores her, colors with full concentration. The box has a hundred-and-fifty-two different colors, along with a sharpener. It came from Harry, as did the coloring book Levi's working in and Pretty Too, the stuffed horse that pokes from the T-shirt beneath Levi's chin.

"I've never seen anything like it," Sue says. Clearly, she wants to know how Mari, who the whole island knows has been begging for any income she can find, could afford to buy new toys. Mari, like her son, ignores Sue. From long history, she knows when it's best to give her friend space.

Alice steps closer to Mari, as if a whisper wouldn't draw Sue and Levi's attention in a heartbeat. She's got on one of the Richardsons' old bib aprons, the print faded, the straps crossed behind her back, pulled around her waist and fastened. Perspiration glistens on her forehead. "Between her sitting there and you with your head somewhere else," she says, "I feel like I'm doing this on my own."

"Sorry," Mari says.

Alice's brows dive, her sea-colored eyes on Mari's face. Mari turns the tap water high to drown further questions. She hasn't told her parents about the sheep yet. Her father will be fine with it; he likes that she's building a life for herself, tying all of them more firmly to Little Great Island. As for her mother—once the details are sorted out, it will be easier to convince her. The timing needs to be right. After a moment, her mother goes back to arranging crackers on a cheese plate, and Mari loads highball glasses into the dishwasher, so tired that her eyes won't focus.

"Cleaning houses and catering the odd cocktail party isn't going to solve your long-term problem," her mother says.

Sue mutters, "But having a sugar daddy sure does, especially if you are thinking of buying a bunch of sheep."

Sue only knows of Mari's desire to buy sheep, not that she's actually purchased them, so that's not what she's referring to. Does Sue know about her father loaning money to Mari? Or is she talking about Harry buying a box of crayons?

"I don't have a sugar daddy," Mari says.

Triscuit still in one hand, Alice side-eyes Mari before turning to Sue. "What are we talking about here?"

Sue points with her chin. "Ask her."

"What's going on?" Alice demands.

The kitchen is so silent Mari believes she hears Levi's breathing. She feels the way his antennae are honed, listening for words that aren't said. She finds room for one more high-ball glass in the dishwasher and busies herself adding detergent to the machine.

"If you're talking about the crayons, Harry bought them for Levi," Mari says finally.

"Oh, is *that* all?" Sue asks, and Mari sends her a glare that clearly says *back off*.

"Mari," her mother says. "What have you done?"

Realizing she's cornered, Mari turns on the dishwasher and decides to reveal her own secret rather than the one Frank asked her to keep.

"I bought some sheep," Mari says and lists the benefits of Columbians before her mother can speak. Columbians are easy to care for, good lamb producers, tender meat, good fleece.

"How'd you come up with the money to buy a bunch of sheep?" her mother asks.

Mari avoids answering by saying, "I got a great price. Don't worry. I can make this work." She picks up the platter her mother had been filling, a distraction and a reminder that they are working here. The Richardsons' kitchen is not a place for a lecture.

But Alice continues, "Where are you going to keep them? In the living room?" The perspiration on Alice's face is dripping now. The cracker trembles in her fingers.

Mari says, "It's going to be fine." It will be. Right at the moment, however, she can't see the steps to get there.

"Unbelievable," Alice summarizes, and Mari is about to make her escape from the kitchen when Sue asks, "Where *did* you get the money? Harry Richardson buy those sheep for you too? Could you ask him to buy me and Bob a new boat?"

Finishing the sea star he's been busily coloring red violet, Levi says, "Mr. Harry is nice. He gave me my pony. His name is Pretty Too." The stuffed horse is brown furred with a white blaze and a thick mane and tail. The coloring is like the real Pretty, Levi's favorite horse at God's Bounty. After Harry had told Mari about Levi being disciplined, she told him everything she could remember from the day they'd fled: the prayer shed, the rope, the stench of urine, the darkness.

"He stuck out his tongue," Harry said, and she nodded. Yes, there had been a sore. Perhaps Levi had cried so hard he'd bitten his tongue. Perhaps he had tripped over something in the shed. Something could have crawled into his mouth and bitten him when he'd been sobbing in the dirt.

"We should get back to work," Mari says now. Her mother is eating the cracker in her hand.

"And here's me," Sue says. "With a husband who's, like, decomposing because he's stuck working for my dad and my dad on my case about how I need to stop working because of the baby. Sit around by myself all day in the middle of the island while Reggie makes a complete mess of the business and my dad nitpicks my husband to death."

"I'm sorry," Mari says.

"Which doesn't change anything, does it?"

"Hush, you two," Alice says. "Honest to pete, I've had about enough of this."

"Hey," Isabelle says, striding into the kitchen. "What's the holdup? Are we out of food already?" She's looking at the plate of cheese and crackers as she asks. Isabelle's got Harry's dark hair and blue eyes, but her hair is straight. She's got it yanked back in a ponytail tight enough to stretch the skin on her forehead and a couple of pearls nailed in her earlobes. Perfect makeup, and the outfit she chose for the party makes her look like she's ready to argue a case in front of a judge. A moment later, Harry's behind her, dressed in a navy jacket and bow tie, looking like an unconvincing actor dressed for a part.

"Had to grab more appetizers," Sue says, dropping her feet from the chair and nabbing a platter. "Great party. People seem to be having a really good time." She waddles for the door, and Mari's mother heads after her with a fresh bucket of ice.

Isabelle keeps Mari in place with her eyes. "You wanted to talk to me?"

Harry's look goes from Mari to Isabelle and back again, clearly surprised that Mari requested this conversation.

"Yes," Mari says. "I'm trying to get full custody—"

Isabelle interrupts. "Here's what we need to talk about. You seem to be opposed to us legally selling our own property to a buyer who is ready, willing, and able."

"I would just like to use a few acres of land—"

"That's a hard no, and there's no *just* involved here. You've made it abundantly clear that you intend to quash this sale. It won't work, and I suggest you stop now before I start lobbing lawsuits your way."

"I think it's wrong for the island."

"And you have the authority to make that decision why?"

Eyes on Levi, Mari keeps her voice level, hoping to steer the conversation back to her son as soon as she can. "I don't have the legal authority. But I do have a conscience, and I do have the freedom to talk with other people who live here all year about what I see as the disadvantages of an executive retreat on this end of the island."

"And what's your plan for replacing income lost in the fisheries?"

"Not turning the people whose home this is into a servant class for summer visitors."

LITTLE GREAT ISLAND · 183

"I didn't ask what your plan *isn't*. I asked what it *is*."

"Start a small local farm," Mari says. "Demonstrate that it's possible. Get others to follow suit. As long as there are any lobster at all, the farms can generate food and supplemental income. There are organic markets and farm-to-table restaurants on the mainland that will purchase meat or produce raised out here. I've already talked to a few, and they're interested. If the fishing collapses totally, we'll at least have something to eat. And we'll still have our independence and pride."

"So your plan is for you and everyone else who lives on this island to starve slowly?"

Oh, how Mari would love to get into it with this woman. But not with Levi here, and she can't risk losing her cleaning job with Harry.

She turns to Levi. "Do you want ice cream?" Of course he does. That's why it's in the freezer. Harry stocks it for him.

"I'll get it," Harry says, and Isabelle and Mari watch him as he fills a bowl and settles Levi on the porch. The moment they're gone, Isabelle leans against the open shelving, her arms across her chest.

"I understand that what you want, fundamentally, is full custody of your son, without visitation," she says. It surprises Mari that Isabelle has pivoted to the subject she'd asked to discuss, but she nods. Isabelle explains that she's a corporate attorney; she doesn't practice family law. She's not licensed in Maine.

"But I can put you in touch with some people who can help and who will give you a reduced rate," she says, "if you stop all this fussing about our business. Stay in your own lane."

Mari doesn't agree or disagree. The force of Isabelle's stare makes the insides of her eyelids ache, and she hates that she's the first one to look away.

"Levi can't go back there," she says as Harry returns to the kitchen.

"You will have to substantiate any claims of abuse or neglect," Isabelle says. "It can't be your word against his. Is there anyone who will speak up about what goes on there?"

Sister Grace? Unlikely. Anything she says that's at all helpful to Mari brings the full glare of suspicion on her for Mari managing to get away with Levi. The rest of her God's Bounty brothers or sisters would be too afraid. Or they've convinced themselves Mari's a liar in the clutches of Satan. There's no way of knowing where the people who've left the ministry are now, and Mari doesn't even know their real names. Everyone was rechristened the moment they became members. Their lay names were erased along with their pasts.

"What about if someone went there?" Mari asks. "Someone from the outside, I mean."

"Private property," Isabelle says. "Which means no one's showing up without a search warrant, and no one's going to issue a search warrant without a very good reason. If someone did show up unannounced, they'd have to catch abuse occurring and secure evidence. Such a thing is so unlikely as to make it not worth trying."

"Then what am I supposed to do?" Mari must have spoken more loudly than she'd intended because she senses a sudden stillness on the back porch, as if Levi's antennae are now trained exclusively on her.

"Prepare yourself for a very expensive court battle," Isabelle says, rocking forward on her feet to indicate she's done here. "And don't get yourself involved in another one."

"Will you help me if I don't fight the development?"

"I told you. I don't do domestic law. I can give you some names. People to call."

But Mari can no longer stomach the idea of accepting a favor from this woman. "I already have a lawyer," she says. Her fury makes her voice tremble.

Isabelle gives Mari a final stare. "You play with fire, Ms. McGavin, you're going to get burned."

In the children's living room, a group bursts into a drunken and off-key chorus of "Somewhere Over the Rainbow."

THE TINY UNIVERSE OF
A CAR AT NIGHT

Harry

There's a particular intimacy to a car at night. Outside: everything. Inside: a cocoon, a capsule, a collection of seeds within the protective covering of fruit.

Intimate, too, is the shared comfort of a sleeping child. Harry, driving far more slowly than necessary, listens beneath all other sounds—the burr of tires on asphalt, the engine's hum, Mari's sniffs, and his own swallows—for the rhythm of Levi's breath. Eons seem to have passed since Harry last witnessed—or listened to—the slumber of another soul. If this island weren't so small, if there were miles of highway they could cruise along, he'd drive all night like this.

After the party, he offered to drive Mari and Levi down the hill because Levi was too tired to walk. Harry wanted to use the time to apologize for his sister's behavior. And to somehow sort out his feelings about Mari having gone behind his back to talk with Isabelle. All that was going to take longer than the short distance down the hill to the McGavins', but when he asked Mari if she was okay driving out to Little

Beach with him, what he wanted most of all was her company and Levi's after the packed bodies and banal conversation of the party. She nodded, head turned over one shoulder to check on Levi, who had already drifted into sleep.

Now, as they leave the village behind, Harry says, "Isabelle can be a bit…" "Ruthless" is the word that occurs to him, but he goes with "blunt" because Isabelle is his sister.

"A bit of a bitch," Mari says, and Harry smiles. There's little trace left of the confused and emaciated woman he'd run into on the road back in April.

"Not going to argue with you on that one," he says, and he catches Mari's glance at his face. "I wish you'd talked to me before talking to her." He's had a lifetime of experience dealing with his sister.

"You told me there was nothing you could do."

Harry grimaces. Guilty. But even he wouldn't have predicted Isabelle would have been quite so harsh.

"She wouldn't really file lawsuits against you," he says, hoping it's true. "She's used to playing hardball with expensive New York lawyers. I like to believe she's got a good heart. But it's gotten awfully buried beneath that prosecutor persona."

"What a horrible way to live," Mari says, surprising Harry, who expected anger, not sympathy.

"No more going behind my back, okay?"

"No more going behind mine."

His conversation with Frank, she means. "Agreed," Harry says.

"I'm not going to stop fighting for my son's safety. But that isn't your problem. I understand that."

Isabelle told him Mari could be accused of parental kidnapping. That the penalties are the same as for any other abduction. "We're talking prison, Har," she said. He didn't tell her about the prayer shed, only that inappropriate punishments were used.

"It's pretty hard to sort out what's what in these situations," Isabelle said, but every time Harry thinks about Levi cowering behind that chair on the front porch, certain of his guilt and terrified, he wants to hop the next flight to South Carolina and pound the daylights out of Caleb and that Aaron fellow.

"Couldn't you get a job at the executive retreat? They're going to be hiring—"

"It's years away from being finished," Mari interrupts. "Never mind whether they go broke in the interim or change their mind and sell or decide they want to divide the land up and sell it in pieces for individual homes. Someone could easily build five or six houses on your land. Or Duncan defaults and the bank takes over the property, and who knows what happens after that? Anyway, I couldn't be civil to those people. I hate everything they stand for."

"In point of fact, I do too."

Mari puts a hand to the bristle of her hair. "Yah, but someone's offering you a boatload of money to compromise your values. That changes the equation."

"Ouch."

Mari's shoulders are hunched, her hands trapped between her knees. Her chin is pressed to her chest. The road unfurls in the headlights. In the back seat, Levi sighs and smacks his lips.

"You think I'm compromising my morals for money?" Harry asks.

"I'm not judging."

But she is. The car goes airless. Mari's movement could be a head shake or a twitch.

"Look, I don't doubt that you're a good person," she says. "But you've got your own problems and your own needs. It's your land. You want to sell it, so sell it. Go do whatever you need to do to make you happy."

What is that? Permission? That's not hers to give. What it sounds like is more of an insult.

"What about your sheep?"

"I don't know. Maybe I can get out of the purchase. Maybe I should take the money I've got and move to the mainland. I'll have a better chance of getting a job there. Or maybe it's not worth fighting Caleb. Levi loves his dad. I think Caleb really does care about Levi. I could find a job on a farm in South Carolina so Levi can see his dad from time to time."

"He tied his son up in that shed."

"Well, he did, or Pastor Aaron did."

"Either way, your husband permitted it to happen."

"I don't know. Maybe Pastor Aaron sent him off on some errand to get him out of the way. Maybe it was someone else from the farm. I don't really know what happened."

When they reach the flattened grass that serves as the parking lot for Little Beach, Harry pulls over and shuts down the car. In the distance, mainland lights sparkle faintly. A waxing crescent moon hangs blanched against the midnight sky.

"I thought you loved it here," Harry says. "I thought you wanted Levi to grow up here."

"I do." Mari's hands tangle and twist in her lap. "But maybe it isn't going to work."

"After Ellie was diagnosed, she wanted to go through IVF," Harry says, surprising himself. He hadn't known he was willing to share this information with anyone. "The treatment would damage her eggs, so IVF had to come first."

"But why? Didn't she know she was dying?"

Harry shakes his head, remembering the arguments. Ellie's cancer was an aggressive type but caught relatively early. The oncologist talked about risk of recurrence and emerging treatment options. What Harry heard was that Ellie might die. What Ellie heard was that she was likely to live long enough to raise a child.

"I want to live a normal life once we get past this," she insisted. "That's what we should be preparing for, statistically speaking."

"What we should be doing," Harry countered, "is everything possible to get you healthy."

"She wasn't supposed to die," Harry tells Mari now. His voice is bitter when he adds, "Statistically speaking."

"I'm so sorry," Mari says, touching him lightly on the back of the hand.

A dozen or so years ago, there was a power outage on a summer evening. The whole island suddenly had to face the inability to cook the rice that was planned for supper, had to admonish one another not to open fridge or freezer, had to scramble for flashlights and candles even though full dark was more than an hour away. People came out of their homes into the gloaming to share whatever news they had. A few years out of college and uncertain whether grad school was the right choice for his life, Harry drove out to the west side of the island and parked to watch the sunset. The sky threw out yellows and reds and purples and a dozen other colors he couldn't name. He followed the path Mr. Estabrook kept mowed across a field and then descended a rocky embankment to a lip of beach. It was the kind of beach that was four feet underwater at high tide, but that evening it was a hem of smoothed rocks and drying seaweed. When Harry finally made it that far, Mari was standing there, her hair a sheer fall of deep brown that ended at her waist. She didn't acknowledge his presence when he stood next to her. Without speaking, they watched the sunset spill its colors into the sea until the air turned inky, and then they climbed back up the rocks and walked across the field side by side. They never spoke a word. To the extent that Harry ever thought about that evening, he recalled how self-possessed Mari was, particularly for a girl of fourteen or fifteen. Silent, when anyone else would have engaged in small talk.

Mari says now, "Missing someone or something puts a hole in you that everyone around you expects you to ignore." She turns to face him. "This island is the only place that fills that hole in me. But I don't see how I can support myself and Levi in a place where even the lobstermen are struggling to survive. It feels to me like this whole community is going to collapse sooner rather than later. No one's doing enough to adapt. No one wants to change. But the Earth doesn't care. It's changing whether we want it to or not."

She's right. There have been otters in the waters around Little Great Island, presumably because of the increase in freshwater runoff into the ocean. More sharks, including great whites, have been observed in northern waters, closer to shores. The ocean off the coast of Maine has risen by eight inches in the past seventy years and is projected to rise by as much as three feet in the next twenty-five.

"I don't think you should leave," Harry says, but what he's thinking is selfish. He feels better when she and Levi are around.

"I don't want to."

Tiny waves rasp the shoreline. The beach rose bushes stand quiet in the night. Whiffs of brine-soaked sand and seaweed invade the car.

"I should get Levi home," Mari says finally. "Thank you for trying to help." Unclipping her seat belt, she leans across the center console. Perhaps she only intends a companionable hug or peck on the cheek, but Harry's head turns of its own accord and his lips find hers. For a moment, it's right. She is kissing him back and he's losing himself in their touch, and then Levi stirs in the back seat and says, "Mama?"

THE GHOST OUT OF NOWHERE

Sue

The ghost appears out of nowhere, standing right in the truck's beams as Sue makes her way home after the party. If she'd been going any faster, she might have hit it, or gone through it, or whatever happens when a vehicle collides with a dead spirit. As it is, she slams the brakes hard. Doesn't scream so much as make the huffing noise of someone punched hard in the chest, and then stares at the logo in the center of the steering wheel, trying not to have a heart attack. Trying to get her breathing back under control for the baby. Trying to convince herself that, when she looks again, there will be nothing in the high beams but dirt road and potholes and trees crowded on either side.

All that takes less than a second, and then Sue gets the truck shifted to park and shuts the radio down before something thwumps the passenger-side window. Holy Mars bars! Sue about hucks up her lungs before seeing it's her own stupid brother.

"Roll your window down," Reggie shouts, making a winding motion with his hand. Honest to God, it takes Sue nearly a minute to figure out she turned the ignition off, not the radio, and that she has to crank the Titan back up before she can power down the window.

"Party over?" Reggie asks.

Twinkling lights have appeared in the back of Sue's brain. Pieces of what happened begin to arrange themselves. She was driving. The radio was on. She was yelling at the whole world because now even Bob is getting on her case about how she should be resting more, but if she's not in the store, Reggie's going to decide he's Bob's boss and start ordering him around. And if her dad would get his head screwed on right about Reggie and let her...

The road was empty because it always was. Only then it wasn't.

"What the hell're you doing out here?" Sue demands. "Other than trying to become roadkill?"

"Going to see Mari." Reggie grins, which is a scary look on him. It's hard to tell how drunk he is, which is also disconcerting.

"Mari's with Harry Richardson," Sue says, by way of reminding Reggie that he hasn't got a prayer with Mari so he should give that shit up now. "Get in the car. I'll take you home."

Reggie says, "Nope. Not happening."

"Reggie."

"Got something for her." Reggie roots around in his pocket and pulls out a fistful of bills.

"Where'd that come from?" Sue knows for a fact that she locked up the cash from the market, but Reggie's a resourceful thief when he's drinking.

"Mari's a bit strapped," Reggie slurs. "Dad gave her some dough, but you know what a tight-ass he is, so I got some more. Thought I'd help her out some."

What the hell? "Dad gave Mari money?"

"Yah."

"How long ago was this?"

"Couple weeks?" Reggie guesses. "Maybe more? Maybe less?"

Mother Mary in a doughnut hole. How many times has Sue seen Mari in the past few weeks? Four? Five? Did they not just spend six solid hours together? Has Holy Mari in her righteousness somehow forgotten that they are supposed to be best friends, and that best friends do not keep secrets? Especially secrets like handouts from Sue's own father?

"Bitch," Sue says.

"Back at you," Reggie replies pleasantly.

"Get in." Sue can't leave Reggie out here, where he's going to get his ass run over by someone or do something stupid like proclaim undying love to Mari. "Seriously, Reggie, don't fuck with me right now. Get in." She already knows it's a lost cause when she says it.

"You drive safe now, you hear?" Reggie taps twice on the side of the car, and then he heads past her, back in the direction of the Richardsons' and the McGavins'. Back where Mari isn't because she's off with Harry Richardson.

So totally not going to end well, Sue thinks as she gets the Titan rolling again. This time, she barely lets the thing crawl, knowing trouble can leap out of nowhere.

FUCHSIA ON AN
INDIGO SKY

Mari

Mari creeps from her bed when daylight is a streak of fuchsia on an indigo sky. Sleep never came or, if it had, it hadn't been restful. That kiss shouldn't have happened. She's married. He's an emotional disaster zone. She's facing what could be a nasty court battle. His sister is part cobra, part tiger hungry for blood. Ten days have passed, and she's barely seen Harry, but they need to talk. The sheep are penned on McGavin land with no place to graze. Feeding them is expensive, and it's not as good for their health. Ever since her mother got done yelling at her about buying the sheep and how rotten it was to have taken money from Frank behind Sue's back, they've barely talked. Caleb is inundating her lawyer with threats and demands. Her lawyer wants her to come into the office on the mainland, which is a day without work. Her savings are down to less than two hundred dollars.

On his cot, Levi breathes wetly, his hands folded next to his cheek. After nearly four months on the island, they have their own socks and combs, sweatshirts and rain gear, and already Levi has acquired the casual habits of ownership. Dirty clothes pile the rocking chair. He begs to watch television with his grandparents. He knows what Pokemon is and the difference between Spider-Man and Batman. Pretty Too is stuffed inside his pajama top. Crouching next to her son, Mari pulls the blanket over his shoulder, presses a kiss onto his scalp. From her parents' room emerges the creak of a bed joist, the whisper of her father's footsteps on the bare wood floors. The water bursts on in the bathroom, and Mari tiptoes to the hallway.

"I'm up, Dad," she says. Today there are no houses to clean, no gardens to weed, and so she'll help her father on the *Alice-Mari*.

Dressed in boxers and a T-shirt, her father turns to her and winks. His mouth is full of brush and bubbles, his cheeks covered with stubble.

Downstairs, Mari measures grounds and water, starts the coffee, and then stares out the kitchen window at the Richardsons' house, still quiet at this hour.

"Mermaid?" her father calls quietly.

"In here."

Her father is dressed now, in jeans and a stained gray sweatshirt. Her mother descends the stairs behind him in a blue terry-cloth bathrobe.

"Levi still asleep?" her father asks.

"Yes."

The three of them in the kitchen in the early dawn is familiar. They are all quiet, trying not to wake Levi. Mari cuts slices from the bread she baked and lowers them into the toaster while her mother cracks eggs into a skillet. At the counter, her father pours coffee.

"Shot that mink," he says. The one that had been after Mari's hens.

"Thank you."

"You hear about Marietta and Linda losing their boat?" her mother asks. Mari's heard. Marietta and Linda were written up in *Down East, Working Waterfront,* and other Maine publications because they were reported to be the only married female lobster crew in the area. The repo spooked people. When Bob and Sue lost their boat, the whole island knew they had a fallback position with the market and boatyard, but Marietta and Linda have nothing. Everyone's talking about how bad the catch is. It's broadcast all over Mari's father's face every time he comes ashore.

"If we sell this place now," Alice says, "we can get a decent price." Back still to Mari, Alice goes after the eggs with a fork. Metal clicks against cast iron. Mari's father clears his throat, but when Mari glances at him, his only response is the half curl of his lip that she's always referred to as his pre-coffee smile. It doesn't indicate pleasure or amusement; it means he's not yet awake.

Alice adds, "Maybe we could ask Isabelle Richardson if their developer will want this place too."

"No." Mari's voice is loud enough that she might have awakened Levi, and her mother scowls at her before continuing.

"Mari, you've got to think about your son."

"He's what I'm thinking about twenty-four seven."

Mari's mother whips the eggs so firmly her shoulders are shaking. "You never should have gone to Frank for money," she says. "I could have told you Sue would be pissed. I don't know why you won't listen, why you always feel the need to upset everyone."

"I don't." Mari stops herself from adding that her mother's the only person she seems to upset one hundred percent of the time.

"You might try listening to me for once." Alice turns toward her, the skillet in one hand. At this hour, her hair is uncombed and unruly. The whites of her eyes are red. If they move now, Alice reasons, they can get a three-bedroom and a yard, maybe in Androscoggin or Cumberland, some place that's far enough from Portland and the coastline that the prices haven't been driven sky high.

"I can watch Levi after school," she says. "You could find work in an apple orchard the way you did in college. Go back and finish your graduate degree."

Mari's father isn't looking at her, but she senses he's tense as he sips his coffee, wondering if the argument is going full scale before the sun has even considered rising.

"I don't want to finish my master's," Mari says. "I told you that already."

"I'm only trying to point out there are options. Maybe you should quit thinking about what you want and start doing things that are going to make life a little easier for you and your son."

There's too much truth in that statement for Mari to have an answer, even if there's no way her mother could be referring to what happened at God's Bounty.

"Why don't you pick up the phone, call your husband, and see if you can't find a way to work this out? Why pay all this money to a lawyer when you haven't even tried talking to him?"

"There isn't a phone at God's Bounty." Her parents know this.

"Well, Aaron has one."

Pastor Aaron, Mari's ear automatically corrects. That phone is closely supervised by Pastor Aaron and Sister Ann. Her mother knows that too.

"If there isn't a phone you can use, then use the computer. Do a video call."

"No." The computer is in Pastor Aaron's office. He'd be the one to answer, and Mari feels dizzy at the thought of seeing his face again, even on a screen.

"You are so stubborn," Alice says.

"Me? What about you?"

"Never mind you getting yourself all involved in the Richardsons' business. You'd think, somewhere along the line, you'd have learned to let the summer people be." A clear reference to one of Mari's mother's favorites of her various transgressions committed years ago. Two cars blocking Main Street, one of them heading the wrong way on the one-way road. The drivers chatting across their rolled-down windows, oblivious to the traffic stacking up behind them. Mari, emerging from the post office, assessed the situation quickly and slammed her hand on the roof of the car whose driver was ignoring the one-way signs.

"You're heading the wrong direction, dimwit," she hollered at the startled female behind the wheel. "Move." The idiot didn't pull forward to a place where she might reasonably have turned around. Instead, she spent nearly five minutes maneuvering her car back and forth across Main Street in the single-lane space between parked cars. When she finally drove off, Mari flashed her middle finger.

How was she supposed to know that the woman behind the wheel was sibling to an ex-president? Even a year later, that story was repeated every time a summer person laid eyes on Mari.

"Mom," Mari says now.

"Those sheep," her mother says and shakes her head.

"I'll find..." If that ridiculous kiss hadn't happened, Mari could have convinced Harry to let her use some land. How much could his brother and sister really care? Duncan's not going to walk away from the sale over a few sheep, and if she can't stop the sale, she'll figure out someplace else on the island for the sheep.

"And then running around trying to convince everyone to vote against the rezone that your father's best friend is

202 • KATE WOODWORTH

working very hard to build support for." The cooked eggs get chopped decisively with the edge of the spatula and divided evenly onto the waiting toast.

Mari says, "But that development is wrong for—"

"In your opinion." Mari's mother punctuates each word with a slap of the spatula to the eggs.

"They would pave the road out here," Mari points out. "Do you know what that would do to the drainage? You want that extra traffic out here? What about the increased refuse in the landfill? Do you think any of those people are going to care about what happens to this island? To you? To us?"

"That boy misses his father something fierce. You're coming between them, and that's not fair."

"You don't know Caleb. What makes you so certain he's a wonderful parent who only has his son's best interests at heart?"

"I don't know him because you never let us meet him."

"So even without having laid eyes on him, you're certain I'm the terrible person here."

"Don't put words in my mouth. All I'm saying is that a boy needs a dad."

"Not that kind of dad."

"Just because you're angry with Caleb doesn't mean he's a terrible parent."

"Mom."

"What?" Alice demands.

"Why can't you ever take my side?"

Her mother shakes her head in a way that means *I'm right. Why can't you admit it?*

"You want me to leave?" Mari asks. "Levi and I can leave today. But that's the end of your relationship with both me and him. Don't expect us to show up at your place for Thanksgiving and pretend we're a happy family."

Alice's shoulders fold minutely inward. The refrigerator motor switches off. Even the faucet ceases dripping. If Mari could reach into the air, grab the tail end of her sentence, and pull it back, she would.

"Look, why don't you tell us what happened, Mermaid?" her father asks from in front of the sink, where he is cleaning out his cooler. "We don't know anything about Caleb. You've left us in the dark here. We're your parents. We want to help."

"Fine," Mari says. "You want to know what a horrible disaster your daughter is, listen to this."

The kitchen itself seems to hold its breath as Mari tells them about the prayer shed, where black widow spiders were found on a near weekly basis and where a copperhead once decided to deliver her young. When she finishes, it's her father who has tears in his eyes, her mother who is gripping the skillet handle as though preparing to use it as a weapon.

"But—" her mother begins.

Mari interrupts. "I know. How could I have let things go so far? How could I not have seen what was going on?" Her mother is shaking her head, but Mari believes her explanation is needed.

"How could I not have put a stop to it sooner?" she asks, her voice rising. "How could I have been so irresponsible and stupid as to marry a man like that?" She's crying herself now. "I don't know," she wails. Both her parents turn reflexively toward the living room, and Mari checks as well to be certain she hasn't woken Levi.

"I made it all make sense at first," she continues more quietly. "I don't know how else to describe it. I felt safe, validated. Like I was in exactly the right place, doing exactly the right thing. I had absolutely no desire to be anywhere other than where I was. And then I had Levi."

Mari glances at her mother, who meets her look. "I didn't dare run after that," Mari admits. "I couldn't take him away from his father and his home. I couldn't leave without him. I had to protect him." Her voice breaks.

Her mother shakes her head, the spatula raised. "One thing I can tell you for damn sure, those people are not getting anywhere near my grandson."

The idea of her fierce mother leading a battalion of islanders armed with cast-iron pots and pans makes Mari smile for the first time in what feels like years.

Alice wraps the waiting sandwiches in foil. Something in the set of her mouth tells Mari her mother understands now. She believes that—in this one instance at least—Mari did the right thing by running away. Mari turns to her father, who's drying the inside of the cooler with a dishrag like it's the most important thing in the world. A tear clings to the side of his nose.

"Dad?" she says.

He waves her off with one hand, and Mari thinks he's still too upset to answer, but then he says, "You got away. You and Levi are all right now. That's what's important."

"I have to prove I can support Levi, Dad, and farming is what I know. It's what Levi knows. There were good parts to God's Bounty. I hope you understand that. I learned hands on about animal husbandry. About crop rotation. How to care for the land so it keeps producing. How to make small pieces of land productive. How to create bounty, really." Turning to her mother, Mari continues, "That's the part I want to recreate here. And Levi needs to be in a small community, at least until he's fully gotten used to life outside of God's Bounty. Here is where it makes sense to raise him."

The cooler hits the floor with a bang. Both Mari and her mother turn to her father, who seems surprised that the cooler has escaped him. His cheeks redden.

"Felt like a damn horse kicked me in the chest," he says. "I don't know what the hell that was about."

WE NEED TO TALK

Harry

"We should talk," Harry says. It's early, not yet seven a.m., but he's been up for hours, chased from sleep by broken images of Levi sticking out his tongue and by thoughts of Mari that go well beyond that kiss. In the years since Ellie's death, his body has retained its own agenda, but he's had no real interest in getting involved with another woman. He still doesn't, particularly with Mari, who has way too much on her plate anyway. Nevertheless, he doesn't want to lose her as a friend.

So when Mari had emerged from the house a few minutes earlier and headed for the barn, he'd thrown on clothes, run a comb through his hair, and headed toward the McGavins'.

"About the other night," he adds.

"We should," Mari agrees. "But right now, I'm in the middle of a manicure." In fact, she's got Houdini tied by the halter, one of the goat's back legs curled over her knee. Each time she touches the trimmers to the animal's hoof, Houdini thrashes, trying to pull free.

"Hold his head," she says, and Harry—who's quite certain he's never touched a goat before—asks how.

"One hand on the halter. He may push his head up against you. It's not butting. It's more like a goat cuddle."

Gingerly, Harry does as he's told. Houdini doesn't butt or cuddle, but his eyes roll and it's impossible to know what the creature's going to do next. "I don't think he likes me."

"Scratch him on the top of the head. Or, if you want a friend for life, scratch him on the front of his chest."

Briefly, Mari looks up at him. There's humor in her eyes, which helps dissipate Harry's anxiety.

"But his absolute favorite thing in the world is if you tickle his armpits," she says.

"You're kidding."

"I'm not."

Houdini goes still in response to Harry scratching his forehead with the tips of his fingers, and Mari gets to work cleaning out the crud in the center of the goat's hoof and trimming the edges. Even though the morning is already warm, she's dressed in stained and worn denim that reaches to her wrists and ankles. On her feet are black rubber boots. Ellie had eschewed fussy feminine clothing, but it's impossible to imagine her with patches of something that's likely to be manure smeared on her backside.

"This is the heel ball," Mari says, using the trimmer to point to something on Houdini's foot that Harry can't see. Holding the trimmers out to Harry, she asks, "You want to do the honors?"

"No. Thank you."

"Coward."

"Guilty as charged."

Releasing Houdini's foot, Mari moves around to the other side of the goat and attends to the next hoof in silence. Houdini makes a sound like a sigh and leans his face into Harry's stomach. The animal's eyes are half closed. Its coat has none of the softness of a dog's or a cat's, and its odor is strong and musky. The horns arch backward from its fore-head. The tips are pointed, though not sharp, and Harry has no doubt that one of those horns, with enough force behind it, could go halfway through his body.

"Done," Mari says and releases the goat. Harry feels her eyes on him, noticing how the goat presses into him. "Looks like you made a friend."

"Probably my kind of guy, given that I'm feeling a bit like an old goat."

"Pfft. Harry. You're not even forty yet, right?"

"Forty-one."

"Okay. Old. And bearded. So maybe old goat works." Untying Houdini, Mari leads him to his pen and releases him.

"Do not run away this time," she instructs as the goat wanders off. "He was behind The Sweet Shoppe yesterday," she adds. "Helping himself to Lydia's trash." Harry's trailing her back to the barn when he sees a cigarette butt, smoked nearly to the filter, on the ground. No one in the McGavin family smokes, to the best of his knowledge. Although he knows next to nothing about farms, he's quite sure that smoking anywhere near a barn is a very bad idea.

Leaning over, Mari grabs the butt and pockets it. "Reggie," she says by way of explanation, and Harry feels a pang as he imagines her standing outside in the starlight with Reggie Clatcher. Irritation, not jealousy, he decides. Reggie's got a reputation, at least among the summer population. She ought to be careful. But then again, it's none of his business.

"I owe you an apology for the other night," he says. "I'm in no shape right now to get involved."

"Me neither. Because, to begin with, I'm married. Not to mention I'm in the middle of a custody battle. Oh, and your sister hates me."

"I'm a mess."

"Truth."

"Ouch." But Harry's not actually hurt by her assessment of him. "We still friends?"

Mari gives him a long, hard look. "If you promise to quit feeling guilty."

"I'll do my best. But just so we're clear, I can't promise you I'm going to get myself into legal trouble by trying to get out of the purchase and sales agreement. Nor will I promise to destroy my relationship with my siblings. Isabelle may not be a prize, but she's the only sister I have."

"This is about more than you and your siblings. It's about more than me. This island has a soul, Harry, and it's going to die unless we can find something other than lobster or tourists to keep it going. Keep us going."

Harry lifts a shoulder, lets it drop. "I don't think I'm the right person to save the island."

"You mean because your wife died?"

Mari's question startles him. She's right, but he didn't think he was being that obvious. "Her death wasn't your fault," she adds. "You can't outrun grief."

"I know," Harry says, although he isn't certain. Everyone talks about battling cancer, as if people who have it are meant to be warriors and not patients. Would Ellie have fought harder if she'd had the possibility of motherhood?

Eyes on Houdini, Mari says, "Look, I know it's not the same, but I feel some guilt when an animal dies on my watch. Perhaps the better word is powerless. I feel how useless all my efforts are in the face of death. I think that's part of the attraction of God. Once you convince yourself there's a power greater than yourself and you imbue it with loving motives, then you get to let go of responsibility."

"Yah, but that only works if you believe," Harry says. "Maybe it worked for you, but it's not going to work for me. And anyway, I can't undermine my siblings."

"You can talk to them. And to be clear, I'm quite certain God doesn't solve our problems. We do. I'm not abdicating my responsibility anymore. I've got an idea for you. Run it past Isabelle and Jonathan. See what they think."

Mari's thought is that the Richardsons sell their property to the Maine Farm Preservation Trust. "The trust will protect it with an agricultural easement so that no one can ever develop it. Then they will either sell it to someone who wants to farm it or underwrite a farming effort."

"We already have a buyer."

"I know, but hear me out. You have a buyer, but not yet a sale. Just back out. Isabelle can find a way to make it happen. Then, if you sell to the Maine Farm Preservation Trust instead of Duncan, Levi and I could live in the house, and I'd do the farming. Or you and I could do it together. I could teach you ecologically sound practices. You wouldn't have to go back to the city, where everything smells like city."

"Mari, I have a job." As he says it, Harry realizes he wants to go back to it. He loves teaching history. He loves his students, or at least most of them most of the time. "And amazing as you are, you can't run a farm by yourself."

"I can try. It's better than cleaning houses."

"What makes you think the trust would even be interested in land on an island? It makes for a limited market, and the challenge of transporting things to the mainland is part of what killed farming here originally."

"Because locally sourced and farm-to-table foods are big right now. Because the trust wants land with good-quality soil. I know you have that. They are looking for farms with enough acreage to produce a decent-size crop. You've got that too. They like buildings that are in decent shape. Your garage used to be a barn. It wouldn't be that hard to convert it back. Your house already is a farmhouse. It's perfect for a farming family. Or for workers. Or it can be rented out and the income used to support the farm. There are built-in customers here year round, but especially in the summer. Climate change is extending the growing season this far north. If your siblings won't change their minds, then all you have to do is make sure the sale to Duncan fails."

"Duncan has prequalified. He can close."

"Doesn't matter. We only need to make sure the rezone doesn't pass." It's not like Harry has to create bumper stickers and advertise in *The Boston Globe*, Mari adds. No one needs to know. Harry just has to stop acting like he's in favor.

"People will find out. You know what it's like here."

"Fine. And then what?"

Then all hell breaks loose. Harry shakes his head. "I'm sorry," he says. "I can't."

Bits of straw dust speckle Mari's shirt. A flake of skin curls from her bottom lip. Fingers tucked in her back pockets, Mari lifts her chin. Harry's seen that pose—all outward "bring it on" while the eyes are full of fear—in his students.

"Well, I can, and I will."

Their conversation feels incomplete, so Harry trails her back to the barn, where she cleans the nail trimmers and puts them away. The barn smells barn-like: hay, manure, animal, island air. There's an overhead light on, but its illumination is dim. Mari thrusts a bucket of grain at Harry. "If you're going to keep following me around, make yourself useful. Help me feed some chickens."

The hens trail them from the barn and surround them, tutting and murmuring near Harry's feet while the rooster regards him with a tilted head, first with one beady eye and then the other.

"Please don't promote the farm trust idea on the island," he says. The repercussions would all come back on him.

"It's not my land. There's nothing I can do." Mari won't look him in the eye. Her tone is flat.

"Listen," Harry says, hoping to say something that will bridge the chasm that is suddenly appearing between them. "That morning I found Levi hiding on our porch. When he was telling me about deserving to be punished. You remember I said that he stuck out his tongue." Young children who stuck out tongues were usually being rude, but Levi seemed to have wanted to show him something and then changed his mind.

"I told you. He got a cut on his tongue in the shed."

"How?"

"Don't know. He won't talk about it." Mari tosses another handful of grain. "But I do know there was a knife sharpener in the shed. The thing with the green handle, like Ellie's brush. It was weird. I still can't think of a reason for it to be there."

"You think they stabbed him in the tongue?" Had those assholes threatened to cut out Levi's tongue? Wasn't there some Bible thing about plucking out offending eyes and cutting off perverse tongues?

But there was no knife, Mari says, and the wound was more of a blister or sore than a cut.

"Nothing else?"

She half shakes her head and then pauses. "There was a weed torch, but it was outside the shed. Around the side of the building." A propane torch, she explains, that was used to clear weeds from the walkways, sterilize some equipment, or, rarely, to de-ice vehicles. "We kept it in the barn. It shouldn't have been down by the prayer shed."

"Did the sore look like a burn?"

Mari stares. When she finally nods, the rest of her body remains rigid. "But what did they...?"

The imagining of it is horrible enough. Explaining to Mari what he thinks happened is horrific. "They could have used the torch to heat the metal of the knife sharpener," Harry says. "Then burned his tongue with it."

"Those bastards," she whispers.

Right now, Harry could easily rip every single person at God's Bounty to shreds with his bare hands. Tears pour down Mari's face, but she doesn't seem aware of them.

"I have to go," she says. "I need to be with Levi." She's already at the door when Harry calls, "Wait."

"What?"

"You can put the sheep on our land. For now."

"Okay. Fine. Thank you."

But he's not doing it for her, or not only for her. It's for Levi. And for Ellie, who had wanted so badly to be a mother. There will be hell to pay with his siblings, but it's the least he can do.

THE CUPBOARD WAS BARE

Tom

Not a thing to eat in the house for Tom's sweet tooth, and it's already past nine p.m. so the market's long closed even though it's late July and the height of the season. Tom peers down at Jussi, who examines the contents of the refrigerator more mournfully than Tom himself: a whole uncooked chicken with its sickly skin, a head of iceberg, a sleeve of tomatoes in a plastic tray, a brick of orange cheese of the sort that's sold in every supermarket in the world. Damn stuff tastes like wax. There's something wrong with Alice McGavin lately, bringing him this stuff. She knows what he likes and what he doesn't.

"But when he got there, the cupboard was bare," Tom says to Jussi. The dog wags his tail. Tom's stomach rumbles. Well, then. Tom isn't stuck here with nothing to eat. He has a car. He can head into the village. There's bound to be someone who will fix him some food. As he opens the front door, he invites Jussi to join him.

When Tom gets to the village, one of those Florida women who runs The Blue Buoy tells him the kitchen's closed even though there are people still sitting at tables and a group hanging around at the bar.

"Sorry," the woman says. "Come back tomorrow?"

"Doesn't help us today," Mr. Estabrook tells Jussi as they wander toward Main Street. There's a light on in The Sweet Shoppe kitchen. That nice Lydia Smith stands there, gazing out. A woman and a kitchen. It's sufficient for Tom to see the solution to his needs. Sure, she's got the *Closed* sign on her door, but that's probably to keep the kids out. He only needs something light to eat. He doesn't want to be a bother.

Lydia answers the door in a bathrobe and slippers, which brings up a wave of nostalgia. Coming home from China or Argentina or even his office in DC and finding Priscilla in the kitchen in that tatty pink robe of hers. When you're young, you think a woman wearing nothing is the best sight there is, but the time comes when what you really want is the woman who's there when you come home tired and beaten and everything that needs saying is right there in her eyes.

"Mr. Estabrook," Lydia says. "You okay?"

"Hungry," Tom says. "That's all." A very fat Siamese cat by her legs hisses at Jussi and swats the dog back to a respectable distance.

"Cat's pregnant," Lydia explains. "Clive across the way there let all the cats out at one point, and now he and Carol can't get them back inside. This one kept getting into my garbage. I figured the only way to deal with it was to let it inside, where I can keep an eye on it." Jussi loses interest the third time he gets swatted, and then the cat jumps its bulk impressively onto a shelf and begins a prolonged session of grooming.

Only when Tom's seated at one of the tables and Lydia's gone off to the kitchen for wine and a couple of slices of quiche does it occur to Tom that perhaps he's being intrusive. That it's close to bedtime for both of them, and here's this woman who isn't his wife and who isn't actually dressed. But Lydia is a businessperson. She's a restaurateur, or whatever they call themselves these days, and the two of them are well past all that other malarkey anyway. Jussi lies against one of Tom's feet, his body warm and soft. The cat's asleep with one eye still on the dog.

When Lydia returns from the kitchen, she has the food and the wine and the dishes and even—bless her heart—a couple of cloth napkins. Tom asks for candlelight, and she strikes a match to one of those bottled candles that emits an odor. This one smells like balsam fir and reminds Tom of his early days on Little Great Island.

"This is lovely," Tom says. "I am really very grateful."

Lydia takes a seat across from him and lays her napkin on her lap. "Me too," she says. "Even in summer, the nights get long."

TWELVE FLAT TIRES

Mari

Thank goodness it's Bob who answers the door and not Frank, who Mari calculated would be at work. And not Reggie, who could be anywhere.

"How is she?"

"Mnh." Easy enough to see how *he's* doing, Mari thinks as she follows him through the familiar Clatcher living room and up the stairs. Bob's face is gray. His eyes look dead in their sockets. The house smells heavily of stale male bodies and cooking oil.

"What did the doctor say?" Mari asks.

"She's got to stay in bed. Not even supposed to come downstairs."

Mari's already done the math: Sue's six weeks from her due date. The baby could live at this point in a hospital, but if it decides to come early, it had better come slowly or there won't be any chance of making it to the mainland. The "boys"—Sue's word choice for her brother, her father, and her doctor—have decided she needs to be in the village for the duration of her pregnancy.

"She pretty bummed out?"

"Yup."

Mari and Bob stop face to face outside the closed bedroom door. Bob wipes his hands against the sides of his jeans. Bob was always *that kid* in high school: kind but shy. Good enough looking but awkward. Sue was the one to figure out that Bob was someone worth dating.

"She's not in the greatest of moods," Bob says. "You know how she gets. She's bored to tears lying in bed all the time, and it's making her nuts Reggie's working in the store and not her."

Mari can imagine how upsetting Sue would find that. Even back in high school, Mari heard the reasons for Sue's fears: Reggie's oldest. Reggie's a guy. According to Frank, Reggie's got some unrealized potential that can only be brought out if he runs the family business. Reggie's going to take over the business no matter what Sue does, and then they're all up a creek.

Her second biggest fear was ending up back under her father's roof. "He needs a maid," Sue always complained. "A cook. A laundress. He still calls me Susie, like I'm four."

"I don't know what's going to happen if we lose this baby too," Bob says.

"It's going to be okay."

Bob shrugs the comment off, but his eyes are grateful.

"I won't stay long," Mari says and turns the knob slowly. The shades are drawn. Opened suitcases are propped against the walls. There's an expensive-looking baby crib set up in one corner of the room and Mari has the sense, from the way Sue's got her elbow crooked over her face, that she's trying very hard not to notice it.

"Hey," Mari says. Bob, who has followed Mari into the room, stands by the window, his fists dug deep into his pockets. Bob and Sue have probably spent hours like this, Mari thinks. Alone together with their terror of the things that can still go wrong.

"Hey," Sue says.

Walking carefully to the end of the bed, Mari examines first the twin peaks of Sue's feet, then the vast mound of her belly, and then the jut of her friend's elbow.

"You should know that Frank's pretty PO'd at you at the moment," Bob says. "He's taking it personally that you're working against him on the development. And I guess he told you to keep that money he gave you secret, so he's pretty mad about that."

Sue adds, "Plus it's got back to him that you think his produce is for shit." Lydia has apparently made matters worse by saying she'd be thrilled to buy her vegetables from Mari if there are ever any to sell. Summer visitors like the idea of organic and locally grown, Lydia said. Also, they think Frank's produce is as pitiful as Mari does.

"You're not actually allowed in the house," Sue says. "On account of you being ungrateful. And a socialist. And the person who turned my brother into an alcoholic, not to mention the so-called best friend who promised to tell me the truth while secretly taking money from my dad."

"I've been banned from this house before," Mari says. "And I've been called a lot of names. Including, if I may say so, by you."

"Well, yah. Always well deserved, bitch."

Deciding to ignore this newest insult, Mari asks, "How'd you luck out and get your dad's bedroom?"

"Double bed," Bob says, but Sue says, "I'm an invalid. I'm fragile."

"Wow. Imagine you fragile. How'd you ever convince anybody of that?"

From where she's standing, all Mari can see of Sue's face is her chin. Still, it's possible there was a brief smile.

Mari contemplates the crib. "Where'd you get that Cadillac?" she asks. "It's even fancier than your truck." The truck that's got a dead starter that no one's got the time to fix. Bob rubs his feet against the floor and looks out the window, as if he's thinking of diving through. Mari wishes she hadn't brought up the truck.

"My dad," Sue answers. Removing her arm, she turns her face to the crib. "He's thrilled I'm back living in the house again," she says. "I think this is what he's wanted from the day I moved out. It's also bribery," she adds. "He wants to make sure Bob votes in favor of the rezone. And you're here to make sure he votes against."

"I am."

Sue turns to her husband. "What'd I tell you?" she asks.

Bob shrugs. In the silence, the sounds of Main Street drift in. Steady traffic. Conversations that blend together: "...her life jacket in the car...", "...until after lunch....", "...reservation on the Saturday morning boat..." Mari, turning to Bob, asks him his thoughts, but Sue is the one who answers.

"You should know that I'm also pretty pissed off at you right now," she says. "And not only over the money. I have enough going on without you stirring everyone on this island—especially my dad—into a frenzy."

"I'm sorry," Mari begins. What she wants to say is that she's barely slept since figuring out what Caleb and Pastor Aaron did to Levi. At her lawyer's suggestion, she had over-ridden Isabelle's advice and hired a private detective to look for evidence of ongoing child abuse at God's Bounty. What Mari had imagined was someone skulking at a distance, viewing her brothers and sisters through high-powered binoculars. In fact, the moron had knocked on the door, and of course the faithful swore that God's Bounty was a safe and loving place to raise children. Mari railed at her lawyer that the detective's visit would have inflamed both Pastor Aaron and Caleb, that all that had happened in return for the fifteen hundred dollars Mari spent—once again bringing her savings to near zero—was to give Pastor Aaron and Caleb incentive to increase their efforts to get Levi back.

But before Mari can get another word in, Sue says, "And then you come in here, not to sympathize with me being stuck in bed for the duration and not to cheer me up over ending up back in this fucking house. No, it's to see if you can use our friendship to get to my husband to be sure that you get what you want, and the rest of us be damned."

"No. Wait. I—"

"Like I care what you have to say right now."

Mari says, "I'm fighting for my son's safety. What they did to him down there is beyond horrific."

Sue says, "Sad. But not my problem. My problem: that you are the worst possible friend in the history of mammals."

"I thought you knew about the loan," Mari protests. "I figured your dad or Reggie would have told you."

"Great. You told Reggie and not me?"

"Reggie walked in right as your dad was giving me the money," Mari explains, but none of that matters to Sue, and even as her friend unloads on her, Mari can see how she could have handled things differently. Should have, in fact.

"Look, I'm sorry I didn't tell you," Mari says. "I'm sorry you guys have ended up living here."

"I don't give a rat's ass if you are sorry or not." Actions speak louder than words, Sue reminds her, and Mari's actions, in her estimation, have always added up to how much she takes Sue's friendship for granted.

"You can be damn sure," Sue says, "that from now on, I'm not your friend. I'm not on your side. Whatever you want, I'm going to do everything in my power to ensure you don't get it unless it's exactly what I want. What I need. That includes this vote. I'm in favor of the rezone. I hope some jerk builds his rich man's playground on this island, and that he hires Bob to build it, and that my dad gets a contract for his building materials, and that it means we can jack the boatyard up so it doesn't get swept out to sea in the next storm, and that we can have day care on this island so I can go back to work without having to have my kid stuck in a playpen behind the cash register. We need this rezone to pass. We want this rezone to pass, and we, in this instance, means me and my husband. And I don't give a shit what that does or doesn't do for you, any more than you've ever given a shit about what you do means for me. Right, honey?"

Both women look at Bob, whose attention is focused on the mountain of his wife's belly beneath the bedclothes.

"Bob?" Sue says.

"Leave me out of this," he replies. "This is between the two of you."

But it isn't. Bob's the one on the planning board. The one with the vote.

"Look," Mari says. "I said I'm sorry. I don't know what else you want me to do."

"Leave."

But how can she? Bob's vote is important, but what's more important right now is making things right with Sue.

"All I'm trying to do is make a life for my son," Mari says.

"So am I," Sue replies.

"I want him to be able to grow up here."

"Ditto."

"Look at us. Somehow, despite our intentions, we've both ended up back on the island, living with our parents."

Sue says, "Fuck that shit," but her tone is rueful.

"I don't know how to fix this," Mari says. "But I do know

that I always wanted us to have kids at the same time, and I pictured them as friends too."

"You want my son hanging out with your son," Sue says, "you're going to need to get him a haircut." Her voice is quieter. Maybe, just maybe, this fight is no different from the ones they had when they were younger. Maybe the friendship isn't over after all.

"Done," Mari says. Levi's been resisting a full haircut—his hair, he's cried, is all he has left from God's Bounty—but it tangles and knots. He hates washing it. The time has come. "Shove over," she adds, giving Sue's hip a gentle push. "Quit hogging the whole mattress."

"I can't. Think tractor trailer with twelve flat tires." But Sue does inch herself in the direction of Bob far enough that Mari can stretch out beside her. Bob looks the two of them over before turning his attention to the window and the view of the shed with its wall covered by lobster buoys.

"You okay?" Mari asks.

"I've got freaking Moby Dick swimming laps inside me. How do you think I am?"

"You hope he's got a moby dick." The words sail out of Mari's mouth before she can stop them, but she's got Sue laughing, and Bob's face is red.

When Sue regains control of herself, she says, "You know better than pretty much anyone how the last thing in the world I ever wanted was to end up back in this house. But sucking up to my dad is the only way I'm going to get a fancy-ass crib, jobs for both me and Bob, and a chance that we're going to have a business left to inherit when my dad retires."

"I know," Mari says. Really, it isn't fair for her to ask Sue and Bob to give up any of that to help her get what she needs. Going to God's Bounty was her choice. So was coming back here. So is the farm.

"I should probably tell you," Bob says. "We've determined we need to open this rezone thing up to an island-wide vote. There are too many conflicts of interest if the planning board tries to decide on its own." People have figured out that Frank's in favor of the development because he sees it profiting his business. Everyone knows—or thinks they know—that Lydia will vote in opposition to Frank to piss him off. Carol's pretty tight lipped, saying only that newcomers using the ferry had better follow the rules.

As Mari listens, she realizes that her task has now gotten substantially bigger; she's got to talk to every year-round resident. Or not. Maybe her plan for Little Great Island was never any more feasible than her ideas for God's Bounty.

"A full vote of the year-round population is the fair way to do this," Bob adds. Summer residents have no vote on the issues that govern Little Great Island, despite being taxpayers, but they are allowed to speak if the town manager—Sam McGavin—gives permission.

Yes, it's fair. But Frank is by far the most verbal person on the island about this issue, and he's only telling people half the story about the development's impact on the island. He's not mentioning the additional pressure on the plumbing and sewage, the further depletion of freshwater resources, and the ways in which the islanders will drop even lower on the socioeconomic totem pole. There's no guarantee that the things he is talking about—the day-care center, the jobs, the possibility of new businesses catering to shorter-term visitors—will ever come to fruition.

"Look," Sue says finally. "You can put your farm somewhere else. Or figure out something else to do. I'm sure my dad will give you a job if you apologize profusely. Maybe grovel a bit. And shut up about growing a bunch of freaking kale when the problem is a whole lot bigger than hopping on the latest foodie trend."

Eyes on the ceiling, Mari clamps her jaw shut. She knows now that working in the market is not what she wants. The thought of being stuck inside there all day makes her want to scream, but maybe it's her only remaining option. It's not as though she hasn't been told her farm idea is nuts. One female farmer she called for advice told her there's no way she can run a viable farm on an island; she needs daily tourist traffic. Another said that pumpkins are the only decent cash crop, and that Mari needs to be prepared to sell hundreds of them throughout October to keep going the rest of the year. A third farmer was full of practical advice—everything from a twenty-four-seven veterinarian hotline to links for state- and federal-level grants and subsidies, but he ended the conversation by reminding Mari that farm work is endless. "People burn out," he said. "Don't make the mistake of thinking you can do it alone. There's no value in saving the cost of a part-time helper if you end up in the hospital."

Instead of listening, Mari'd dug deeper. But now it's time to let go.

"Seriously," Sue says, as if she could read Mari's mind. "You're the most indestructible person I know. You'll find work. You're still adjusting to being back here."

"Are you and Bob really going to be happy answering to your dad for the rest of your lives?" Mari asks. Could Sue make a life kowtowing to Frank? Could Mari herself ever have been happy beholden to Caleb? She now knows the answer as far as Caleb goes, but she's also asking for her friend's sake. Sue always wanted her own life, free of her father and brother. Even the idea of taking over the businesses someday had ultimately been, for her, the booby prize after her father had ordered her back to the island. She'd finished her EMT training. She'd been in nursing school. Bob had been willing to move to the mainland to be with her. From what she's told Mari, she was happy.

Mari adds, "You're a grown-ass woman. You get to do what you want."

Sue gives her a long look before saying, "Look where that got you."

Fair enough. "Where it's gotten me is a need to go home," Mari says. "Mom and Levi are making brownies, and she is not a believer in limiting sugar intake. He's going to be bouncing off the walls." Mari's working herself to standing when she hears footsteps and male voices downstairs. Frank's home, along with Reggie.

"Oh shit, Mari," Sue says. "He really does not want you here."

"It's okay. I'll tell him I forced my way in."

Frank, like Sue, has a temper. When he used to watch Sue, Reggie, and Mari after school, he yelled if they played hide-and-seek among the market aisles, knocking over endcaps and running into customers. Mari was banned from the house after the girls engaged Reggie in a water fight that soaked the kitchen.

There's heavy clomping on the stairs. "Susie-Q," Frank's voice calls from outside the bedroom door.

"Shit," Sue says. "Shit, shit, shit."

Knuckles on the door. "Who're you talking to?" Frank asks. "What's going on in there?"

"Wait one sec," Sue calls, but her father doesn't listen. The door slams open.

"What in the name of Jiminy Cricket is she doing here?" Frank sputters, his finger directed at Mari, before adding, "Get the hell out of here and don't ever even think of coming back."

HOW MANY ENDINGS?

Little Great Island

August settles onto Little Great Island. Bees, butterflies, ants, and beetles move from here to there, leaving pollen grains in their wake. Crows holler, seagulls complain, a bald eagle lands for breakfast on the carcass of a fawn revealed by the ebbing tide. Chickens scrabble and tut, while in a bathroom overlooking a kitchen garden, Levi stands at the mirror, regarding the strange boy who looks back at him. One eyebrow lowers as he considers how, with his new haircut, he looks like the other boys on the island, but is that a good thing or a bad thing? In the bedroom next door, an old woman reads with a hand cupped on her husband's hip, as if reassuring herself he is still by her side. The softest of moans slips from his peeling lips.

Across the island, far from her home above The Sweet Shoppe, Lydia sits in an unfamiliar chair in an unfamiliar patch of light and watches an unfamiliar sight in an unfamiliar bed: an old man emitting the most harmonic of snores. At her feet, a dog lifts his nose and gives the woman a long and soulful look. Upstairs in the yellow house on Main Street, someone's pissing like a horse in the bathroom while Sue, crammed in her own childhood bedroom, reads the empty ceiling for promise that her life will improve.

The buckthorn spreads here. The garlic mustard spreads there. A spider descends a filament to examine its most recent catch.

Mari, seated by the potbellied stove in the living room, holds the newest missive from God's Bounty. Children cry that their mothers will rip their families apart as Mari has done. Pastor Aaron, who loved Mari like a daughter, suffers now as only the righteous and loving can. Caleb spends hours prostrate in the prayer-shed dirt, praying for guidance.

Across the street, atop The Knuckle, Harry stands with his hands in his pockets. Sheep graze the fields below. His sister berates him. His brother runs and runs. Inside the farmhouse, most rooms are clean and devoid of memories. Ellie's toothbrush has moved to a cupboard, her hairbrush to a drawer. Her voice, her footsteps, her almost-presence, are gone. How many endings, Harry wonders, can occur before there is nothing left? If the past crumbles, does the present crack and the future disappear?

The *Alice-Mari* is tied to her mooring. There's a rumor the lobstermen will be asked by the state to stop fishing. The remaining lobster should be left alone, in the hopes they can replenish. Everyone calculates the cost of regearing for scallops or haddock, commuting to the mainland for work, whether mainland work must eventually mean leaving the island for good. In the cabin of a dock-tied lobster boat, a fisherman takes the fishing log that was left to him by his father and hurls it against the wall.

The air is still. The sun is hot. Clouds, mounded like whipped cream, lie flat-bottomed across the sky. Out on the water, the post-larval lobster sail with the currents, dive for the shallows, fall victim to seagulls, cod, flounder, eels, sharks, and crabs, while the few that make it settle themselves down in rocky nurseries to molt and grow and molt again.

WHITENER

Sam

East of a submerged ledge of granite known as the Furies, Sam opens a trap, tosses back a juvenile lobster the length of his palm and two green crabs. It's the height of the season. The lobster are elsewhere. Or maybe they're gone.

A friendly shadow, foraging in the *Alice-Mari's* cabin, lifts the jar of instant coffee from the metal holder that keeps it from sliding when the waves are high.

"Whitener?" the shadow asks, and Sam responds silently because the conversation takes place only in his head.

"Under the sink."

"Expired two years ago."

"Best I can do."

The presence joins Sam on deck. The air takes on a note of coffee along with salt and bait and fuel. Together, he and the formless shadow gaze forward through the windscreen, at the scrim of heat haze laid out across the water, at the distant humps of the mainland and, above it all, contrails dispersing in the sky.

"Nice day," his companion comments, and then he turns, faceless, to Sam, who understands with no surprise that his shipmate is his own death. Soon or eventual? he wonders. Fast or slow? Is he going to stand on numb feet and pitch sideways off the deck a minute or two from now, or can he hold his wife again, his daughter, his grandson? Does his own will matter?

Sam looks at his guest, wondering if questions are allowed. Shifting the *Alice-Mari* into neutral, he shuts down her engine. Lets her drift.

His death takes a sip of coffee.

"It's just, there's the boy..." Sam says. He can't leave Levi. Not yet.

"Damn shame," Sam's companion says, or maybe doesn't, because he's seeming less there now, which makes Sam think there's an important question he wants to ask, if he can remember what it is. He pictures that mink, shot right through the middle, blood running into its shiny fur. Despite all the damage the critter could do to the chickens, that mink had given him pause. Killed for trying to fill its belly. Its only crime was doing what it was born to do.

Sam's visitor is gone now. There's only a seagull perched on the roof, peering beady eyed at Sam's empty traps. Rubbing his forearm, Sam discovers there's neither pain nor numbness. He takes a sip from his own cold cup of coffee. He will buy fresh creamer next time he's at the market. He will make up his own mind about what's best, and then he'll make sure Alice and Mari are prepared. That Levi will remember him. He will go when he has to.

The tide is ebbing. The day has passed. The gull tips its head, opens its beak, remains soundless, and then gives Sam another glare, causing him to recall the question that keeps fleeing his brain. Did he put the gun away in its lockbox after shooting the mink? Levi had come screaming from the house. Mari had barreled down the driveway toward him. Harry Richardson, from up on the road, had called out, wondering if there was anything he could do. But what about the gun? Sam needs to ensure that thing's under lock and key the moment he's back on shore.

LIFE IN THE GRAY

Harry

Harry shows up for yacht-club cocktails because not attending would cause more trouble than being there. The club room is packed, filled with loud voices, ruddy faces, tinkling glasses, the smell of open ocean and salted air. Sweatshirts and windbreakers are thrown over shoulders or tied around waists. He spots the Hanovers, Pete and Abby Shaw, Mack and Missy Worthington, a handful of Peabodys, and a mop-haired man with distinctly Kennedy features. In the far corner, by a wall of windows, Mr. Estabrook holds court from a window seat.

Drink first. Do his best to mingle after.

Arguably, three forty is early in the day to start drinking, but the yacht-club tradition is that the bar opens the moment the winner of the Saturday sailboat race crosses the finish line. By the time the last skipper straggles in, at least some of the yacht-club members are already a few sheets to the wind.

"Short course today," a woman near Harry's elbow says. She's got the greenest eyes he's ever seen. Colored contacts? Why doesn't he know her? A newcomer or somebody's guest?

Harry asks, "What's up with that?"

Thrusting her wine glass in the direction of the bartender, the woman laughs like Harry's cracked a joke. Ellie was the better skipper—more strategic, more competitive. Harry never really cared about winning, but he loved the intensity with which she studied the wind and currents, the random insights she had into the forces at play around them. He'd learned to listen to her in a sailboat. Why not on land, where the stakes were so much higher?

"Scotch," Harry tells the bartender now. He knows for a fact there's some nicely aged single malts stashed somewhere. "Can you break out the good stuff?"

"You celebrating a win?" the bartender asks.

"I am." *Somebody* won. It doesn't matter that it wasn't him.

The green-eyed woman beside Harry tsks. "I didn't see you at the starting line," she accuses and walks away.

The bartender selects a bottle and pours liberally. "Bruichladdich Port Charlotte ten year," he says. He hands over the glass. "Award winning. From Islay."

Harry nods, understanding only that he's been informed of his drink's pedigree. The liquid sears his mouth, ignites the tender flesh of his nostrils, leaves a faint taste of ash on his tongue. Shaking his head to clear the flames, Harry drinks again. Damn Isabelle, who'd scoffed at the idea of jeopardizing the sale to Duncan in any way, and who is now peppering him with emails, texts, and phone calls about whether he's found a therapist, notified the school he's returning, talked with a real estate agent about his condo. Someone, probably Frank, told Isabelle that Harry had requested permission to speak at the town meeting—because how could he not do something to help Mari after what those people did to her son?—and now Isabelle's fighting him on that.

Jonathan hasn't wavered from his assertion that he's not speaking to Harry until he "shapes up," but lately Umeko has been calling and putting Charlie on the phone. Charlie hates telephones, refuses to speak, which puts Harry in the position of nattering at his poor, defenseless nephew. The whole business is meant to make him feel closer to Charlie, Harry understands. In fact, it makes him feel vaguely slimed.

It hasn't escaped his notice that many of the year-round residents are a lot less friendly than they were in previous years. Most of the summer visitors have little to say to him as well. He's been invited nowhere. But who cares? He has nothing in common with them anymore. They live a life insulated from true loss.

He should go home. Or no, he should stay. Maybe Isabelle will see attendance at the post-race cocktail party as a sign of improved mental health.

After a third swallow of scotch, Harry hears Mr. Estabrook's foghorn voice above the general burbling of conversation and decides the safest harbor in this roomful of people is over in the corner, with The Butterfly Diplomat. Getting through the crowd is like threading a sailboat up a rock-strewn river. Dickie Vydell, as if in response to Harry's thought, becomes one of those obstructions, turning from his conversation and body-blocking Harry's progress. Then he stares without a word.

"Excuse me," Harry says. He's known Dickie since they were in the novice sailing class together. Dickie took to the job of skipper readily, especially the bit about yelling at his boatmate when Harry was crewing.

Dickie doesn't move.

"Can I help you?" Harry asks finally.

"Yes, you can. You can quit trying to turn this island into goddamn Fort Myers. What's next, Harry? A Starbucks?"

Harry takes a drink and swallows, does his best to channel his sister before he speaks. "Ease up, Dickie. There's a legal contract in place. Besides, the final decision is up to the people who live here, not you and me."

"And what's with that McGavin girl running around, putting posters up like she owns the place?" Dickie says. "Who knows what kind of drugs she did on that commune?"

The urge to punch Dickie is nearly insurmountable. "Listen, you piece of—"

"Harry!" Mr. Estabrook calls from his seat by the windows. "How's my favorite historian?"

Harry pushes past Dickie, intentionally jostling the other man.

"Watch it," Dickie says, and Harry wheels, free hand already clenched in a fist.

"Harry," Mr. Estabrook calls again. "You're a very elusive young man. I've been trying to track you down since Monday."

Dickie gives Harry a final shake of the head before turning away.

"Seems as though you've caused quite the kerfuffle on the island," Mr. Estabrook says when Harry stands before him. The man's cleaned and well groomed, Harry notices. He seems happy.

"The Shaws and I were just talking about the plans your Mr. Duncan has for Little Great Island," Mr. Estabrook adds.

"Can we not talk about this?"

"A venture of this sort could save this island," Abby says. "I do not understand what the objection is."

"It seems not everyone agrees with your perspective," Mr. Estabrook tells her.

Pete jumps in, saying, "This place needs to move forward. All this opposition is really about resistance to change, but the world is changing. Little Great Island must adapt. Evolve. Or go extinct." There's something smug in the way Pete lifts his glass to his lips, tips his head toward it, his demeanor saying he's scored the winning point but is too much the gentleman to gloat. All Harry's anger surges toward Pete, who built that ridiculous energy suck of a house. Who bulldozed Harry's concerns about whether an executive retreat was right for the island and who completely ignored Harry's repeated statements that he wasn't ready to sell. Who has always, Harry realizes now, been the sort of man who thinks himself superior. Opposition to his actions, Harry recalls Pete saying, isn't his problem. It's up to those he leaves flailing in his wake to figure out how to swim. If they sink, it's their problem for not getting on board. Harry gives the liquid in his glass a sardonic smile, recognizing that Pete is exactly the sort of person who would take a metaphor and torture it like that.

"Listen," Harry says. "I never asked, but what's in it for you if this executive retreat goes through?"

Pete waits a millisecond too long before saying, "Me? Nothing." He will not look Harry in the eyes. Some kind of finder's fee? Harry wonders. A pile of cash or a favor that shoots Pete ahead some number of spaces in his career?

"How are you *doing*?" Abby interrupts, wrapping her fingers around his wrist. "Out there rattling around that big old house all by yourself. We never see you. You must be so lonely."

Not that Pete and Abby have reached out to him. Since the offer was signed and Isabelle took over handling communications with Duncan Development, the only contact Harry's had with his old friends has been superficial conversations if they happened to see each other in the village.

"I'm not," Harry says. "I'm fine other than this development thing." There's a nasty edge to his voice, which he's certain both Mr. Estabrook and Pete notice.

"We cannot believe the way that McGavin girl is running around, trying to stop a project that is clearly good for this island. And now she's put sheep on your land." Abby's eyes go wide. She taps Harry's forearm, drawing attention to the glittery bits of jewelry on her hand. "I know she's taking advantage, with you grieving and all. We don't hold it against you, do we, Pete? But honey, the thing is, you've got to stop acting like you are against the sale. You were the one who said you wanted to sell as quickly as possible, remember?" Abby leans a few inches closer so that a strand of her hair catches in Harry's beard. "We care for you so much, Harry. We hate to see you getting manipulated by a woman who, well, we both think is only after your money."

Harry downs his drink. Wonders what the chances are of getting another. The room's still packed, so navigating to the bar's going to take some effort. Abby and her husband are like a matched set. Both are brown-haired, brown-eyed, with unnaturally white teeth. Abby's mouth's a bit too large for her face. Pete's is a bit too small.

"I think it's great you're coming out of it, getting interested in women again," Pete says and shakes his head. "But a word to the wise here, Harry: not that one. She's trouble. Who even knows who that child's father is?"

Is Harry's revulsion for these people clear on his face? How could it *not* be? He needs another drink. Mr. Estabrook is watching him, clearly expecting a rebuttal, but Harry's eyeing the door. Go now, before his fist lands in Pete's face.

"I would like a word with young Harry here," Mr. Estabrook tells the Shaws. "If you don't mind." Summarily dismissed, Pete and Abby drift away, a mutter passing between them. Both give pitying glances back at Mr. Estabrook, and hatred surges through Harry once again. *You, too, will get old*, he wants to tell them. *If you're lucky*. It's not a personal failing; it's a fact, and someone who has contributed as much to the world as Mr. Estabrook has deserves respect.

"I do not believe this executive retreat was ever what you wanted," Mr. Estabrook says. "You may have convinced yourself, at some point, or let someone else convince you. Grief does funny things to us. I can see that you have changed your mind and that you are trying to ensure that the sale fails.

However, your actions, both for and against, have engendered a great deal of animosity on this island." Everyone, it seems, has a problem with everyone else at the moment. A summer visitor has contacted the animal control office on the mainland to complain about the Stanleys' Siamese cats, which have gone feral in the village. Never has an animal control officer been summoned to the island. Frank Clatcher is threatening legal action against Lydia Smith, who is apparently behind on her rent. She has talked to an attorney about forcing Frank to make whatever renovations are needed to protect her business from the next storm tide. Year-round residents might have feuded in the past, but legal recourse has never been sought. Some members of the summer population are calling for parking meters on Main Street to stop the fishermen from using spaces all day. A coalition of year-round residents, in retaliation, is calling for a priority reservation system on the ferry.

"These sorts of ruptures have never, in my experience, been this contentious."

"I should never have gotten us into the deal with Duncan Development," Harry admits. Pete Shaw has never really been a friend. Rather, Harry's been a bit player in Pete's network, the kind of friend worth staying in touch with in case he becomes useful someday. Bastard.

Mr. Estabrook says, "You have a diplomatic negotiations problem on your hands."

"I don't know that there's a lot more I can do at this point."

"Nonsense." Mr. Estabrook wraps his arms across his knee. Even with hair on his ears, he is transformed to the senior statesman. "You remember how I used to tell you that people like to reduce all issues to black and white?" Up come the fists representing opposing positions, just the way they had the first time Harry heard this talk.

"But in point of fact," Mr. Estabook continues, "much of life occurs in the gray." Harry's heard this soliloquy before too.

Life in the gray area is complex, challenging, and rewarding. Those who confine themselves to black-and-white thinking miss what it means to be truly human. Still, Harry isn't sure where the gray area is in this instance. The island approves the development because the majority want the benefits of increased tourist trade, greater tax revenue, and the possibility of jobs. Or else they turn it down because they recognize the impact such a business would have on the culture and atmosphere. Your siblings either get what they want, or they hate you. You can't have half a Swedish sauna or a brother and sister who only despise you six months out of the year.

"Do you remember the fundamental principle of dispute resolution?" Mr. Estabrook asks.

"I do." Over the course of his career, Harry's read any number of books and articles by people claiming to know the most critical aspects of successful negotiation. With each one, he's held it up to Mr. Estabrook's first principle and determined The Butterfly Diplomat knew his stuff.

Mr. Estabrook says, "Tell me."

"Find the common ground and negotiate from there," Harry says. "Although in this instance, I don't see what the common ground is."

"Love," Mr. Estabrook says.

"Love?" At the moment, it seems more as if hate is the common denominator.

Mr. Estabrook plants his hands on his thighs and stands. "Love of this island," he says. "Which you and Ms. McGavin are tearing to shreds."

Without another word, Mr. Estabrook takes the glass from Harry's hand and leaves him sitting by the window while, behind him, rowboats nestle and jostle the dock, and sailboats, in their various classes and sizes, bob at their moorings, all of them with their bows to the wind.

ON THEIR KNEES

Mari

Mari, seated atop Leah's Knuckle, has her knees pressed to her chest, her face against her thighs. Constellations spread above her, the occasional star cut loose from the firmament, but their beauty means nothing. She made it here thanks to their illumination and that of a sliver of waning moon but noticed neither. She'd ignored the lightning bugs flashing in the bushes and the thin claws of brambles that scraped her naked legs, climbing until she'd reached the island's highest point. It's well after midnight but also well before dawn.

She'd been awakened by the ringing landline snaking its way into her dreams: a school bell persisting, but she could not remember what class was next; a God's Bounty summons that must be answered, but her legs would not respond; a timer screaming that a meal was burning, a deadline was passing, a crisis was set to explode.

Her eyes had snapped open. The room was dark. Levi's curled form was still, his breath the gentlest of comforts. Her parents' bedroom doorknob clicked. Still, the phone rang. Barefoot in a T-shirt and panties, Mari met her mother in the hall. Alice's face was sleep-creased, her eyes alarmed and questioning: Middle-of-the-night phone calls could only be explained by Mari. Anything else, if it couldn't have waited until morning, would have merited a knock on the door.

"I'll get it," Mari said. "You go back to sleep." But Alice followed her down the stairs, the floorboards creaking beneath their bare feet. The kitchen was lit by the vigilant eyes of appliances. The faucet held a bright reflection of barn light. The stovetop bulb they used as a nightlight had burned out. The landline, propped on the counter the way it always was, gave off a sense of malice and, for a moment, Mari believed it had gone silent. Maybe a wrong number? Someone else's turn for terrible news? An instant later, the phone rang again, and she was no longer saved.

When Mari lifted the receiver, she said nothing. Let Caleb—because who else could it be?—speak first. Let him say what he had to say and be done, and then she could hang up and begin doing what she needed to do. Sell the sheep. Find a home for Houdini. Notify the granting agencies that she was withdrawing her proposals. Apologize to Frank, pack the new clothes and the toothbrushes and Pretty Too, tell Harry the harvest is all his now, hug her parents and Sue. Tell them goodbye.

But what she heard through the receiver wasn't Caleb. It was a woman struggling for breath on the shore after a near drowning. Alice stood in the doorway between kitchen and living room, a silhouette with crossed arms, propped against the jamb. Watching. Closing her eyes, Mari tried to put a location to the gasping to help her identify the caller. In her nose was the pungency of South Carolina in the summer, and her ears rang with the chirps and whistles of southern night. God's Bounty. It had to be from there. But God's Bounty had one telephone; it was in Pastor Aaron's office, as accessible to the brethren as a crater on the moon. The closest usable phone could be the booth outside the Food Lion over on Route 321. It was a place of cracked glass and graffiti that had merited less than a glance the handful of times Mari had passed it. Surely, even if one of her brothers or sisters from God's Bounty wanted a phone and was able to get to that ancient booth, they would have found the phone itself long gone. Besides all that, it was after two a.m. No one from God's Bounty could be off the compound at that hour and have any thought of ever going back.

"Mummy?" came a small voice through the receiver. "Mummy?"

Joanna, Mari realized. The daughter of Sister Grace, her best friend at God's Bounty, Joanna was a timid girl whose eyes watered when her mother wasn't nearby.

"Sister Grace?"

In the kitchen, Alice shifted her weight. Cleared her throat. At the other end of the phone line, Sister Grace's breathless sobbing had turned to sniffling.

"Are you safe?" Mari asked, watching as her mother made her way to a kitchen chair and sat.

Sister Grace said, "I have—we have—a friend. He left this phone hidden for me. There's a ride coming. They will take us. We will be safe."

Mari nodded against the receiver. Her mother's eyes were fastened on her face. Sister Grace, who had made Mari's Christmas socks and given her the few bills that she must have stolen from somewhere, had fled God's Bounty with her daughter. Sister Grace must have found Mari's parents' phone number on the Internet.

"It's okay," Mari mouthed to her mother.

Sister Grace inhaled deeply. "They are coming," she said on the exhale. "For you. It's so horrible here." Another deep breath before Sister Grace could start again. "They cracked down after you left," she said.

"The men?"

"Pastor Aaron. Sister Ann. And Caleb." In broken sentences, Sister Grace told Mari the rest of it. Caleb's heartbreak over Mari and Levi's disappearance had morphed into a bitter anger under the tutelage of Pastor Aaron. The brothers and sisters had spent hours on their knees in the prayer circle while the sun shone or the rain fell. Sisters were dragged by their hair, given half rations, forbidden to speak during meals. Brother Daniel had been caught talking to a heathen in town and his tongue had been seared. Twisting the phone wire, Mari began to cry. It was true, what they had done to her son.

Sister Grace continued, "A man showed up, claiming he was lost. Pastor Aaron wouldn't let him in, but the guy kept trying to peer around the door."

That stupid private detective. Firing her lawyer was one more thing Mari had taken too long to do.

"After he left," Sister Grace continued, "Pastor Aaron said you'd hired people to kidnap all the children. He made the children sleep in one stall in the barn. The men took turns standing guard. We were only allowed…" Sister Grace's voice faltered, and Mari pressed her head against the wall. Her fault. All of it.

"A half hour a day with our children," Sister Grace added. "I ran."

"What does he want?" Mari spoke as quietly as she could, wishing her mother couldn't hear. Wishing the full repercussions of her screwup didn't have to be on display in front of the woman who had always told her she'd fail.

"What will make him let the children go?" Mari already knew the answer, so it was no surprise when Sister Grace said it.

"Caleb wants Levi back."

"Only Levi?"

"Pastor Aaron won't allow you near us." They both knew Pastor Aaron's refusal meant Caleb wouldn't either.

Mari asked, "Has he left yet?"

"They. Pastor Aaron's coming too. And no, they haven't left yet. But soon."

Sister Grace murmured to Joanna. When her voice came again through the receiver, she told Mari that Pastor Aaron still needed to pick someone to lead in his and Caleb's absence, and then they were heading to Maine.

"There are headlights on the road," she whispered then. A car in the parking lot. Mari's heart pounded while Sister Grace's breathing quickened, and then Grace said, "It's okay. It's my ride. We'll be okay. You and Levi go somewhere they won't think to look. I love you."

"You too," Mari said, but the connection was gone. As she replaced the receiver, Mari imagined Sister Grace holding Joanna's hand. The four or five steps they had to take together to the car and the searching eyes of the driver while seat belts were fastened and tears of relief were shed.

Alice, at the kitchen table, asked, "What was that about?" Fear fogged her voice.

"Caleb's coming." Her mother must have seen that she was shivering. That her skin had risen into bumps. "We're going to go," Mari said. "First boat in the morning."

Her mother shook her head. Her eyes glinted. "No," she said. "You're not going anywhere. No more running. This time, you stay here and clean up your own mess.

"You didn't see what happened to Reggie after you went off to college, but the rest of us did. It nearly destroyed Frank. And then Sue, losing all those babies. Needing a friend. Your father. His heart broke when he found out he couldn't even call you. Never mind you leaving grad school."

"But I—"

"It's not a question of changing the outcome. It's a question of noticing what you do to others."

"But if I stay—"

"Face him, Mari, and resolve this for once and for all. Lord knows how hard it is to win an argument with you once you've made your mind up about something." The buoy saltshaker was clasped in her fingers. "The last thing in the world you are is a coward."

"We'll talk more in the morning," Mari said, which was sufficient to get her mother to go back upstairs. She waited ten minutes, watching the second hand rise and fall around the clock, before letting herself out the door.

A rustling on the path below her, too large to be a field mouse or mink. Mari lifts her head and hopes it isn't Reggie, the last person in the world she wants to see right now. Reggie, who her father is convinced took his gun from the barn, although Reggie denies it. Frank claims he's searched the yellow house and found nothing. But gun thief or not, Reggie stands in the road outside the house at night to watch her. Sometimes he comes as close as the edge of the garden. The glow of his cigarette gives him away, along with the smell of smoke.

"Piss off, Reggie," she says. "I am so not in the mood for you right now."

"It's me," Harry says from the darkness. In a moment, he is standing beside her, two denim-covered legs a few inches from her shoulder.

"I saw you come up here," he says, and she realizes he was looking.

"Stalker," she says.

"That's me. Okay if I stay?"

Mari unfurls her body, waits while he sits. "Couldn't sleep?" he asks, and she tells him about Sister Grace's call.

The suggestions he makes are ones that have occurred to her already: notify the cops, but what good will it do when the closest officer is on the mainland and Caleb is still at God's Bounty? Ask people to keep an eye on arriving ferry passengers? But that's next to useless. Caleb and Pastor Aaron could hire a boat and captain anywhere on the coast. There are docks and beaches all around Little Great Island where a boat might land. Many are private, unsupervised. Anyone could slip ashore. Talk to another lawyer, who will do nothing but give bad advice, file papers, send bills? There's nothing for her and Levi on this island but dead ends.

"Levi and I are going to leave in the morning," she says.

"You're afraid of him?"

"I'm afraid of me." The real truth: She doesn't trust herself. She had loved Caleb too much to see he was dangerous, and she hadn't even wanted to imagine a life that didn't include her sisters. The work was what she'd always wanted. The mission made much more sense than capitalistic greed. She'd been happy when she should have been aware. Should have been a good mother rather than a contented farmer.

"I'm never going to get grant money without land, and I'm never going to be able to get land on this island."

"You'll get funding somehow. You're smart. You're articulate. You're persuasive."

"I put my son in danger."

"You got your son out of danger."

"My mother doesn't want to show it, but she's afraid of Pastor Aaron and Caleb."

"Well, you can be a wee bit terrifying yourself," Harry says. "But in a good way. You stand up for what you believe in. You do what you know is right, no matter what other people think.

"And you're an amazing mother," he adds. Harry, as it turns out, has researched cult recovery just as she has. For children born in a cult, transitioning into society can take years. In a matter of months, Levi has made huge progress.

"Stubborn might be a better word," Mari says.

"Tough, not stubborn. Women have to be more forceful about standing up to authority. Particularly male authority." He reminds her of how much she knows about farming, the factors at play in climate change and nutrition, and that she's come up with a good plan for her future and Levi's. If she can convince everyone to vote against the rezone, he might have a better shot at convincing Isabelle and Jonathan to consider selling to the trust.

"The idea of selling to the Maine farm trust is brilliant. Keep at it. Knowing you, you'll make it work somehow."

"None of that matters." What matters is Levi's safety. "I don't suppose you want Houdini?" she adds. She needs to be able to promise Levi that someone he knows and trusts will take care of the goat, and her mother is unlikely to want him.

"I've got to go back to Boston in a couple of weeks. I don't think Houdini would take well to condo life." Harry does want to help, though. Mari can feel it.

The Milky Way leaves a dusty path across the sky. There's mineral in the night air, and dirt and vegetation. A skittering, a squeak, the sound of Harry's breath. In her mind are the worn floorboards of Clatcher's Market, the hoot of the *Abenaki Princess*, the sight of the barn light through a dripping fog, toppled spruce trees decomposing into the dirt, and even Reggie Clatcher striding Main Street in his work boots as if there were someplace he needed to go.

"Don't let them ruin this island," she says.

Harry's face turns toward her. Has the sky lightened, or have her eyes adjusted? There are his lips, nestled between his beard and mustache; the smooth, pale skin across his cheek-bones; the sour of his breath; the length of his legs stretched out now across the rock. The land beneath them is distinguishable from the overall darkness.

"I have to take care of Levi now. I can't keep pissing off everyone on this island if I expect to make a life for us here. But you said yourself the farm is a good idea. I know it is. I know what I'm trying to do. I know I'm the one to do it. But you're the one with the land. So please, Harry. Do the right thing."

Mari maneuvers sideways, so that she is facing Harry. A streak of orange has appeared in the eastern sky. She can make out the silhouettes of the trees by The Cliffs' edge. A door slaps shut, and her father, with his uneven gait and blue cooler clutched in one hand, heads across the back lawn and down the dock. Her mother's voice calls, "Be safe out there, old man," and her father lifts his free hand in promise. A ewe bleats. Bayberry scents the air.

"Fight this thing."

"I will, but only if you will," he says.

Mari hesitates, then nods. Her mother was right. It is time to stand and fight. "Okay. But I need you one hundred percent on my side."

LOADED

Reggie

It's World War Twelve twenty-four seven in the house ever since his dad caught Mari talking to Bob and Sue, so Reggie's got himself out of there. Decided to get himself a drink. Well, *another* drink, because he's got a bottle stashed behind the washing machine, but the point is, he deserves to have a drink someplace where people aren't yelling at each other. All he's got to do is get into his dad's office, figure out where the key to the liquor room's hidden this time. Not like there are that many options for hiding places. The safe combination is right there in the desk drawer, after all. But the sight of The Blue Buoy's lit-up windows grabs his attention. Why shouldn't Reggie have his drink right there? He's got his pay, which his dad forked over without complaint because at least Reggie's smart enough not to invite Mari into the house.

"Help you?" the summer girl standing inside the door asks.

"Going to get some food."

"You mind sitting at the counter?" the summer girl says.

"Fine by me," Reggie answers, but wouldn't you know, he ends up next to Harry Richardson. Guy's all "aren't I cool?" in one of those sweaters with a little zipper up by the neck and his trimmed beard. This island is too damn crowded in the summer. People like Richardson coming in demanding this, that, or the other. Sucking up to Mari and her kid and giving them stuff like a place to put sheep and stuffed animals and crayons when Reggie can't even get her to talk to him long enough to give her actual useful cash. Her own damn fault he spent it. Now she won't give him the time of day. Meanwhile, Reggie gets to be gas monkey for people like Richardson, filling up the tanks on their damn Boston Whalers because they're too stupid to remember how the pumps work.

"Good evening, Reggie," Richardson says, all la-di-da.

Reggie ignores him because if it weren't for this douchebag, he and Mari might be back together by now. He tells the woman behind the counter he wants a cheeseburger and fries. Plus a Budweiser. Jack Daniels on the side.

Richardson's got a pad of paper next to him, and he's scribbling away. Spiffy nails and clean hands of a guy who couldn't grease a propeller shaft or jack a tire if his life depended on it. Who does he think he's trying to impress?

"Your girlfriend turned my house into a war zone," Reggie says.

"My girlfriend?" Richardson's eyebrow goes up like he has no idea who Reggie's talking about.

"She came over, trying to get my sister and her husband to go for your farm idea."

"Are you talking about Mari McGavin?"

"'Are you talking about Mari McGavin?'" Reggie makes his imitation come out all prissy and likes the anger he sees in Richardson's eyes. His drinks land on the counter in front of him, and Reggie gets his hand around the beer can. Likes the way it feels against his palm.

"Can I get my bill?" Richardson asks. He hands his credit card over without even waiting to see what he owes. Gone practically before Reggie gets his beer to his mouth. Reggie grins, imagining how Richardson would whimper and shake if Reggie had his gun pointed at him. His gun, the one he found on a hay bale in the McGavins' barn. Took it because, hello? Mari's spread the word that her weirdos might show up looking for her. Reggie's the one who lives right by the ferry landing. The one who keeps an eye on how things go down on this island. Sam's an old man and he's out on the water all the time, so what use does he have for a gun?

Cheeseburger arrives, along with a massive pile of fries. Reggie grins again, holding the burger in both hands. Sure would be fun to see Richardson shit himself, and anyway doesn't he deserve it? Screwing with Reggie's old man's deal to get rich. Getting into Mari's pants. Lucky for Richardson Reggie's not really the vengeful type.

LEMON COOKIES

Harry

"Hello, Harry," Lydia says, emerging from Mr. Estabrook's kitchen, a plate of cookies in her hands. Her presence, her ease as an apparent member of this household, throws Harry. As he takes one of the cookies she offers, he puts it all together: Mr. Estabrook's frequent presence in The Sweet Shoppe. His neatened appearance. Lydia's cheerfulness this summer, an abrupt change from the worries she had about the island's future and her own when Harry first arrived. It seems The Butterfly Diplomat and The Sweet Shoppe Lady have managed the improbable. They have kept a secret.

"These are lemon," Lydia says. "Our favorites."

"Along with chocolate chip, macaroons, shortbread, and a few others." Mr. Estabrook smiles fondly at Lydia and then breaks a corner off his cookie and gives it to Jussi. "We're all eating quite well these days, courtesy of this wonderful young lady."

"Oh, you," Lydia says. She sits in the wicker chair beside Mr. Estabrook, both of them opposite Harry on the love seat. This glass-walled porch, one of the last "updates" the prior owners made before the Estabrooks bought the house, is the one place that gets decent sunlight, Mr. Estabrook says.

"An architectural misstep," he adds. "Yet it's my favorite room in the house. I can see nature from here. Every place else, I feel as though I'm wandering in the dark. Such a shame on an island with so much beauty." There's no ocean view from the windows. No scenic vista that would be considered worthy of note by most people.

Mr. Estabrook's teacup looks absurdly dainty in his long fingers. Harry's heard from Mari that Mr. Estabrook plans to leave the island for good right after Labor Day, which is only two weeks away. She and Alice have been helping him pack, and already the living room, dining room, and front hall are lined with boxes.

"I imagine you are here about this whole development kerfuffle," Mr. Estabrook says. A new note has entered his voice. Jussi must notice it too, because he whimpers in his sleep. A front paw twitches. On the plant stand in the far corner, a coleus sheds a leaf, which drifts to the floor.

"Yes." Harry hears the question in his reply and scrambles to recover. He and Mari have poked and shaped their plan until it feels not only viable, but necessary. But before he can speak again, Mr. Estabrook continues.

"Your agricultural diplomacy seems to have led this very small country to the verge of a civil war." One unruly eyebrow has lowered. Although Mr. Estabrook is dressed in a polo shirt and sweater, it's easy to imagine him armored in an impeccably tailored suit, ready to do battle with the likes of Kim Jong-un, Jair Bolsonaro, Vladimir Putin, or Donald Trump.

Harry nods, recognizing the reference to their earlier conversation, when they talked about Mari's garden. "I think we've found a possible solution," he says. If Harry can get his siblings and the trust to agree, the Richardsons will sell their land to the Maine Farm Preservation Trust, which would then—with some luck—sell the land to Mr. Estabrook.

Although Harry doesn't go into details with Mr. Estabrook, Isabelle has said they can talk about the idea as a backup plan if the rezone doesn't pass. *If* Harry notifies the school that he's returning to his job in the fall and *if* he goes back on medication. Jonathan's said he just wants the place sold. He and Umeko need the money sooner rather than later, and every month they still own the property is a month with additional expenses. It's all far from being a done deal, but Harry doesn't need to admit that now.

What Harry does tell Mr. Estabrook is that Mari's been working on a plan for the trust that would allow the land to be turned over to Little Great Island for management. With Mari's help, the island could create community gardens that could be rented for a fee or a CSA. She would help develop farm-to-table markets, including The Sweet Shoppe and restaurants on the coast. The school could rent a community garden to teach children about growing food. Perhaps internships could be offered through agricultural programs at Maine colleges and universities. Every part of the business would be based on sustainable practices. All of it would be overseen by Mari, who could hire help from other islanders as finances allowed.

Mr. Estabrook scoffs, "My suggestion was a conservation trust. Not a farm."

"A farmland trust provides a much more direct benefit to the year-round population," Harry says. It promotes self-sufficiency. It has the potential to offset some of the income lost to the diminishing lobster catch. A conservation trust, which protects views and birds as well as taking the land off the tax rolls, is a summer-visitor priority. The island natives are more interested in finding a way to survive.

"A farm destroys natural habitat. It disrupts migratory pathways. It involves fertilizers and pesticides and noise, all

258 · KATE WOODWORTH

of which upset the environment." Mr. Estabrook is simply stating facts, all of which Harry is prepared to rebut. Yet Mr. Estabrook's tone seems dismissive. Is something else on his mind? Well, of course: the fact that his time on the island is coming to a close. Leaving the island is always hard, no doubt exponentially harder when you do it for the last time. But Harry and Mari have a solution for that issue as well.

"Or else," Harry continues, "we wondered if you'd be interested in buying the property outright. We leave the trust out of the equation." Mr. Estabrook has always said it's the nicest spot on the island. The hope is that he would allow Mari to farm a few acres in return for her acting as caretaker for the house and land during the offseason.

"It's way too late for me," Mr. Estabrook says. Leaning forward slowly, he sets his teacup and saucer on the table in front of Harry. Lydia clears her throat, plucks at the hem of her sleeve, and Mr. Estabrook turns to her, his expression concerned.

"There are people on this island who need housing they can afford," she says, and the dog whimpers again. A crow squawks in the distance. Inside the room, the silence stretches. Why does Harry get the feeling he's unwelcome here? A month ago, he would have made his excuses and left, but now he hears Mari's voice: *Be in this one hundred percent.*

"If the fishing collapses, the community collapses," he says, startling the dog so that it lifts its head and peers around. Harry lists examples: abalone off the coast of Southern California; Pacific salmon; Atlantic cod. Collapses lead to moratoriums, and moratoriums create massive layoffs. Joblessness on an island this small means a mass exodus of the island natives, no one to caretake the island in the offseason or the summer visitors when they're around.

"Protecting natural beauty and wildlife is important, but as Mari points out—"

"Are you aware of the trouble you and your Mari McGavin have caused on this island?" Mr. Estabrook doesn't wait for a reply before continuing. "I spent nearly an hour listening to Abby Shaw tell me all sorts of gossip and speculation about how Ms. McGavin is trying to bed you in order to secure a new father for her son."

Harry starts to protest, but Mr. Estabrook raises a hand.

"I am perfectly capable of ignoring gossip. I defended you. I gave you the benefit of the doubt. But then this whole rigamarole cost this fine woman her home."

Harry glances at Lydia, who won't meet his look. Mr. Estabrook is the one who tells the story. Sue moved out of her father's house after Frank accused Bob of stealing from the market. She stood on the front walk, big as a barn, in full view of Main Street and hollered, "Wake the fuck up, Dad. Reggie's been stealing from you all summer." She also added that her father could take the fancy crib he purchased for his grandchild and shove it up his—

"Well, you get the gist," Mr. Estabrook finishes. "Sue came right to Lydia, who used to look after both her and her brother back when they were small."

"She just needed a place to sit," Lydia says. "And calm down."

"And out of the generosity of her heart, this lovely lady offered Bob and Sue her guest bedroom."

"That was nice," Harry says, still not understanding what this has to do with him, with Mari, or with the Richardson land.

"Frank promptly notified Lydia that he was terminating her lease," says Mr. Estabrook.

"Now, Tom," protests Lydia. "I was behind on my rent."

When Mr. Estabrook cants forward, Harry leans back. He's never seen his friend angry. He's never even seen him ruffled.

"Frank Clatcher refused to capitulate after the situation was made whole."

Which means, Harry understands, Mr. Estabrook paid Lydia's back rent, and Frank still refused to let Lydia stay. The Sweet Shoppe will be closed at the end of September, and Lydia will be without a place to live on Little Great Island. Bob and Sue are apparently talking about moving off island once the baby is born. She's making noises about finishing nursing school. He's talking about working in construction.

"Surely Frank will relent," Harry says. Frank has thrown Reggie—who clearly has a lot more problems than Sue—out of the house any number of times and always let him back in. He's not the kind of man who will force an elderly woman he's known his entire life into the streets. But Mari will be devastated by all of this, which is clearly Frank's intention.

"It seems you are not the man I thought you were," Mr. Estabrook says.

For a moment, Harry feels found out, revealed as his true self rather than the more worthy person Mr. Estabrook believed him to be. When Ellie died, Harry was on a chair in the hallway outside her room. Face in his hands. Unable to sit at her bedside when she wouldn't look at him. The nurses were kind, telling him many people preferred to go alone rather than know they were leaving behind someone they loved, but they didn't know Ellie. They didn't know how angry she'd been with him when she'd finally given up the idea of IVF.

Lydia places a hand on Mr. Estabrook's thigh. Jussi whines and twitches. Without glancing down, Mr. Estabrook lays his hand across Lydia's and clutches it.

"Very soon," he says. "I'll be gone from here." Harry's unsure if Mr. Estabrook means from the island or from life, but then he realizes it doesn't matter. One way or the other, The Butterfly Diplomat has given up.

"The one thing I wanted to do before I shuffled off this mortal coil was to protect this island," Mr. Estabrook says.

"Preserve it. I never imagined I'd be fighting you. Losing to you." He doesn't look at Harry when he says, "It's time for you to go now," and he doesn't stand to shake Harry's hand or walk him to the door. There's no silver dollar slid across the table. Harry's already in the hallway when he hears Mr. Estabrook say, "It's the rats that eat the butterflies, Harry. The wasps and the snakes and the rodents," and Harry, knowing he's been called the most reviled of creatures, snaps back, "Maybe it's you that's wrong, not me. Maybe there is a way to protect the land *and* its people."

He hesitates for an instant, hoping his mentor will call him back and ask him to explain, but the house is silent except for the sound of Jussi's collar jangling as he scratches a troublesome itch.

CHIAROSCURO ON THE FOREST FLOOR

Mari

L ight and shade paint the leafed and dusty ground. A for-
ager rustles among last autumn's leaves. Levi walks a few
feet before Mari, his head bent and his arms close. His fists
are tight. If Mari takes her eyes off him for an instant, there's
a chance he could disappear.

"Do you understand what I'm saying?" she asks.

"No," Levi says. "I don't want you and Papa to do a
divorce. I don't want to not see him."

They are walking in the strip of woods that separates the
peninsula where the house sits from the village, a space that
was magical to Mari as a child. Back then, she built tiny houses
here out of sticks and pine needles. Examined the soft clusters of moss with its threadlike stalks full of spores. Climbed
down the rocks to the shore and studied the sideways creep
of crabs and the probing stalks of sea urchins. So much life
happens all around, if only you take the time to observe. Mr.
Estabrook is right that all this needs protecting, but so do
the people who live here. Why is it so hard to make everyone

understand that? How is it possible to take all these competing life forms and weave them into a cohesive community, particularly when her own life is unraveling?

"Sweetie, it's important," Mari tells her son. "I'm not saying you can't love your papa. And I'm not saying that he doesn't love you. But for right now, if he should happen to show up here..." More than a week has passed since Sister Grace's call. Mari's tried calling God's Bounty, but no one answers the phone. Reggie's been after her constantly, smelling of booze and telling her he loves her. Frank's announced she's *persona non grata* at the market. Both Sue and Bob refuse to speak to her; whenever she's made it as far as Sue's new bedroom above The Sweet Shoppe, she's been greeted with two middle fingers extended like cannons from the hilltop of Sue's belly. Apparently being evicted from the home she didn't even want to be in has caused Sue to revoke her forgiveness. For five hundred additional dollars, Mari's learned from her new lawyer to "document, document, document," which seems to mean keeping track of all the hours Caleb doesn't arrive and noting her phone call to the mainland cops, who'd said they'll come as soon as they can if something happens. She has finished the proposal for the farmland trust, but Harry has asked her not to submit it. It's enough to present it as a viable alternative at the meeting, he said. He wants a little more time to work on convincing Isabelle and Jonathan. But those are excuses. What's really going on is he's been a mess since his conversation with Mr. Estabrook, furious one moment and devastated the next.

If it were humanly possible, she would have put off this conversation with Levi for months, but Caleb could show up any time.

"Papa doesn't love *you*," Levi spits. "Because you're mean, and you fight with everybody."

They walk in silence, sunlight trickling between the trees. A bird sings a two-note song.

Levi snaps a stick from a branch that brushes him, and Mari can tell by the action of his elbows that he's breaking it into tiny pieces.

"Maybe, in a little while, you can…" she begins. But what can she promise her son with regards to his father that is likely to ever occur? That Caleb can be trusted to know the difference between setting limits for a child and inflicting damage? Unlikely, because Mari can now see some of the things Caleb told her about his childhood in a different light. His idea of appropriate discipline was deeply rooted in his past. All Pastor Aaron had needed to do was give him permission.

Levi throws aside the remains of his twig and picks up another to demolish.

"There are going to be some people we have to talk to," Mari begins again. Lawyers. Social workers. How does she begin to explain all this to her son? "They'll ask questions about whether you like living here." She won't be with him. She's not supposed to coach him, can't tell him to point out that he's now registered to go to an accredited elementary school, that no one limits the amount of food he eats, that his Grandma Alice is cleaning junk out of the small room at the end of the hall so that he can have a bedroom of his own.

"I have a day off next week," Mari says. "Maybe you and I can go to Little Beach. If it's not too cold, I can teach you to swim."

Levi begins humming, making it clear he has no interest in whatever his mother has to say. When he crouches beneath a tree, Mari stops to wait. A foot scratches in the dirt. Pine cones collect in small hands. A branch snaps in the trees behind them, but Mari sees nothing except shadows and the lacy dance of ferns in mottled sun. Her heart thumps inside her ears.

"I need you to stay close to me or to Grandma Alice when I'm at work," she tells Levi. "No running away, okay? Not even hide-and-seek, at least not for the next little while."

Levi hums. He rises to his feet and walks off.

"Don't you want to stay here with Grandma Alice and Grandpa Sam and Houdini? Don't you want to go to real school? Do you really want to abandon your garden right now when it's producing, after all the work you've put in? What about Mr. Harry? Don't you think you'd miss him if we left?"

"You said we were going to go on his motorboat, but we never did."

True. There are more things to do in a day than she can accomplish.

"We can do it soon," Mari tells Levi. "If you promise to be good."

Another twig breaks, and Mari wheels. Once again, there's no one there, but Caleb could be. Or Reggie. Any minute. Behind any tree.

"Levi," Mari says, "Let's run back to the house."

Levi ignores her. He throws a pine cone into the ferns.

"Come on, I'll race you." Three jogged steps and Mari's past him. Still, Levi refuses to budge. Is that a person hiding behind that tree? Were the sounds she heard human footsteps or the passing of a squirrel?

"Levi, now," Mari says, grabbing his arm. "Run now. Run as fast as you can."

DON'T LET GO

Harry

Harry, in his childhood bedroom above the kitchen, regards the bed that was his as a child and remembers lying there with Ellie. Making love carefully to keep the springs from squeaking. Falling asleep with her head on his chest. Waking up hours later, both of them drenched with her sweat.

"Let's have a baby," she said. "Let's do it now."

Amazing how easy that had seemed at the time.

Back downstairs, Harry spins the washing-machine dial to the proper cycle. Water cascades into the drum. Tomorrow he's got to head to the city for his first classes. In less than a week, he'll be back on the island with his brother and sister for the vote. If the rezone passes, they'll celebrate, or at least Harry will do his best to appear pleased. If it fails, they'll discuss what's next. Mari is certain he handled the conversation with Mr. Estabrook poorly, that she should have been there to explain all the ways her farming approaches are good for the environment, but Harry knows the next move is his. He just hasn't a clue what it is. Ellie's no help. Memories of her are everywhere, silent and remote as photographs, but the sense of her proximity has ended. Her footsteps are gone, along with her whispers.

Come back, he pleads with her sometimes. *At least long enough for me to say that I'm sorry.*

But it's Mari he really needs. Her conviction can be exhausting, but it's also energizing. Her clarity reduces the muddle that comes from life in the gray. When she berates him, it feels like a challenge to do better rather than a reminder of what a mess he can be. Then there was that kiss, the thought of which still causes his body to react.

But there is so much going on. Gearing up for the semester. Talking with real estate agents about the condo. Preparing simultaneously for his sibling visit and for returning to work. Maybe it's time to quit worrying about the vote, the sale of the house, the future of the island. The rest of life is closing in.

The sounds come all at once: footfalls on the back steps, the kitchen door thrown open, Mari calling him with a voice that sends blood rushing to his ears. When he gets to her, she's sobbing, her face a mess of dirt and wet and her breath jerking from her throat. Arms around her, Harry feels the long bones of her arms and the press of her chin. Her arms are across his back, and briefly he touches his cheek to her hair. She smells like sea salt and soil, like pine and sunlight. She smells like Little Great Island.

"Is it Levi?" he asks. "Is Levi okay?"

"He's okay. With. Mom." Her words are wrestled out between sobs. Ellie never once cried like this. If she had, he would have known how to comfort her, but Ellie was a scientist, not a crier. Crying, she told him, didn't change facts.

Harry gathers Mari closer. "It's okay. It's okay," he murmurs, rocking her slightly. "You're safe."

"I'm sorry." Pulling away, Mari runs a palm across her face. Her skin is blotchy. A mosquito bite domes in the center of her left cheek. There's a cooling emptiness in the space where she'd pressed against him.

"Don't be. Please," he says. "There's no reason."

"I need a minute."

"Take all the time you need."

Mari's still shaking. Her skin has browned over the summer. Her frame has filled out. Less than a month ago, they had played Old Maid in the children's living room, and when she lost, she rocked back on her tailbone with her hands and feet in the air and fake cried while Levi giggled and called her Old Maid. Harry laughed because he couldn't not. When Harry lost, he ground his knuckles into his eyes and said, "Boo-hoo," while the two of them ridiculed him. Levi, when he lost, smiled with his one wiggly tooth showing. Those were moments of pure joy.

"Your dad okay?"

"It's not him."

There's a tiny indentation in Mari's earlobe from a piercing that must have healed shut. The swoop of skin down her neck begs his touch. When Harry's about to ask if she wants a glass of water or if she'd like to sit down, she speaks again.

"Everybody's upset at everybody else, and it's all my fault. I keep thinking Caleb is everywhere. Frank blames me for Reggie's drinking. Reggie thinks you and I are having a mad affair. Sue hates me. Lydia is furious with me. My mother is barely speaking to me. I can hear her and my dad arguing in whispers at night. I've ruined everything. I'm falling apart."

"You haven't," Harry says. "You aren't. Just tell me what happened."

"Levi and I were coming back from the village. We were in the woods." Mari stops speaking, gasps for breath. "I heard something. I panicked. I couldn't get Levi to run so I grabbed him."

"Was there someone following you?"

"No." Mari's voice is practically a howl. "I *grabbed* Levi, Harry. Hard. And I dragged him. I'm turning into … I'm becoming like…"

"You aren't," Harry says. "You're nothing like him. Them." Mari's back is to the fridge door, sunlight landing on the tip of her nose. She glances at him and then away.

He shouldn't.

He should.

He wants.

It's not fair. He's going back to Boston. She's upset.

"Caleb may come after Levi," he says. There's a small, round mole low on her chest, barely visible, and a chasm between her breasts that needs to be explored. Mari's eyes are on his, and Harry wishes he could read what's in her mind.

"But he isn't going to get him," he continues. "I promise."

"I never know what I'm doing. What good is belief? It can't be trusted. Look what happened to me at God's Bounty."

"Look at you now. How hard you're working for something you believe in. How well you have protected your son. What viable plans you've laid for the farm and for the island."

"Levi's angry with me."

"Kids do get angry with their parents."

"I shouldn't have grabbed him like that." Mari's tears have stopped. The sunbeam has travelled to her arm. Her shirt is tight across her breasts. The round of her hip would fit like a ball in the glove of his hand.

"You didn't put him in some shed without food or water," Harry says. "You didn't burn his tongue. You got him away from danger. You're doing everything you can to keep him safe and healthy. You're a good mother. A great parent."

A puff of wind lifts a paper from the table and blows it to the floor. The *Abenaki Princess* hoots, announcing its final arrival of the day. A crow caws and Harry has Mari in his arms again, and this time they don't let go.

ALONE IN A ROWBOAT

Mari

When Mari opens her eyes, her back is pressed to the wall in the downstairs bedroom, her head on her arm. The sheets are twisted, the windows are closed, and the room is stuffed with old air and recent sex, but that's not what woke her. Harry is beside the bed, fastening his shorts at his waist. She wants to say his name. She wants to reach out a hand and bring him back onto the mattress with her, but some knowledge tells her that speaking could ruin it all. Harry won't look at her, but she knows what he's thinking. This is Ellie's house. He is Ellie's husband. Mari's a hot mess. Saying his name aloud would only be the last tap that blows him apart.

Harry leans over and feels for something on the floor. A shoe, Mari realizes as he raises an ankle to the opposite knee to slip it on. Perhaps she should get dressed without speaking and go home. Her parents and Levi will be worried. But if she leaves now, without a word between them, she will have ruined one more good thing.

The truth is, she's only sorry if she's hurt him. For everything else, she is glad.

If Harry sighs or glances, she will meet his look. And then what? Perhaps he will lean to kiss her. Perhaps she will put her fingers against his skin. Their first few minutes had been a slow exploration: the edges of her shirt pushed from her neck and lips across her skin. The knobs of his backbone. The pebbled nubs of his nipples. The trailing of her fingernails from his chest, down his abdomen and then the slightest tickle on his balls. After that, they'd gone for each other with an unfamiliar hunger. A grasping and clutching that she hopes hasn't bruised him, although she doesn't mind in the slightest that she feels bruised herself.

Harry slips on the other shoe.

I want…Mari thinks to say. But what? Too much. Absolution for her past. Forgiveness for who she is. A husband who loves her. A community that embraces her. An island to call home. Her hands in dirt. To grow food without damaging the Earth. Also: nothing. Her life is more than she can handle already. There is no room for a grieving man who will soon be leaving her in more ways than one. She slides her hand across the mattress, but the movement must be too subtle because he doesn't look. Or doesn't want to.

Harry pulls his shirt over his head, then takes his sweater from the floor and puts it on. Fully dressed now, he stands again by the window. The sky is completely dark. Across the room from where Mari lies is a bureau with a mirror. Her own reflection regards her with blank eyes. Also visible in that image are the skin of her chest and shoulders, her outstretched right hand. Her left hand, the one with her wedding ring, is out of sight behind her head. The moment she's near the water, she'll throw that ring into the sea.

Harry glances in her direction, but when he doesn't speak, she says she'll go home.

"We fought," Harry says.

Mari, suddenly understanding, laughs inwardly at herself, at her assumption that his behavior is all about her. Of course. It's Ellie. She pats the mattress once with her fingers.

"Sit," she says, and he all but collapses. Freeing the sheet, she sits with her chest to his back. His breathing expands and contracts the space between them. His misery is palpable, a force against his skin.

"Tell me," she says and wraps an arm around his waist. *I will keep you here*, she thinks. *I will keep you from flying apart.*

While he speaks, Harry keeps his gaze on the spot where the floor meets the wall.

"All I knew was that she had to get better. I promised I'd be there for her every step of the way. She wanted a baby. Finally. Badly." But the doctor strongly urged her to start treatment right away, Mari discerns from his broken sentences. Ellie wanted time, at least, to retrieve eggs, which could be kept frozen until she was cured—a necessary step because the cancer drugs would damage her eggs.

"Her doctors said it was a bad idea. The cancer was aggressive. She needed to start fighting right away, and fertility treatments take time." But despite the doctors, Ellie was determined.

"The stats are in my favor," Ellie told Harry. She wanted to resume her normal life when the cancer was behind her. "Light," she said. "At the end of the tunnel."

"I fought her and fought her. I thought she didn't understand, didn't realize she could die. She finally gave in, but then it was like the will to live went out of her."

Mari feels his sweat against her chest, although his hands are ice. His voice shakes. His body quivers hard enough that Mari's moves with it.

"She needed that promise of motherhood to fight for survival. I wasn't enough for her."

"You were. You can't think like that."

Harry shakes his head vehemently. "No. I wasn't. I went to hold her hand that last day. It was like holding an empty glove."

Mari lays a cheek against his back, remembering from her early days at college and grad school all the ways loneliness can eat a hole in your soul.

"She made her own decision," she says.

"She didn't. I forced her."

"No." She wasn't there, Mari admits. But from everything Harry has told her about Ellie, she wasn't the kind of woman to change her mind for someone else's sake. If she decided against retrieving her eggs, it would have been because she didn't want to become a mother when the possibility of a relapse would always be hanging over her. Didn't want to leave Harry with unfertilized eggs that he'd have to agree to dispose of and didn't want to leave him with a motherless child if she died before their child was raised.

"You said yourself that women have to be strong to stand up to men," she adds. "And you know Ellie was strong. Female scientists have to be. She stood up to you. She stood up to her family and to her entire medical team." After that, Mari explains, Ellie could face her cancer without the distraction of other people's opinions. "That's when she did the strongest thing of all. She changed her mind."

"But she...she..."

An hour before Ellie died, Harry had laid beside her with his arm around her, telling her he was sorry. Telling her how much he loved her. But she wouldn't turn her face to him. Wouldn't forgive him, is how Harry has interpreted it. Wouldn't say she loved him back.

"Maybe she couldn't," Mari says. She's seen animals die, how the look in their eyes speaks of withdrawing to a place where the living cannot follow.

"It was as though she launched herself alone in a rowboat and headed off without me," Harry says. "She never once considered letting me on board."

Mari's hand has found his, and he's gripping her so tightly it hurts, but she will not let go.

"The thing is," he continues, "You can love something or somebody, you can fight for that love, and that can end up being a very, very bad idea."

Shifting positions, Mari gets her other arm around him. "Harry, please don't blame yourself for Ellie's death. She was dying, and there was no way you could stop it. Her withdrawing doesn't mean that she didn't love you back. That's the way dying is. There are some things you can't change. The point is, you fought for what you believed."

Harry shakes his head, but she can feel him struggling to accept her words.

"I know it hurts," she continues. "But love is never a bad idea. Pain doesn't mean failure, and we can't let it stop us from trying to do what's right for Little Great Island."

Tightening her grip on Harry, Mari lays her cheek against his back. "I do understand. I feel as though I've made enough mistakes for a lifetime." She shifts and then adds, "It's past time for both of us to learn that we have to do what we think is right, whether it means learning to accept death or to fight for life."

Proverbs she once would have quoted waver at the edge of her awareness, but Mari ignores them. Life is always a better teacher than the Bible anyway, so she tells Harry that you learn the same thing growing up on an island that you do in a Christian farming ministry: It's always easier not to do things alone.

THE FLESH IS WEAK

Little Great Island

L abor Day has come and gone. September has claimed Little Great Island, dropping the first yellowed leaves on streets and rooftops. Moorings sit empty off the yacht club. Kayaks and tennis rackets are stored and summer homes closed for the season, while just offshore from the gray-shingled Cape with peeling white trim, the *Alice-Mari* rests at her mooring. Inside the house, on a sheet-kicked bed in a braided-rug room, Sam lies on his back in his old-man's body with his hand in the hand of the woman he's loved for fifty years.

"The flesh is weak," he says, although the more accurate word is flaccid.

Alice kisses his chest and lingers, heartbeat and blood flow precious beneath her lips. "The heart is strong," she replies.

The porch-wrapped farmhouse up the hill is empty, its wicker loveseat and wooden rocker pushed back against the walls. Within the garden fence, kale and chili peppers are exuberant in their growth.

At The Sweet Shoppe, the shades are drawn. Chairs are tipped forward against tabletops as though deep in prayer.

Upstairs, the bed where Sue has recently lived and labored is rumpled, the overnight bag she packed to take to the hospital forgotten when the time had finally come to leave. Bob's fleece jacket remains draped on a chair. There's a hole in the plaster outside the bedroom door, made by Frank when he discovered his daughter went off to have her baby without telling him. Outside, the Siamese kittens are exploring the joys of blowing leaves and shifting shadows. The Blue Buoy is closed with a *For Sale* sign taped to the window.

Poking among the dock pilings beneath the boathouse, Levi discovers the mud and barnacles and seaweed and sunglasses and Coke cans revealed by the ebbing tide. He's escaped his mother and grandparents because all they ever do anymore is tell him not to wander, and he's found a world of his own where the rocks are slippery. The mud smells yucky. He finds a dry place and a flat rock, on which he sits and smiles.

The school auditorium is ready for a crowd: more than a hundred chairs, pressed side by side with aisles up the sides and middle; two six-foot tables set facing the room; a microphone standing ready for anyone called upon to speak.

A squirrel scales a tree. A house sparrow hops two steps one direction, cocks its head, hops two steps back. The tiny lobster in their cobble-bottom ocean homes settle in to grow. When they emerge, they will be large enough that their greatest predators are human.

ASS OVER TEAKETTLE

Lydia

Tom is wrong, Lydia tells herself. Frank turned her out because he's a vindictive man and there were years of animosity between them. It had nothing to do with Harry or Mari. But what's worse is that Tom's broken his own heart by treating Harry Richardson that way. Since Harry left, her sweet butterfly has barely spoken. He ignores the dog. In the middle of supper, he pushes his plate aside and seems to slide away from her, leaving a withered old man in his place.

But how, she asks herself as she checks inside the oven to see if the potatoes are done, can she tell him he's wrong? How can an old lady who spent her life selling muffins tell an internationally renowned gentleman that he's got his head stuffed up in a place where the sun doesn't shine?

Well, she can't.

But he is wrong.

He'll be fine, Lydia reassures herself. He's chosen a retirement center that has sunny windows and a choice of restaurants and card games and book groups and concerts.

Her own definition of hell.

Lydia herself would rather take her chances with the island's cancelled ferry runs and spotty electrical service. It's what she'd planned for and imagined for herself, and maybe retirement wasn't her choice, but it's here now and the truth is, she's tired. Exhausted by the cooking and cleaning. If she can find a place to live—and she doesn't need much, just a room and access to a kitchen—she can be content sitting still.

But, on the other hand, she never imagined a man like Tom in her life. Right from that first night, when he came to the café like a supplicant, believing he only needed something to eat when it was so clear to her what he needed was a relaxing dinner with a woman, he had seemed—and there was no less cheesy word for it—like her soulmate.

But goodness, he's been down in the dumps since young Harry's visit. He loves that boy—man—like a son. Like a favored son, to hear him talk. He'd had a certain respect for Mari up until the whole business with Frank Clatcher. Well, that wasn't really Mari's fault. It had been a long time coming.

Three more days, and Lydia will have to say goodbye. Three days, and right now a clock stuffed away in a box is tocking off the minutes with a sound like something solid tossed about in a can.

There's been talk of visits between them; her there, him here. But those are plans that can't be counted on. Her wandering into a candlelit dining room, surrounded by Harvards and MITs and Wellesleys and a Yale or two? Deadly.

Him on the ice-encrusted ferry in January, visiting her here? But where's here? As soon as he leaves, she'll have no place on the island to live.

Upstairs, the bathroom door opens and closes. Lydia gazes around the kitchen. Supper's nearly ready. They'll eat at the little table with the glass top and the wicker chairs with plump pillows in the sunroom. Both of them like it better there than in the dining room. Both of them like candles lit and a glass of wine and Jussi sacked out cold beside them.

And then, during supper, she'll say to him: Let's stay on Little Great Island. Plenty of old people do. The mainland and its doctors and hospitals are only fourteen miles away. Let's buy Harry's house. Maybe Tom's children will object, but their dad won't be alone; he'll have her and the whole community to care for him. All the money he paid the retirement center will be lost to them, but a house on Little Great Island will retain some value. Tom's kids spent their summers here. Surely the island means something to them.

But is it too late? Can she talk him into buying the house out from under that developer like Harry suggested? Is there something he can think of that can help poor Mari? Even though Lydia's never had children of her own, a mother trying to make a living for herself on a tiny island is something she feels in her chest.

I'm going to do it, Lydia tells herself. Because there is no end to the things that a woman knows better than a man, no matter how smart and well travelled he is.

"Tommy," Lydia calls up the stairs. "Supper's ready."

She's in the front hall when she calls him a second time and hears the rattle of dog tags that means Jussi is hauling himself to his feet. Then another noise, a short grunt and a thump, like a hand slapped on plaster. Lydia turns as fast as she can toward the staircase and sees Jussi scamper as Tom Estabrook, her friend and her dinner companion and The Butterfly Diplomat, lets go of the towel he's got wrapped round his nakedness and comes ass-over-teakettle down the stairs.

THE BUTTERFLY EFFECT

Harry

"There's a kid on the porch," Isabelle says. She's still in pajamas, coffee mug cradled in both hands.

"Levi?"

"Mari's kid? Maybe. With a haircut. And an attitude. We've got to leave soon," she adds as Harry heads for the porch.

"Is Jonathan even up yet?"

"Up, ran ten miles, showered, dressed, and gone into the village to try to get cell phone reception. He'll meet us there."

In the seventeen or so hours Harry's brother and sister have been on the island, Jonathan has spoken fewer than a dozen words to Harry. He went running the moment they got to the house, showered, ate supper with his siblings, and then retired to his room with the door closed firmly behind him.

Outside, Harry expects to find Levi curled in a porch corner, but the boy is ensconced in Mr. Estabrook's rocking chair, which he's pulled back to its original position. Mr. Estabrook broke his hip and received a mild concussion in his fall and is now in the hospital on the mainland, where he'll remain for at least a week. Lydia reported the likelihood of a rehab facility after that: a long road, lots of physical therapy, but a decent chance of full recovery.

"Darn all the stairs in that old house," Lydia'd said, and then she told him she thought Mr. Estabrook should buy Harry's house. Harry barely listened. Mr. Estabrook had already said he didn't want the house. The time is up. The vote is in less than an hour.

"Good morning," Harry says. Levi pushes hard against the floor with both feet, rocking in short, hard jerks. Watching him, Harry thinks that so much of what the world has to offer is disappointing once you're old enough to notice. It's unlikely, given the mood the boy seems to be in, that Levi's told his mother or grandparents he's here. It's clear that Levi won't tolerate being told to go home.

"Want to go for a walk?"

Levi acts as if Harry hasn't spoken, so Harry ups the ante. "I saw a monarch yesterday. On the path to The Knuckle. Shall we go look?"

Abruptly, the rocking stops, and Levi heads down the stairs with Harry behind him. He's not running, but he's moving quickly, fists clenched at his sides. There's no time to call Mari to let her know Levi's with him or even to ask Isabelle to call. No chance Levi is going to pause and wait for anything. The garden is thick with produce, but Levi doesn't give it a glance. It's hard to tell if he wants Harry's company or merely tolerates it. Harry sees a small blue butterfly, which he's certain is an eastern tailed-blue, perched far enough off the path that it's not worth pointing out to Levi, plus a brown-winged moth that he can now identify as some type of sphinx moth. Thanks to Mari, he's become interested in the island's pollinators. Thanks to Mr. Estabrook and his touchstone of the Butterfly Effect, he's become increasingly curious about what moths and butterflies can be found on Little Great Island.

Suddenly Levi stops. He rubs a foot against the back of a leg, then extends a finger and runs it across a thistle. The struggle between whatever it is he wants to say and his stubborn silence is visible on his face.

"There's one." Harry points. The monarch's perched about a foot off the path, its colors so bright Harry can practically smell them. Its proboscis taps an aster, looking for nectar, while its wings quiver and flex. Levi is utterly still, watching it. A flock of gulls squawks and caws.

"How do they go from caterpillar to butterfly?" he asks.

There's the whole explanation about the chrysalis, but the truth is, that transformation is something Harry has always taken on faith, like some form of naturally occurring magic.

"Don't know," he admits. "We can look it up on the computer when we go back, though." The slightest of nods seems to indicate Levi's relaxing some. Harry puts a hand on the boy's shoulder: those growing bones, still birdlike. His shoulder blades, the shape of wings.

"Does your mother know where you are?" he risks asking.

"I hate her."

"You don't, though."

"I do so!"

Harry crouches so the two of them are eye to eye. "You're angry at her. That's not the same as hating someone."

"She's mean." Lower lip jutting, Levi details his mother's latest meanness: Even though Levi's been promised that Sue and Bob's baby is going to be his best friend for life and that they can see each other every day, he hasn't met the baby yet. No one will take him to the hospital so he can see his new best friend, but he's even more upset that there's been talk of Bob and Sue needing to move to the mainland to find a place to live.

Levi says, "My friend came too early, and now his mama and his papa don't know where to live because Mama went into Aunt Sue's house when she wasn't supposed to. It's not fair. Even the sweet store has gone away, and it's all Mama's fault for making everybody mad at her." Levi's scowl deepens. "She promised I'd have friends here like at God's Bounty, only I can't have any friends at all anywhere because she makes everybody mad."

Mari and Sue were apart for a decade with no communication, yet they resumed their friendship as soon as Mari returned, Harry tells Levi, trying to explain to the boy how the past can feed the present without necessarily hurting it; how unknowable the impact of our mistakes is on that other unknowable thing called the future. Levi makes it clear he's in no mood to listen.

"But Mama's always been mean, and she's always going to be mean."

"She stands up for what she believes in," Harry corrects. "That's not the same as being mean."

"You're supposed to be nice," the boy responds, hurt in his voice, and goes on about how his mother made him leave God's Bounty and now he can't be the baby's best friend and it's all his mom's fault. As Harry half listens, aspects of Mari's plan for the land begin to fall together in a new way somewhere in the back of his brain. A configuration that makes sudden and complete sense to him. It's not a simple shape; God knows, it's all a long shot. But it is a solution in the gray area, a collaboration that can work if all the parties agree to cooperate. If the rezone fails—or if Harry can delay it long enough for Mr. Estabrook to recover sufficiently—and if Harry can get Isabelle and Jonathan to agree, at least conditionally, to a sale to the farmland trust, then Harry can broach the idea of Mr. Estabrook and Lydia renting the house. Mari has told him renting the house is possible under the terms of the trust, and the income could be used to support the farm. Until the sale to the trust is final and the siblings have the proceeds, the rent could go to Jonathan. Harry's brother might start receiving the extra money he needs as early as the first of October. Mari and Alice and Sam could look in on Mr. Estabrook and Lydia, help with the cooking, the cleaning, and any repairs.

Mr. Estabrook would have company and support, Harry imagines telling Mr. Estabrook's children. Their father will be in a familiar place, a place that he loves, surrounded by a close-knit community. Harry won't tell them how important it is to hold on to love when you find it because it's not his place. In the end, the most compelling argument would be Mr. Estabrook wanting to stay on Little Great Island, and to make him want that, the natural habitat on the Richardson land needs to be protected.

But that can be done. Under the umbrella of the farmland trust, portions of the land could be set aside for pollinators. Leah's Knuckle, for example: It's land that can't be used as pasture or garden anyway. It's too steep and rocky to be farmed and should always be accessible to people who want to climb it. Another protected parcel might be the acreage from the house to the island's end, which, in addition to being critical habitat for birds, is home to a wide variety of insects. Yet another might be the wide swath of woods between the McGavin and Richardson houses and the village. It's probably close to fifty acres, which will appeal to Mr. Estabrook.

"And now it's too late," Levi says, jerking Harry from his reverie. "She ruins everything."

Harry checks his watch. Twenty-five minutes until the meeting begins. It's a miracle Isabelle hasn't driven off without him. Mari's voice is clear, calling for Levi from the other side of the barn. Harry crouches further, invites Levi to climb onto his shoulders.

"It's not too late," he says. Too late comes after the last beat of the heart. It comes when the last breath has already passed.

LOVE YOU, OLD WOMAN

Mari

"I can't find him," Mari says. Of all the times for Levi to have wandered off. The meeting starts in less than twenty minutes.

"We have to go." Alice is already behind the wheel, the door still open, one foot planted on the ground. She's wearing a skirt, something Mari can't remember happening more than once or twice before, but her feet are snugged into sneakers crusted with dirt. Mari's dad, in the passenger seat, is also in holiday best: a collared shirt that could have used an iron. A pair of jeans that are nearly new.

Mari herself is stiff and sore from a sleepless night, but at least she feels ready. Don't worry, she tells herself, but hears "please" whispered in her brain. It's hope, not prayer. It's understanding that she's done all that she could, and now the outcome is out of her hands.

Alice continues, "Your dad needs to be on time." The meeting can't begin without him.

Panic sears Mari's skin. "LEVI!" she screams, and there he is, riding on Harry's shoulders down the path from the

Richardsons' house as if she hasn't told him a hundred times not to leave the property without her permission.

"I told you not to wander off."

"I didn't. I went to see Mr. Harry." Levi's mouth snaps shut. His brows descend.

Whatever, Mari thinks. *You're here now.* She steers him into the back seat and buckles his belt.

"I can do it myself," Levi insists. Mari ignores his protests.

"I have an idea," Harry says. "I'll see you there." He squeezes her hand quickly before sprinting toward his driveway, where Isabelle is now waiting in the car.

"This is going to be a very tense meeting," her mother reminds Mari for the umpteenth time as they turn onto the dirt road. "There's really no need for you to say anything else at this point. Let things take their course."

"I'm opinionated and stubborn. I stand up for what I believe in. I believe I have you to thank for that."

Her mother's mouth twitches into a quick smile, and her eyes meet Mari's in the rearview mirror.

"Thank you for taking us in," Mari adds. "For putting up with me. For all of it."

Her mother's chin dips. There's a softening in her cheeks. "Of course," she says. "You're my daughter."

The car bumps onto the pavement, and Alice steers them right, around the outskirts of the village on the one-way road. The silence crawls back. Time is running out. What else does Mari need to tell her parents? Is there anything left she can do to protect the island?

"I need you to recognize Harry so he can speak," Mari reminds her father. It will send an important message that Harry, as co-owner of the property, talks about the idea of putting the land in the trust. While he hasn't exactly convinced his siblings, they've given in to the idea of him speaking as long as he's clear the plan is Mari's, he doesn't specifically endorse it, and that it's no more than an idea.

"Bottom line," Harry told Mari when they talked last night. "The sibs are focused on selling the place and pocketing the money. I've told them the trust is unlikely to be able to offer the same amount as Duncan, but that it's the ethically and morally right thing to do." Apparently, Harry's siblings are convinced the rezone will pass, that Duncan will build his executive retreat, and that nothing Harry or Mari do will change that. Harry hadn't bothered to argue.

"Yup," her father says now. His fingers grip the handle above the window.

"Just don't go dragging your father into some huge blowout," her mother says and then, to her husband, "You okay? No horses kicking you in the chest?"

"I'm fine," he says.

"Nothing's numb?"

"I'm fit as a fiddle," he says. Mari's father's voice is far away. Mari, studying his new-shaven cheeks, reaches across the distance between them and lays a hand on his shoulder. Her father briefly covers her fingers with his own.

"I love you, Dad," she says.

"I know, Mermaid," he says. "I know." As Alice parks by the town office, he adds, "One way or the other, it's all going to be behind us soon."

"Let's hope," Mari says.

Once they are inside, Alice surveys the room. "Big crowd," she says. Most chairs are occupied, and there are clusters of people gathered at the back and along the walls. Mari sees two men in too-new L.L. Bean gear and guesses it's Tim Duncan and one of his sidekicks. At least they are smart enough to stay in the back. They don't have permission to speak during the meeting, and it's clear from the way most people glance

292 · KATE WOODWORTH

and walk past that no one intends to so much as greet them. Pete Shaw, however, lurks near them and gives Harry a wave that he doesn't return.

"Jerk," Mari mutters. Harry joins her, runs through his plan quickly, nods when she makes a single suggestion, and then has to go. Jonathan and Isabelle still need final updating, as does Lydia. Frank's not here yet, Mari notices, which is surprising. Maybe he plans to show up late so no one has a last chance to tell him what they think. Levi pulls free of her hand.

"I want to see Mr. Harry," he says when Mari tries to object. Mari lets him go. He'll be easy to keep an eye on. The room is full of people, so no stranger from God's Bounty is going to sneak up on them. Behind the long table at the front of the room, Lydia hovers, her face worn from the nights at Mr. Estabook's bedside. Clive shakes the hand of Bob, who wears the beam of new fatherhood. The baby, as yet unnamed, weighed in at nearly eight-and-a-half pounds.

"Totally hale and healthy," Bob says. "I swear he was looking at me. I swear he recognized my voice." Bob's words travel proudly in the hubbubbing room. Mari, as she stands by one of the seats Alice has saved for them, smiles in Bob's direction. She flashes a thumbs-up. That's a different Bob than the one she'd seen dragging his ass up the stairs in his father-in-law's house. A different Bob, even, than the shy shuffler from school. Bob turns to another well-wisher, and Mari scans for Levi, who is still standing near Harry on the other side of the room. Harry catches her eye and nods; he's watching out for Levi. He points at a seat near where Isabelle and Jonathan are gathered and raises a shoulder. Mari nods her approval. Levi can sit with them.

Carol taps her watch in the direction of Sam, whose responsibility it is to call the meeting to order.

"Well, then, here we go," he says. He glances first at his wife, and then at Mari, then heads for his seat at the table in the front of the room. After a few steps, he turns long enough to say, "Love you, old woman. You too, Mermaid."

When he reaches his seat, the only person missing from the table is Frank, and he's on his way up a side aisle now. The way Harry stands by his brother and sister, Mari notices, you'd think tension could be a family trait. When he catches Mari's eye, he smiles, but his eyes are worried.

"Everything okay?" she mouths, but Harry has already turned away and is studying the numbers of people pouring into the room.

PAPA

Levi

Under the dock smells like mud and seaweed. There's one of those plastic tabs for keeping bread bags closed and a very sharp piece of clear glass. Levi takes the glass between thumb and finger and sets it far away from his favorite rock. The water's a little closer to him today than it was the other time he came to his secret house. It's clear and green, and through it he can see a crab skittering sideways through the mud. The meeting was stupid and boring, and so when Mr. Harry was talking, Levi told Mr. Harry's brother he was going to the bathroom, but then he decided he'd rather go outside. Sometimes there are cats and kittens wandering around in the village and they let him pat them. But there weren't any kittens, and The Sweet Shoppe was closed, and the market was locked, and no one was around, so Levi went to his secret place beneath the boathouse.

Once upon a time, when this island was even younger than you are now, Levi begins in his imagination. That's the way his grandpa starts his stories. Grandpa Sam's also told Levi that your imagination is your own playground where all your friends are, and that you can take it with you wherever you go and play there whenever you want. When Levi tells his own stories, he uses the schools of silver fish that sing and dance across the sky at sunrise and the wise, whiskered harbor seal with only one eye from Grandpa Sam's stories, but he adds his own characters: his papa and some of his sisters and brothers from God's Bounty and a kitten named Hershey and another named M&M, who are at the center of every adventure. Hershey and M&M have a friend named Pretty who's always hungry and one named Houdini who gets them out of all sorts of jams.

Mama's going to be mad. He should go back. He will, soon. But.

Levi picks up a rock and tosses it. It's too round and jagged to be a skipping rock, but when it hits the water there's a satisfying plunk. From where he's sitting, Levi can see the town dock with its motorboats and rowboats and lobster boats tied up every which way. He can see the pilings that hold up the yacht club and the yacht club itself, which he's not allowed into because it's *Members Only*. The huff of a boat engine gradually draws his attention even though he can't, at first, see the boat itself.

Hershey didn't go with M&M when M&M went on an adventure, Levi tells himself. *Hershey went off all on his own because—*

The boat putts into view. It's one of the longish ones with no cushions on the seats and a motor on the back, and Levi knows now that this kind of boat is called a skiff. The man in the back with his hand on the tiller wears a visor that shields his face. One man sits in the bow with his back to Levi, but the one in the middle seat's looking forward, and Levi knows for certain it's Pastor Aaron. The engine noise cuts out, and the man in the bow turns to push boats already tied to the dock out of their way. Levi's on his feet, his heart thumping and his torso bent so he doesn't slam his head on the underside of the dock, but it's hard walking through the mud. A shoe comes off and he has to get it. He falls and his legs get dirty. When he gets out from under the dock, his father and Pastor Aaron are already at the top of the stairs, almost to the street.

"Papa," he calls. "Wait up! I'm coming."

THE FUTURE'S A PATH

Harry

When people shuffle and glance at the back of the room, Harry sees two latecomers whose faces are obscured by wide-brimmed hats making their way through the crowd. He turns his attention back to the audience. Shakes the tension out of his hands. The first time he stood in front of a classroom, he realized how much he loved it. He loves it still, or perhaps again, but what matters is how good it feels being back at work. It feels good being back in relationship with the world. He owes all that to Mari. After thanking Sam for allowing him to speak, he acknowledges Mari. Mari and her fierce determination to do what she believes is right. Mari and her love of the natural world. Mari and her love of the people of her community. Mari, who nodded enthusiastically as he told her his thoughts for modifying her plan, and who then suggested that Bob and Sue might even move in with Tom and Lydia to care for them. Sue has a background in health care, she reminded him, and Lydia, despite her energy, is nearing eighty. Bob and Sue and the baby need an income, they don't really want to leave the island, and they could benefit from living closer to town than their trailer.

Finally, Harry thanks the island's year-round inhabitants.

"For sharing this beautiful island with us. For all you do every year to ensure our vacations go smoothly. For all the lobster dinners and sailboat picnics, scraped hulls, filled gas cans, mowed fields, and the sight of your faces each summer that have made us who we are. Thank you."

The amplification of his voice feels wrong for the tone he's trying to set, so Harry pushes the microphone aside and says, "You came here today to vote on the zone change that would allow a corporate retreat center to be built on what's currently my family's land."

There's an outbreak of murmuring and shuffling in the room. The latecomers are pushing their way across the crowd standing at the back. If those guys had been students, Harry would have knocked a point off their grades for being both tardy and inconsiderate. Instead, he continues.

"But in fact, the conversation we've been having, or trying to have, over the past few weeks isn't about an executive retreat," he says. "It's about preserving the past of this island. Its beauty, its history, a way of life, and our memories. And it's also about what we want for the future of Little Great Island."

"Not up to you summer people," someone calls from the audience. Another voice adds, "You got no vote."

Harry nods. "I don't have a vote, but my actions have repercussions, just as yours do." As he explains the Butterfly Effect, he imagines Mr. Estabrook in the audience, nodding his patrician head and fingering a silver dollar in his pocket, even though Mr. Estabrook is recovering and doesn't know yet about Harry's plan. He smiles at Lydia, who was even more grateful that Sue and Bob would have jobs and a place to live than she was about an opportunity to stay on the island with Mr. Estabrook. There's some shifting and conversation in the back rows. Reggie Clatcher's come into the room, and even from a distance, Harry can tell that he's far from sober. He follows the other men up a side aisle toward the front of the room. *Ignore them*, Harry tells himself. *Don't let them derail your train of thought.*

"Mari McGavin has come up with a proposal that promotes self-sufficiency rather than dependence on a business with no roots on this island," he continues, returning his attention to the crowd seated before him. "It's a complex plan but a solid one. Mari has the knowledge and expertise to create a farm that serves all of us. She knows this island and loves it the way we all do." Harry pauses long enough to glance again at his brother and sister, neither of whom look happy. But there's no going back now, he wants them to understand, just as there is no do-over on what happened between him and Ellie. But mistakes in the past don't mean you have to give up on the future.

"You can, if you choose, postpone this vote. Give yourselves the opportunity to consider whether you want fresh, healthy meat and vegetables for your family or a minimum-wage job that could be taken from you any time some manager in New York City decides to slash a bottom line." If they proceed and the land is rezoned, he adds, then not only will the executive retreat be built, but a precedence will be set. Other old farmland—the open spaces of Little Great Island that are privately owned—may be sold to developers who build exclusive inns, multiple cabin-style rentals, boatyards that cater to the shower-and-laundry needs of yacht traffic along the coast. None of it bad, necessarily, but all of it bringing, along with tourist dollars, an impact on the island way of life. Is that the life the people who live on Little Great Island truly want?

People shift and whisper. There are a few raised voices saying no summer person should be in the middle of this. The latecomers are slow working their way toward the front, seemingly looking for empty seats. Who are they? And is that Levi behind Reggie? Harry glances first at the empty chair next to Jonathan and Isabelle, and then at Mari, whose face reflects terror. Suddenly Harry knows who these latecomers are.

One of them points.

Levi screams.

Sound explodes everything.

HERO

Reggie

Jesus. The noise. The kick. The smell. What the hell just happened? Everybody's pushing and shoving. Nothing makes sense.

Reggie came out of the yellow house on Main Street less than five minutes ago with a burning certainty that he had a right to show up at the damn meeting and vote, no matter what his father thought about his sobriety or lack thereof. Shouldn't have been anyone on the street, but there were a couple of men in those stupid brimmed hats that only off-islanders wear. Had to be Mari's husband and the other cult weirdo. The ones she warned everyone about. This was Reggie's chance.

He ducked into the shed to retrieve a half-empty bottle of Uncle Jack and the loaded gun. He wasn't going to shoot anyone. Only scare them off. He drained the better part of the bottle and left it behind. Tailed the a-holes to the town office, the two of them so full of themselves that they never noticed him. Older guy had stringy muscles, a shirt buttoned all the way to the top like he expected spiders might come crawling. The younger one went through the town office door like he'd have been more than happy to forget about it altogether and rip a hole in the wall. Four steps behind them, Reggie pictured Mari's face when she saw what he was made of. Imagined her in his car with him again, him talking about building boats and her hair snapping everywhere in the wind as she told him he could do it.

That was how it was supposed to turn out, except...then what the hell happened? One of the Jesus freaks pointed at Mari and shouted. Someone behind Reggie screamed, surprised him so he flinched. Suddenly a huge noise. Something slamming his hand so that it hurt all the way up to his shoulder.

Now someone's behind him, trying to push him onto the ground.

Get the fuck offa me.

"Don't let him go," someone shouts. Women scream. Chairs flip over. Reggie's hand hurts something fierce. His face is on the floor and someone's sitting on his back. The floor smells like ass.

How, he wonders, did someone fire the gun that was in his own hand?

THE SMELL OF FRESH COFFEE

Sam

People shouting. Chairs overturned. A body crashes to the floor nearby, and from where he lies, Sam sees that it's Reggie with a half-dozen men on his back. But then Reggie's hauled upright, and Sam's vision is filled with feet scuffling every which way and a tangle of chair legs.

Reggie. He was always wrong for Mari, but Harry Richardson will make her happy. Sam's seen what's changed between the two of them. He'd like to tell Alice not to worry. He'd like to tell Mari he's glad.

He'd like to turn his head.

It takes a few tries to get the message through, but then he's facing the ceiling, and the pain comes like it's somehow related to where he puts his eyes. Something's spilled. Sam's lying in the spill. It's wet. Clive's face hovers over him for a moment, and then it's replaced by Frank's. Frank's mouth is moving, his expression panicked. The words are clear, but their meaning won't process. Sam can see that one gold tooth Frank was so proud of. He would tell Frank he remembers when that tooth was new, but the words keep drifting away.

"Jesus H. Christ," Frank says. "Jesus Christ, Sam. I'm so sorry. Jesus. Reggie. I never thought. I'm sorry."

Right now, it would be great to smile. Great to give his old friend a hard time because with all those "Jesus Christs," he sounds like he's praying. Like Frank, of all people, got religion. Well, Sam had never seen it coming with Mari either. But Frank's face is gone now. Alice is there. Old woman. His old woman, whom he's loved for so long he can't remember another time. Something's off with her face. Something's very wrong. Darkness wavers at the edges of Sam's vision, but he fights it because he needs to understand. Alice is screaming. Over and over, she's screaming, and the last thing in the world he'd ever expected his old woman to do is scream. Behind her head, the air ripples as if something has come closer, and Sam discovers that, miraculously, he smells fresh coffee. He's quite pleased with himself for having remembered to buy new creamer.

YOU. AND YOU.

Lydia

Lydia has the sense she's corked in a bottle shaped like her body. There is noise that should be loud—people shoving to get out the door, voices raised, shoes squeaking and banging against the wooden floor—but they are muffled. Distant. Her eyes take in sights that she knows, numbly, are upsetting: Levi on the side of the room, sobbing in Harry's arms. Alice screaming while Mari holds her. The younger of the strange men—Mari's husband, Lydia has figured out—standing like a statue with blood on his face. Other than that, he's whiter than a bedsheet on laundry day. The older guy waves his arms in the air, his head thrown back. Lydia knows he's praying. She wonders if he's the one who caused all this, whatever this might be. But Reggie has played a part in it too. Right now, he's backed in a corner with his head bent while one man winches an arm behind his back and another shouts. Frank is crying actual tears. Clive and Carol are hugging, which Lydia might have said was impossible for those two. Isabelle Richardson paces with a cell phone.

Silly woman, Lydia thinks. *There's never a signal inside the town office.*

She's grateful Tom is safe in the hospital, where there are no guns and no bullets.

Mari's husband looks like he might faint. He seems, to Lydia, like a boy who's realized he's in over his head. Then his eyes connect with Mari's, and he mouths something. Was that *I'm sorry*? Lydia can't be sure. Mari turns away. Lydia looks down. Sam blinks. There is such an astounding quantity of blood.

When Tom rolled down the stairs in his house, there was no blood, but his eyes were open like Sam's are now. For what felt like a longer time than it probably was, she and Tom stared at each other. The understanding that she needed to summon help crashed into how long it took to get medical help on Little Great Island and paralyzed her.

"You," Tom said finally.

The word poured her back into herself. She might be old and on the verge of homeless, but it was up to her to get help, and she realized exactly what she needed to do to get The Butterfly Diplomat from the rug to the hospital on the mainland just as she realized Tom wasn't going to die. Not yet. They still had some good years together.

"Yes," she said. "And you."

Lydia leans forward, taps the microphone to get everyone's attention.

"People, please," she says. There's no magical response, but Isabelle and Jonathan Richardson come closer, along with Carol and a few of the others. Lydia points at them, one by one, and tells them to get blankets from her bedroom for Sam and for Alice, who is shaking so hard her hair wavers. Get the first-aid kit from the office. Get anyone who took EMT training or a first-aid course or anything up here for Sam. Get a helicopter. Get some cops. Get Reggie coffee and a trash can in case he vomits. Make sure those strange men don't leave. Get Alice and Mari—what? Tea and a scone? The two of them are gathered in a knot with Harry and Levi, and Lydia doesn't need to look down at Sam to know that he's gone. Whatever she and Tom are going to be able to do for that family, it's going to have to come later.

THE FORGIVENESS OF
HIS SON

Caleb

I intended no harm.
   I have not broken Thy commandments. I did not murder.
And yet...

I sought only what was right and just and that which would please the Lord.

A child belongs with his father, who can lead him on the path of goodness and right.

And yet.

If I had listened to the voice of my conscience and not of the man whom, deep in my soul, I doubted. If I had listened to my wife, my helpmate. If I had not come here. If I had not come with vengeance in my heart. If I had not, then would that gun have been fired?

From half a room away, Caleb tries again for Mari's attention. Prays she can read his thoughts in his eyes. She looks up. He knows that expression: hatred.

Mari was beautiful. She was smart. Right from the start, Caleb loved her. What a miracle that she loved him back. How could that not be a gift from God? An answer to his prayers?

But there was also allegiance to Pastor Aaron and to the needs of God's Bounty. There were the demands of the fields and the coffers and the spreading of The Word and a son who needed raising to be a good and faithful man. The behaviors of a woman who would not mind her tongue nor curb her actions were his fault, as her husband. Her transgressions were punished with words shouted down at Caleb's bent head by the righteous fury of God's chosen leader. By Pastor Aaron's hands that slapped him over and over. And Caleb knew. He sees that now. All along, his own voice had cautioned "don't follow," yet he hushed it. And he followed.

Mari glares her accusations at all the ways he has failed.

This Caleb understands now: His intentions became twisted. His thoughts poisoned by the devil.

A man was shot. A man was killed.

My father-in-law. Caleb tries the phrase on. It doesn't seem right, but it is. Levi's grandfather was killed and might have lived if Caleb hadn't come to this place.

A child belongs with his mother, who loves and nurtures. Who guides and teaches.

Who knows what is right.

Who worships neither man nor idol.

Who does no harm.

His son does not belong with a father who has lost the difference between right and wrong.

Caleb bows his head. When men take his arms, he does not heed them. When Pastor Aaron commands him with his eyes to resist capture by these heathens, he does not obey. With all his attention focused on Mari and Levi, he prays for the forgiveness of this woman who was his wife and whom he did not honor or respect.

He prays for, someday, the forgiveness of his son.

THANKSGIVING

Mari

Late November sunrises are cold and slow. The air remains night-spiced with wood smoke and frost. Mari, climbing the path toward the red farmhouse in her father's weathered winter coat, his red-knit hat, and his thick, too-large gloves, hears the minute crunch of her footsteps in the frozen grass and, behind her, the uphill breaths of her mother. A crow's caw splinters the air. A second crow calls back.

When Mari and her mother reach the front porch, they both stomp as if there's snow on their feet, but there's none. The storm door, unlike its screened counterpart, is silent when they pull it open and close it behind them. As Mari heads for the kitchen, she glances left at the children's living room, which is filled with round tables and folding chairs. To the right is the dining room, the table pushed to the wall to act as the buffet. Down in the McGavins' own kitchen, the turkey is already roasting in the oven. For now, the farmhouse and land are still owned by the Richardsons, but Mr. Estabrook and Lydia live here and pay rent to Jonathan. The sale to the farmland trust is in process. When it's complete, the island will lease the land back from the trust, and Mari, as farm manager, will receive a small salary. The rent money will be applied to farm expenses. In the meantime, she and her mother are paid by Mr. Estabrook to handle the cooking and the housework at the farmhouse, while Sue and Bob get a small stipend and free housing. Mari's grant from the state education department to teach animal husbandry and sustainable farming to schoolchildren, plus her court-ordered child support from Caleb, will help keep her going. She's still waiting to hear on some other grants, but the news should come quickly once the trust owns the land.

"I'm going to use that old cutwork tablecloth," her mother says.

"Sounds good."

It's an act of defiance against Harry's parents, many years past due. That table covering was always saved for "special occasions." It was never used. Perhaps, hidden in the table-cloth remark, is a comment about Mari's relationship with Harry but, in this moment, her mother passes no judgment. Maybe she trusts Mari now to make her own decisions, or maybe she's still too devastated to care.

The kitchen is spotless, the pies lined up and covered on the counter: Sue's doing. Sue, as the house's manager and accountant as well as caregiver for Mr. Estabrook, has also left a sticky note with the breakfast menu attached to the spiral notebook where his medications and other health indicators are tracked. There's another notebook where Sue records rent income and utility payments and a third where Sue and Mari leave notes for each other. Sue's last entry, at four o'clock in the morning, is in all caps: *WHEN WILL HE SLEEP THROUGH THE NIGHT?*

Samuel Franklin Greggs is a healthy eater. He's a big boy who has spent much of the last two-and-a-half months in the arms of one of his parents or, for a few precious hours here and there, cuddled against Mari's own chest. Levi loves to peer into the baby's face from inches away and say, "Hi Sammy! I'm Levi!" Lately, Sammy's given a gummy grin in response.

"You do breakfast," Alice says. "I'll start setting things up in the other rooms."

Mari agrees. These days, her mother is self-contained, self-sufficient, and silent. Not a barnacle but a molting lobster, Mari thinks. Shedding a shell. Growing another. This business of living exposed and vulnerable between one self and the next is something that the two of them share, and sometimes now, in the evening, they sit in the living room together with the woodstove lit and everything quiet and motionless and peaceful enough that her father could come to them if he wanted. Every now and then, she feels him near.

Caleb and Aaron are gone now, she tells her father when she senses him. Caleb and Aaron had to wait for the police to arrive, just like everyone else, and they were asked to give statements before they could leave. In the chaotic aftermath of Sam's death, Caleb's presence on the island seemed like a nightmare, but then she received his written apology, which was disjointed, long, and heartfelt. The signed divorce papers arrived from a small town in Colorado. Turned out Caleb's real name was Jamie Nunn. Someday, he asked, could he write a letter to Levi? Maybe give him a call? Mari has full custody of their son; she still hasn't decided on her answer. God's Bounty is in tatters. Sister Grace called to say she'd heard Pastor Aaron spent three days in the prayer shed, and when he'd emerged, more than half their brothers and sisters were gone. Word is that Sister Ann left as well. No one, including Mari, knows where Sister Grace and Joanna are, but Mari knows in her heart they are safe.

"I'm okay, Daddy," Mari whispers to her father. "You don't have to worry."

Breakfast today is scrambled eggs, vegetarian sausage, toast with the blueberry jam Mari preserved when her father was still alive. There's a creak behind her: Levi's standing at the threshold to the secret staircase leading up to Harry's childhood room. He spent the night up there while Harry slept beside him on a mattress on the floor. Jussi stands by Levi's side.

"You're up early."

"He farted." Levi gestures at the dog and makes a face. "It stunk so bad it woke me up."

"Let him out, then you can feed him," says Mari, laughing.

Opening the kitchen door, Levi urges the dog outside and then stands and watches him pick his way down the stairs. Mari used to stand right there at his age, impatient for her mother to finish working and take her home. Time, she thinks. Harry's right. The past is never very far away. Neither is the future.

"You sleep okay?" she asks.

"Yes," Levi answers.

Harry arrived yesterday on the afternoon ferry, and much as Mari had wanted to be the one to have a sleepover with him, she let Levi have the first turn. Every day in Harry's absence, Levi had checked the calendar to see if it was a day Mr. Harry was coming back. He's been so excited about this visit that Mari worried he thought Harry was returning for good.

"It's only a long weekend, for Thanksgiving," she'd told him. "And for saying goodbye to Grandpa Sam."

"I know *that*." Levi had actually rolled his eyes. He's also told Mari that even though she's sometimes mean, Pastor Aaron's even meaner, and he doesn't think God likes Pastor Aaron. God does seem to like Pretty, Pretty Too, Houdini, and the kittens that roam the village, two of which he's been allowed to bring home. God also likes Grandpa Sam and ice cream and chocolate in all forms as long as it's not the dark kind, because that's yucky. Levi's not so sure God likes Papa, but he'd wanted to see where Colorado was on a map. He'd listened carefully as Mari'd read him his father's apology, his face in a frown, and then he nodded at the end, as if the fate of his father made sense to him. No doubt it didn't. Levi will be coming to terms for a long, long time with everything that has happened since that moment his fork dropped. When Mari asked Levi whether God liked Mr. Estabrook and Mr. Clatcher and Uncle Bob and Aunt Sue, Levi laughed and said, "He doesn't even know them." She still doesn't know if Levi was parroting something he heard about people knowing God or if he believes God is just another adult living somewhere on Little Great Island. Someone who rarely comes to the village but who would not finger wave all around if he did.

God is mad at Mr. Reggie, Levi's informed her, because he smokes and because he shot Grandpa Sam. Mr. Reggie has to live in jail now because he was bad, but God probably still loves him because Uncle Frank and Aunt Sue and Uncle Bob say they love him even though they're upset at what he did. Grandma Alice doesn't hate Mr. Reggie, according to Levi, because she knew him when he was little like Levi, and Grandma Alice loves little kids, even when they grow up and do bad or stupid things.

"Why don't you get Jussi's food ready?" Mari asks.

Levi, clad in a pair of fire-truck pajamas and a flannel robe that Harry bought him, rinses Jussi's bowls and fills them with fresh water and kibble. When the dog comes in, he beelines for his breakfast and sucks it down, his tags clanking against the bowl.

"Morning," Lydia says. She, too, is in a robe and slippers.

Mari replies, "I hope we didn't wake you."

Lydia and Mr. Estabrook have the room that once belonged to Jonathan, right next to the kitchen. Nice and warm. No stairs.

"No, no, I was up." Lydia looks around. "We'll have breakfast in here, then?"

"I think we have to." The other rooms are filled with tables and chairs, and they still won't have enough room for everyone to sit once the memorial gathering is done. "Let me get the coffee started."

Mari's been pleased by how well she and Alice and Sue can work together in the barn and the market and even in this kitchen without getting in one another's way. Her sisters at God's Bounty had also mastered the art of kitchen choreography, but that kitchen was nearly four times the size of this one and designed to feed a group, whereas this one was built for a family.

Bob's the next one up, followed by Harry, still rumpled and bleary from sleep. Harry's eyes seek her out. He's had his hair cut and his beard trimmed, and his clothes fit him now rather than hanging as they had over the summer. Even though he doesn't come across the kitchen to kiss her, he smiles in a way that's almost as good. It puts them alone in a space that's theirs in the midst of everyone. Later, when the Thanksgiving meal is finished, Mari will stand with Harry while he buries his wedding band next to Ellie's deep in the center of the vegetable garden.

"Baby's still sleeping," Bob says. "Sue had kind of a long night."

Bob and Sue and Sammy have Isabelle's room for now, because it's at the top of the staircase where they can hear Mr. Estabrook or Lydia if they call. They'll move to the yellow house on Main Street as soon as Mr. Estabrook is steady on his feet. The other bedrooms were used by Mr. Estabrook's children when they helped settle their father into the house and worked out responsibilities and payments with Bob, Sue, Alice, and Mari. Frank also spent a few weeks in one of the rooms on the third floor, awaiting Reggie's sentencing. His own house was impossible, he said. It was full of ghosts. As soon as he heard there was a chance Reggie would get a life sentence, he gave all his property and the businesses to Sue and Bob, including the little boathouse behind The Sweet Shoppe that Bob uses now to build and restore model three-masted yachts when he isn't running the boatyard.

Once Tim Duncan and his cronies gave their statement to the cops and hightailed it back to the safety of their offices, Duncan Development withdrew the offer to buy the Richardsons' property. Isabelle had made noises about suing them for breach of contract. "For the joy of jerking their chain a bit," she confessed to her brothers, before all contracts were shredded.

Rumor has it that Pete Shaw lost his job. No wine tour, no trip to Vieques. Speculations about business practices that weren't all that legal. Abby is purportedly not at all pleased.

"Sue says she feels like the baby's going to suck her completely into his mouth and swallow," Bob says now.

"I remember those days," Mari says.

This is the morning news now, she thinks as she scrambles a bowlful of eggs into a froth. Not the tides or the bait costs. Not God's commandments or global economies, not new viruses or the carnage of war. There may be record-breaking storms ahead but, for now, there's Mr. Estabrook's first steps and Sammy's smiles. There's Lydia's oft-repeated gratitude that baked goods appear without any effort on her part and that others who are younger are willing to wait on her when she's tired. The garden is plowed under for the season. The next big event will be snow. Next year, there's promise of a larger garden and spring lambs. There will be flowers chosen to bring the pollinators, and the land between the house and The Cliffs will be closed during nesting season. If Mr. Estabrook agrees, there will be pigs to uproot the buckthorn. The farm and, eventually, others like it, will help keep the islanders fed for a little while. It will teach them skills they can use off island, including making cheese and honey or spinning and dyeing wool. Perhaps someone will have the wherewithal to turn The Sweet Shoppe into a farm-to-table café and specialty market. If those measures aren't enough, they will at least help until a better solution is found.

Lydia goes off to wake Tom, who's graduated to a walker now. Alice enters the kitchen with her head down and counts out forks and knives into her hands.

"Mom," Mari says. "We'll do all that after breakfast."

"I want to get it done and out of the way."

Her mother leaves the room, and Mari hands the eggs to Harry. "Can you finish these for me?"

"Sure."

When he takes the fork from her, their arms graze and Mari tips her face for the briefest of kisses. His breath is warm on her face.

"Don't overcook them," she says.

"What? You think I don't know how to cook eggs?"

"My recollection is that your specialties in the kitchen are hot ice cream and chocolate-chip pancakes."

The exchange makes her buoyant, despite having no idea how to help her mother through this day. Maybe Harry didn't teach her cooking, but he has taught her that there's no changing the past. She can, however, change the way she understands it. She's taught him that silence isn't anger and that mistakes don't define who you are. Together they've learned that some qualities can strengthen. Others can weaken or even fade away.

Mari leaves the kitchen and finds her mother in the adults' living room, carefully wrapping napkins around cutlery. Levi and Mari and Sue have made table decorations out of pinecones and driftwood, and in the center is the small wood-carved mermaid that Mari's father gave her when she was not much older than Levi. The sight of it makes her heart hurt. Her mother must have put it there, but it almost seems as though it was placed by her dad.

"Mom," Mari says. "You okay?"

"Yah."

Ask a stupid question, Mari thinks. She got the answer she deserved.

"I'll help," she says. Standing next to her mother, she lifts a fork and then a knife, their heft recognizable to them both from their years washing Richardson dishes. Mari presses the handles together, then wraps the whole thing tightly in a white paper napkin. She and her mother aren't okay yet, but they will be. Until then, they'll just keep on going.

EVERYWHERE, NOWHERE

Harry

Levi comes running toward them the moment Harry rounds the corner on the road from town. Surrounding Harry and the rest of his family, fresh off the ferry, are groups of people, all heading for The Cliffs. The way Levi flaps his elbows when he runs reminds Harry of a chicken, and he smiles. Levi has none of Mari's grace, but all her firm convictions and love of animals. Cocoa, in his way of thinking, is the real hot ice cream. Coming to a halt in front of Jonathan's son, Charlie, Levi says, "You are sleeping in my bed tonight."

Charlie freezes, and the small band of Richardsons stops with him. Something like a veil drops over Charlie. He's wearing khaki pants, a collared shirt, a tie, and a blue ski parka that appears brand new, a marked contrast to Levi's jeans and heavy sweatshirt. The difference between them goes far beyond clothing, and Harry finds it amazing that Levi seems not to care that Charlie has only the slightest ability to relate to other children. The rift between Harry and his siblings isn't healed, but at least they are speaking. At least they and their families are here. Mr. Estabrook's children laughed when Harry offered to return the silver dollars to them.

"He told us from day one those were for you," they said.

"Levi," Harry begins. "Why don't we let Charlie and his mom and dad—"

But Levi talks on. "You can see my kittens, only they can't sleep in the house. Pretty and Pretty Too sleep in the house, but that's because they're not real. M&M and Hershey sleep in the barn—they're the kittens—but they like it there. Also, Wolf. Actually, Wolf's a ewe and not a wolf, but Mama says sometimes wolves put on sheep clothes. Wolf sleeps in the barn too. And there's Houdini. He's our goat. He escapes all the time, so that's why he's called Houdini. And also, there's Jussi. He farts really bad. Look!"

Levi points. Charlie stays rooted.

"Houdini's right here! He came to say hi!" Before anyone can stop him, Levi's grabbed Charlie's hand and is towing him to the pasture fence, where Houdini gazes out at them with his slit-pupil eyes. Surprisingly, Charlie allows himself to be led.

"I'll get Levi," Harry says, but Umeko stops him. His sister-in-law is ordinarily quiet, but there's a new lilt in her voice now when she's on the phone with him. She has thanked Harry, with tears in her voice, because the rent money has enabled her to spend more time with Charlie.

"I thought it would take forever to sell that house," she said. "And every day counts when you have a child like Charlie who needs help."

"He likes animals," Umeko says now. "So maybe it's okay. If it isn't, we're trying to help him learn to speak up for what he needs."

Isabelle has Riley, their three-year old, by the hand. Her husband Zach's got eight-month-old Cayden strapped to his chest. Jonathan's in wind pants and running shoes but hasn't so much as mentioned going for a run.

As Levi chatters to the other boy about Houdini's famous escapes, Mari joins them on the road. She stands close enough that Harry feels the shopping bag between them. The weight and heft of it from the two Ziplock bags of human ashes inside. No, not just ashes. It's Ellie, and it's Sam. But also, it isn't. Ellie and Sam are here, on Little Great Island. They are in the extended wings of eagle and osprey, the salt tang in the air, the ooze of sap in the tree bark and in the thousands of minute glistenings in the granite rocks. They're gone and they're here. They are nowhere and everywhere.

Mari says nothing, but Harry feels the comfort of her presence. He enjoys his classes and colleagues, but he also looks forward to the times he can return to the island. Whatever the future holds beyond those pleasures, he'll find it as he and Mari choose from among their various paths.

"Seems like we're always saying goodbye to something or someone," Alice said when they asked if she minded distributing Ellie's ashes at the same time as Sam's. "Might as well do it together."

The back of Mari's hand brushes Harry's. She smells of cooking, and he imagines that if he kissed her right now, her tongue would taste of coffee. Working side by side, they have packed Ellie's clothing into boxes now piled in the farmhouse's laundry room.

"Whenever you are ready," Mari's told him, "you can take everything down to Boston and donate it to women in need." Harry isn't ready yet, but he understands that the time will come when he is.

"You can touch him," Levi tells Charlie. Harry can't see his nephew's face, but his posture indicates there's no way he's touching the goat. His arms are rigid, his hands clenched in fists. The adults and even Cayden and Riley all watch this tiny drama as if it's the most breathtaking event they've ever witnessed.

"Don't you want to touch him? He's soft on his nose, but the hair on the rest of him is kind of wiry. It's still nice, though. I like the way he smells but not everybody does."

Beside Harry, Umeko stirs. Jonathan gives the smallest of nods, and then Harry sees it too: Charlie's right hand is unfurled. His palm is pressed tightly to his thigh.

"You don't have to be scared because of his eyes," Levi continues. "That's the way they're supposed to be. Sheep have eyes like that too, and I used to think they were devil eyes, but that's just how their eyes are. Ducks and chickens have different eyes from goats and also from people. So do cats and dogs."

"Okay." Charlie's hand moves fractionally from his pant leg, and Harry realizes he's holding his breath.

"Don't let him eat your clothes, though," Levi says, and Charlie repeats, "Okay." Almost imperceptibly, his hand raises.

From Harry's vantage point, he can't tell if Charlie makes contact with the goat, but he does feel the sudden release in his brother and sister-in-law, and when he turns to the others, Jonathan is studying Harry like he's seeing him fully for the first time.

The sound of Alice's car bumping from the Richardsons' driveway brings Harry back to the business at hand. Sue and Bob leave the farmhouse with Sammy in his mother's arms.

"We should go," he says. Mr. Estabrook and Lydia are riding with Alice out to The Cliffs. The people who were behind them on the road from the village have passed them now and are visible as a cluster at the edge of the island. As they head *en masse* toward the others, Levi falls into step beside Charlie.

"Have you ever seen a sea star?" he asks. "Mama says they used to be everywhere, but they're gone now, like maybe the lobster and like my Grandpa Sam for sure. They might be in Heaven, but maybe they aren't. But there are still crabs, and my grandma makes frozen custard from the eggs we get from the ducks she got. The chickens are okay, but the ducks are mean, so don't get close to them." Charlie doesn't answer, but over the boys' heads, Jonathan gives Harry a smile.

Out at The Cliffs, the group stands in a rough semicircle with the ocean laid out beyond. Mr. Estabrook and Lydia sit side by side on a picnic bench, her hand with its new gold band resting on his knee.

"We don't really have a program or anything," Mari says. Her hair's long enough now that the breeze stirs it as it grabs the hem of her dress and plays.

She continues, "Mom and I thought we'd let anyone who wants to say something go ahead and speak. But before we do that, I wanted to thank Mr. Estabrook and the Richardsons for all that they've done to help preserve the beauty of this island while also helping to ensure that the community survives." Mari leads a round of applause for Mr. Estabrook, who manages to convey the dignity of the elder statesman from a decrepit picnic bench with a walker standing vigilant nearby. When Mari thanks Harry's family, it surprises the hell out of Harry that his sister turns pink with pleasure.

"Would anyone like to say something?" Mari asks. People sway and scuff, consider the ground at their feet. Maybe it's okay if no one says anything, Harry decides. Maybe that's how Sam would have wanted it. He'd never been much of a talker himself. But then Frank clears his throat and says, "I will."

Frank takes a minute to collect himself. He's living in Augusta now, near the incarcerated Reggie, and has shed twenty pounds and the twinkle in his eyes.

"Sam was my best friend," he says. "Our moms used to say we'd known each other from the time we were a couple months old, but the first time I remember Sam was kindergarten. He was this chubby little kid with a buzz cut and red suspenders. Same as me, only I didn't have the suspenders, and I thought they were pretty cool. The moment we got outside to recess, I went right over to him, and I shoved him hard, like this." Frank pushes the air, and there's laughter in the group.

"Well, damned if Sam didn't come flying up off the ground and beat the living daylights out of me," he continues. "We were best friends after that."

There's a hush when Frank falls silent, as if no one is certain he's finished his remarks. "So now he's gone," he says finally. "Reggie's gone, and I'm gonna go too. Different places, for sure, and I'm glad about that."

A few people twitter in appreciation of the joke, but there's no real laughter. Frank shakes his head, as if embarrassed by his own attempt at humor, before continuing, "I guess what I'm saying is that things change. I mean, we all know that, but it's easy to forget all the same. So appreciate the people and the pleasures while you've got them. Protect them if you can. Because...I'm just—" he stammers, pressing his fingers to his eyes. "I'm just so damn sorry."

Alice, in her black slacks and shapeless barn coat, strides across the circle. She takes Frank's hands in her own.

"He was my best friend too," she says, her voice quiet. They don't so much embrace as fall into each other, and when they step apart, Alice stands next to Frank, one hand clutched firmly in his.

"Loss," she says to the gathering. "And forgiveness. Letting go. Getting back."

She's asking the community to forgive Reggie, Harry understands, and he will work on it. So far, it seems very out of reach. His fingers find Mari's. The shopping bag is in her other hand.

"Okay," Mari says. "It's time."

DEEPER WATER

Little Great Island

This early in the morning, at this time of year, silence has the texture of glass, the odor of fecundity encased in crystals of frost. Breath lingers as vapor. Smoke curls. Kettles whistle. The *Abenaki Princess* churns and turns, heading for the mainland. Along the Little Great Island shoreline, proud lawns lie buried in snow. The summer houses are empty again. Moorings bob empty in the ferry's wake.

Outside the village, a red farmhouse preens in a new coat of paint while inside, a woman whose hair roots are in need of a touch-up holds her baby to her breast. Her husband is in the upstairs shower, singing just loudly enough for her to hear. In the adults' living room, the island's first female business owner, now retired, works her sudoku while enjoying her scone and coffee. Beside her, The Butterfly Diplomat dozes over pictures of a beached whale dead from an overabundance of plastic.

Down the hill, a woman who once watched her hitch-stride husband walk to his boat stands at a window that faces east, remembering the sight of a lobster boat heading out to sea. A Christmas tree sheds needles while the sun picks shine from the ornaments. A boy with his mother's mouth and his grandfather's penchant for tall tales swings his legs as he eats his breakfast of eggs and toast and new potatoes fried in herbs. In the little alcove at the top of the stairs, a bearded and curly-haired high-school teacher taps madly at his keyboard, utterly absorbed in what might be, someday, a book on Woodrow Wilson, the Red Scare, and the Fourteen Points. Barn-kept kittens stalk imaginary prey around a bale of hay. A ewe blinks and chews while a short-haired woman in rubber boots mucks stalls and hums a Christmas carol.

A ram bleats. A goat chews at the wooden door of its enclosure.

Gulls huddle in a sunspot. A column of light spears from a cloud. A bell buoy clangs the waves. Fish shift through the ocean, while far beneath the surface, the lobster have shed and grown and shed again. Together and alone, they head offshore, seeking deeper water.

Enjoy more about
Little Great Island: A Novel
Meet the Author
Check out author appearances
Explore special features

©2024 Bill Truslow

ABOUT THE AUTHOR

KATE WOODWORTH is the author of the novel *Racing Into the Dark*, hailed as "a compelling exploration of mental illness" by Booklist and as an "auspicious debut" by *Publishers Weekly*. Her short stories have appeared in *Cimarron Review, Western Humanities Review, Shenandoah*, and other literary journals, and her essays on the craft of climate fiction have been published by the Climate Fiction Writers Association. A retired medical writer in addition to fiction writer and essayist, Woodworth has received numerous awards and recognition for her writing, including a Pushcart Prize nomination, multiple Utah Arts Council and Dalton Pen Communication Awards, and an International Association of Business Communicators finalist recognition. She received her MFA from Boston University.

ACKNOWLEDGMENTS

There have been highs and lows along the path, and I have been tremendously fortunate to have a group insightful, compassionate, kind and committed people who have supported me along the way. I am grateful to all of you…including those I've inadvertently left off the list.

I lucked into the perfect publisher with Sibylline Press. Vicki DeArmon, Julia Park Tracy, Alicia Feltman, Anna Termine, and Sang Kim: Thank you over and over for devoting your superhuman energy, your creative talents, and your wealth of experience to my novel and for developing a publishing model that brought joy and collaboration into the process. Thank you, Suzy Vitello, for your editorial eye. Thank you as well to my Sibylline Sisters—Diane M. Schaffer, Jennifer Safrey, Pamela Reitman and Vicki DeArmon (wearing author hat as well as publisher hat)—for being such a great pack to run with.

Huge thanks to my accountability buddies, David Houpt and Margot Kadesch, and to my creative cheerleaders Betsy Burton and Kate Bender, who kept me working no matter how much or how often I wanted to quit. Your willingness to poke, prod, shore up, talk (and talk, and talk) and inspire hauled me out of the muddy pothole of despair more often than you know. Or at least I hope you weren't always aware.

And to my patient and willing fact finders. Truth: I didn't know squat first-hand about lobster fishing, lobster migration, conservation easements, farming, or the kind of religious belief that can blur the obvious when I started writing *Little Great Island*. I am indebted to Margot Woodworth, Patsy Lannon, Sam and Doreen Cabot, Becky Bartovics, and

Henry Morren for never making me feel stupid when I asked stupid questions and for always getting back to me quickly... even in lambing season. I also got great bits of information from Eleanor Motley Richardson's *North Haven Summers: An Oral History,* Trevor Corson's *The Secret Life of Lobsters,* Lydia Webster Brown's *On Solid Ground: Farming on North Haven Island from Early Settlement to Present Day,* and Norwood P. Beveridge and the North Haven Bicentennial Committee's *The North Island: Early Times to Yesterday.* The efforts of these individuals made my job a whole lot easier.

The luckiest of writers have supportive and thoughtful writers who help them on their path, and I am one of the luckiest of all. Thank you to the amazing and wonderful members of my writing groups and workshops in Salt Lake City, New York City, and in the Boston area. You are too numerous to name, but that doesn't make me any less grateful for all the time, attention, and helpful suggestions you made. Over the years (decades!) I have benefitted greatly from your friendship and insight.

I will always be indebted to my beta readers, including Betsy Burton, Teri Holleran, Kate Bender, Whitney Scharer, Femi Kayode, Kate Lee-DuBon, Patty McCracken, Sophie Powell-Westra, David Houpt, Shari Goldhagen, Karen Day, Patsy Lannon, Jenna Blum, and Henriette Lazaridis. Oh, you lovelies! Your insight and suggestions helped untangle the mess I'd created for myself and set me on the path toward writing the book I hoped to write.

Once I knew my manuscript was going to be a book, I decided I wanted the journey to include playtime with friends as much as possible. And so...

Thank you, thank you, thank you to Kevin Healey, who supplied timely and necessary legal insight for the price of lunch because he is just that nice a person.

Hugs and gratitude to Michael Schoenfeld and Bill Truslow—both photographers extraordinaire when I worked with them on the safe side of the camera, and who then made me comfortable when I had to be on the scary end of the lens.

Thank you to the owner of the world's best hands, massage therapist Rachel Baynesan, who worked the knots out of my neck and shoulders innumerable times, making it possible for me to return to the keyboard.

Thank you THANK YOU to the booksellers and librarians across the country who keep showing up to put books into the hands of readers...and to the readers who keep reading even with all the other distractions today's world offers. I think of you as friends even though we may never meet because we share a love of books.

Thank you times everything to my amazing family: Joe, Angela, Xander and Isaak Houpt; David Houpt, Loren Bahor, Mattea Bahor Houpt, and Emmeline Houpt; Danny Houpt and Shawna Cuan. You are the stars by which I navigate even the darkest night. Thank you for listening. For supporting. For making me laugh. For telling the truth. For being such awesome human beings.

And thank you to George Kocur, the brightest star of all: You are my home, my heart, my rock, my life companion, and my favorite knowledge source on pretty much everything. Thank you for leaving me alone on manuscript shredding day (and for putting up with my howls of anger and grief), for celebrating my successes, for standing strong in the face of my failures, and for keeping the walks shoveled and the cat groomed while I wandered imaginary worlds. You are the love of my life.

BOOK GROUP QUESTIONS

1. What aspects of the natural world are important to which characters? Are there characters who don't have an affinity for the natural world? Do you think children have a natural affinity for nature, or is that something that must be taught? What needs or wants might interfere with appreciation of the natural world? Is there an outdoor place that is important to you? How do you feel when you are there? Have you ever had a close relationship with an animal?

2. The threat of change disrupts the fabric of the Little Great Island community, causing ruptures in long-standing relationships. Do you relate more to the needs and concerns of the year-round residents of Little Great Island or to those of the summer visitors? Do you think one group has more valid concerns than the other? How do you feel about the wants and needs of individuals within each group? Are one character's needs more important than another's?

3. This story is told from eleven different points of view, including omniscient sections that can be seen as the island's point of view. Why do you think the author chose to tell the story this way? Did you find it disruptive or confusing? Are there any points of view you thought should be included? Any that you didn't think needed to be included?

4. Do you understand why Mari joined God's Bounty in the first place? Do you understand why she stayed as long as she did? Do you agree with her decision to flee with her son? Do you think she is a good mother?

5. Do you think Mari's plan for farming to help offset the income lost by the decrease in the lobster catch will work? Would allowing the executive retreat be more likely to save the future of the island? What would be gained and what would be lost if the island voted in favor of the retreat?

6. While Little Great Island takes place in the present, the past and the future play a role. Why is history important to the telling of the story? Where is the future mentioned or alluded to, and why do you suppose the author chose to include these sections?

7. Mari promotes the use of sustainable farming practices and is opposed to the use of pesticides and herbicides. What do you know about sustainable farming practices? Do you have a small, local farm near you? Have you ever shopped there? Did you like the products you purchased? Why or why not?

8. Has your community—or a community you are familiar with—undergone destruction as a result of weather or disasters attributed to climate change? What sort of measures are being taken to ensure the community survives? Do you think enough is being done? Do you know how to find out what your local climate issues are and what you can do to help? Are people coming together to bring about change? Do you experience a sense of loss when you remember the natural world of your childhood?

9. Many of the characters in Little Great Island are grieving a loss, a death, or a mistake they feel they made. In what ways are these forms of grief different, and in what ways are they similar? How does personal grief relate to climate grief? Do you think grief changes people? Does grief help form a bond with others or force the grieving person into isolation?

10. Mr. Estabrook is called The Butterfly Diplomat, a reference to mathematician and meteorologist Edward Norton Lorenz's butterfly effect theory, which points out that small changes can have a large effect. Do you believe small changes can mitigate climate change? If so, what small change are you willing to make to help the planet? If you need suggestions, turn the page to see a list of climate authors and their suggested environmental nonprofits.

MAKE A DIFFERENCE
...BE THE BUTTERFLY

"Be the Butterfly" refers to the butterfly effect, which states that a small act can have large consequences in a complex system. We invite you to perform one small act or behavior change to help mitigate climate change. Choose the butterfly act that works for you or, if you need ideas, check out the suggestions made by the following climate authors:

OMAR EL AKKAD is an author and journalist whose books have been translated into more than a dozen languages. His debut novel, *American War*, was listed by the BBC as one of 100 books that shapes our world. Nonprofit: Oil Change International, **oilchange.org**

LILY BROOKS-DALTON is the author of *The Light Pirate*, which was the runner-up for the Dayton Literary Peace Prize, a #1 Indie Next title, and a *New York Times* Editors' Pick. Her previous novel, *Good Morning, Midnight*, was the inspiration for the film adaption *The Midnight Sky*, and her memoir, *Motorcycles I've Loved*, was finalist for the Oregon Book Award. Nonprofit: Indigenous Environmental Network, **ienearth.org**

JULIE CARRICK DALTON is the author of *Waiting for the Night Song*, a New Hampshire Writers Project People's Choice award winner for best novel, and *The Last Beekeeper*, long listed for the Massachusetts Book Award. A former farmer, beekeeper, and journalist, she is a frequent speaker about the intersection of literature and climate science, a faculty member at Drexel University's MFA program, and a visiting professor at Tufts University. Nonprofit: Conservation Law Foundation, **clf.org**

JANE EKSTAM, PhD is Professor Emerita at Halden University College, Norway. She is the author of a trilogy on climate change, *Katja's World Game*. Nonprofit: Trees for the Future (sub-Saharan Africa); **350.org** (USA), **trees.org**; **350.org**

NICK FULLER GOOGINS is the author of the novels *The Great Transition* (2023) and *The Frequency of Living Things* (2025). He lives in Maine and works as an elementary school teacher. Nonprofit: The Half Earth Project, eowilsonfoundation.org/what-is-the-half-earth-project

PETER HELLER is the bestselling author of *The Dog Stars*, *The River*, and *Burn*, among other novels. He lives in Colorado. Nonprofit: American Rivers, americanrivers.org

WREN JAMES is the Carnegie-longlisted British author of many young adult novels (writing as Lauren James), including *The Loneliest Girl in the Universe*, which Amazon MGM Studios is developing as a feature film. They founded the Climate Fiction Writers League, edited the anthology *Future Hopes: Hopeful stories in a time of climate change*, and work as a consultant on climate storytelling for museums, production companies, and major brands and publishers, with a focus on optimism and hope. Nonprofit: The Pelorus Foundation, pelorusfoundation.org

BARBARA KINGSOLVER is a Pulitzer Prize-winning author of fiction, nonfiction, and poetry. She is a trained biologist and lives on a sustainable farm in southwest Virginia. Nonprofit: Earth Justice, earthjustice.org

BILL MCKIBBEN wrote what's generally regarded as the first book for the general public on climate change (*The End of Nature*, 1989) and has gone on to found the global grassroots climate campaign 350.org and Third Act, which organizes people over the age of 60 for action on climate and democracy. Nonprofit: Third Act, thirdact.org

LYDIA MILLET has written more than a dozen novels and short story collections, including *A Children's Bible*—shortlisted for the National Book Award—and *Love in Infant Monkeys*, a finalist for the Pulitzer Prize. She also writes essays, opinion pieces, and book reviews and is the author of a new nonfiction book called *We Loved It All: A Memory of Life*. Nonprofit: The Center for Biological Diversity, biologicaldiversity.org

CATE MINGOYA-LAFORTUNE is a trained biologist, teacher, and climate adaption planner and is the author of *Climate Action for Busy People*—a how to guide on intervening locally in the climate crisis. Nonprofit: Groundwork USA, GroundworkUSA.org

PITCHAYA SUDBANTHAD is the author of *Bangkok Wakes to Rain*, a *New York Times* and *Washington Post* Book of the year. Nonprofit: Climate Action Network International, climatenetwork.org

Mortal Zin: A Mortal Zin Mystery
BY DIANE SCHAFFER

MYSTERY
Trade Paper, 412 pages (5.315 x 8.465) | $22
ISBN: 9781960573933
Also available as an ebook and audiobook

A crusading attorney's death. Sabotage at a family winery...As threats mount and the winery teeters on the brink of ruin, Noli and Luz must navigate a treacherous landscape of greed, revenge, and long-buried secrets. Can two fearless women from different worlds unravel the truth before it's too late?

After Happily Ever: An Epic Novel of Midlife Rebellion
BY JENNIFER SAFREY

FICTION, FANTASY
Trade Paper, 388 pages (5.315 x 8.465) | $22
ISBN: 9781960573179
Also available as an ebook and audiobook

Princesses Neve, Della, and Bry are sisters-in-law, having married into the royal Charming family, and for the last thirty-plus years, they've been living a coveted happily-ever-after life in the idyllic kingdom of Foreverness. As they each turn 50 however, they begin to question the kingdom's "perfection." Can each of the women create a new happily-ever-after and will the kingdom of Foreverness survive it?

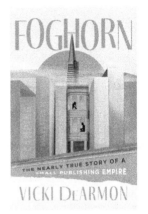

Foghorn: The Nearly True Story of a Small Publishing Empire
BY VICKI DEARMON

MEMOIR
Trade Paper, 320 pages (5.315 x 8.465) | $20
ISBN: 9781960573926
Also available as an ebook and audiobook

The heyday of small press publishing in the San Francisco Bay Area in the 1980s and 1990s lives again in this never-before-told story of how small presses—armed with arrogance and personal computers—took the publishing field. Vicki Morgan was an ambitious young woman publisher, coming-of-age while quixotically building Foghorn Press from scratch with her eccentric brother to help.

Charlotte Salomon Paints Her Life: A Novel
BY PAMELA REITMAN

HISTORICAL FICTION
Trade Paper, 392 pages (5.315 x 8.465) | $22
ISBN: 9781960573919
Also available as an ebook and audiobook

This historical fiction depicts the encroaching terror of the Third Reich and the threat of psychological disintegration of the artist Charlotte Salomon as she clings to her determination to become a serious modernist painter, to complete her monumental work "Life? Or Theater?" and get it into safekeeping in a race against time before capture by the Nazis.

For more books from **Sibylline Press**, please visit our website at **sibyllinepress.com**

Sibylline Press is proud to publish the brilliant work of women authors over 50. We are a woman-owned publishing company and, like our authors, represent women of a certain age.